faded sunset

faded sunset

rachel blaufeld

Mick and Margo
Copyright © 2021 Rachel Blaufeld
All rights reserved

ISBN: 978-1-7340017-5-4

Edited by
Pam Berehulke
Proofread by
Virginia Tesi Carey
Cover design by
© Sarah Hansen, Okay Creations, LLC
www.okaycreations.com
Interior formatted by

emtippettsbookdesigns.com

Warning:
This book is intended for mature audiences.

Clouds come floating into my life, no longer to carry rain or usher storm, but to add color to my sunset sky.

— Rabindranath Tagore

Author's Note

This book features a couple who follows an ugly path, only to arrive at their happy ending. Trigger warnings include abuse and cheating. Not every road to love is a smooth path, but I understand if this story isn't for you. While the characters in this book are products of my imagination, if you or someone you know are involved in an abusive relationship, you can call the National Domestic Violence Hotline at 1-800-799-SAFE or find them on the web at www.thehotline.org.

prologue

margaret

"Another round?" James asked, his emerald-green eyes staring directly at me, but he didn't really *see* me.

Yes, he saw me—the prettied-up, fun-loving, fake version of me—not the broken-down woman who lived in hell. This came as no surprise because it was exactly the look I'd been trying for before I cozied up to the bar at the Oak around ninety minutes ago.

I'd been hungry—no, *desperate*—for someone to take a good look at my facade and roll with the person they freaking got.

You get what you get, and you don't get upset. For a moment, I remembered the teachers saying those exact words in my daughter's preschool a few years ago, and thinking it was a perfect mantra.

I'd already spent a lifetime searching for the person who would know me deeply and understand me. A partner who got me in ways I didn't get myself. When I found that person, I'd decided I would hold on tightly. But I'd failed at finding someone on my first attempt, and had lost my way on the second attempt.

Smiling at James, I said, "Definitely," and he signaled for the bartender.

At that moment, I'd classify myself as tipsy, but not wrecked. I knew the bartender's name was John, and he was adorably cute in his almost too-tight plaid vest buttoned over a white dress shirt, his sleeves rolled up to his elbows. He made a mean French 75, and attended graduate school here in Boston. He'd been behind the bar both times I'd been here before, but not in charge of my drinks. Now, John was my drug-of-choice dealer.

James, an established lawyer, traveled between here in Boston and New York for the law firm where he'd made partner close to a decade ago. I placed him to be around four or five years older than me.

"Divorced," he'd told me earlier in the evening. "Wasn't a good match." She couldn't handle his travel schedule, or so he'd claimed.

"Me? I'm a writer," I'd told him and left it at that.

"*Journal*? *Times*?" he'd asked with an eyebrow raised.

His question felt less about where I worked and more about my political party. Personally, I didn't think we were at that stage of a relationship, or ever would be.

"Freelance. I write a lot for *Adweek*. My life's not that serious. Lifestyle and social media pieces, mostly," I'd said like I meant it. I wished it to be true.

As we waited for my drink, James's hand grazed my back, sweeping under my hair and caressing the back of my neck. More than anything, I wanted to slap his hand away, but I just met his gaze again, confirming he was still seeing me. James was into me, at least for the night, which was enough at the moment.

I'd told him I was separated. And in my heart and soul, I *was* separated, despite wearing my wedding band. But in reality, I wasn't.

I was fully aware that made me *public enemy number one*, but everyone had a skeleton or two in their closet. Mine were neither pretty nor organized. They were a messy bag of bones that not even the most dedicated paleontologist could put back together.

John slid a fresh drink toward me as I relaxed into the high-backed bar chair. Standing behind me, James reached out to take his. Like most nights, the Oak was packed, and I'd been lucky to snag a chair when I arrived. Relieved, I'd hung my fur-trimmed jacket on the back and saddled up for a drink. James appeared moments later and had been keeping me company ever since.

"Cheers," he told me now, tipping his lowball toward my glass.

"Cheers." I returned the sentiment, taking a sip and closing my eyes for a few seconds.

"You probably end up in New York often," James said, more like a statement than a question.

"You say that like you already know."

"I assumed," he said. "Writing, lifestyle, it's all connected, and I was thinking we could meet up there," he said, sprinting rather than leisurely walking from this meet-up to a potential next one.

His left hand now rested on the back of my chair and I took it in, confirming there was no wedding band. His body was turned toward me, his posture confident as he leaned a bit closer.

"You know, you need to be careful in this," he said, caressing the collar of my coat. "I heard the animal lovers are attacking people who wear fur."

And just like that, whatever false connection I was imagining between us evaporated. This man and I had nothing in common.

After taking a sip of my drink, I asked, "Tell me, what kind of car do you drive? A Tesla?"

He shook his head. "BMW Seven Series," he said proudly, like this was a selling point.

"With leather seats? Guzzling gas?"

Rather than taking offense, he threw his head back in laughter, exposing the cords of his throat. Under different circumstances, I would have thought it was sexy, but I was just about over James. Not to mention, I suspected he was married with all this wanting to meet up in New York.

Then again, so was I.

"Ouch," he said, raising a finger in the air, pretending to be burned, before settling his hand onto my thigh.

I shifted my leg slightly, trying to shake James loose as the street entrance door opened, allowing in a burst of cold air. It had been opening and closing all night, but this was the first time I'd noticed.

When I glanced at the doorway, my head started to swirl, and I tried to blame the latest drink. But it was the blacker-than-black gaze focused on me that left me off-kilter, the unzipped leather jacket, the cashmere sweater covering the body I knew better than any other.

His expression hard, the man approached, wedging himself between James and me without even bothering to say *excuse me*.

Breathless, I met his eyes. "Mick."

Nodding at me, he said, "Margaret."

I wilted a little when he didn't use the nickname he'd given me, and so did my heart. Hearing my given name rumbling from him now, I noticed it held a mix of tension and relief.

Silently cursing at myself, I wished I hadn't used his nickname just then. I wasn't supposed to call him that anymore.

"Pardon me," James said snidely, obviously not appreciating another man pushing his way between us.

"Pardon yourself," Mick spat out as he gave me his back and stared down James. "You in the business of picking up women who are taken?"

Of course, at six foot three, Mick had a few inches on the poor guy, and I was surprised James didn't wilt under Mick's glare. Most people did. Instead, James tossed his credit card on the bar, making desperate eye contact with the bartender and gesturing for his tab.

"Dude, she said she was separated," he said matter-of-factly to Mick.

"First off, don't fucking *dude* me," Mick said. "Second, I'm not her sorry excuse of a husband. Either way, if I were you, I'd get the hell out of here."

I wished James would just do as Mick said, but instead he leaned around Mick and asked me, "You okay? Want me to drop you somewhere?"

For a second, I wondered if he had his BMW Seven Series, and then shook my head against the idea. There was nothing humorous about this current scenario, or my life, for that matter.

Mick glowered at James. "She's more than fine. I'm here, so she doesn't need you to drop her anywhere. Now go."

As James stepped back, Mick turned to take me in. Cupping my cheeks with his warm hands, he not only saw me but looked deep inside me. His dark eyes singed me as they took me in, seeing all my emotions play out on my face.

"What did he do?" Mick simply asked, and we both knew he didn't mean James.

Shrugging, I reached for my drink, but he pushed my hand away from the half-filled glass.

"No, Margo, first tell me what happened, then I'll get you a new drink that stuffy piece of shit didn't buy you. After that, I'll take you back to my place and make you forget both of them, if that's what you need. Do you need a reminder of how we work?"

I glanced behind me, noticing that James had slunk away quietly.

"Mick, please," I said with a sigh, not wanting to get into it with him.

In a short time, Mick had gathered enough ammunition on my husband to start a world war, which was why I came to the Oak instead of calling him. I was trying to break the cycle. Although, I didn't want to examine why I picked *our place* to escape to.

"No." Mick's response was firm, and his determined gaze continued to burn through me. "Talk."

"Same as usual," I whispered, knowing his imagination gave him a pretty good idea of what the usual was. "How did you know I was here?"

"Fucker," Mick muttered under his breath.

It didn't escape my notice that he'd ignored my question.

He cleared his throat. "Let's go take care of it," he said matter-of-factly, knowing there would be something for him to put back together. "You need to push forward and get out like you said you would. If not for me, then—"

His words were interrupted by the shrill ring of my phone. I pulled it from my purse without looking at caller ID, already knowing who must be calling.

"Is everything okay?" I said in a panic.

"Yes, everything's under control, but we're at the emergency room. Priscilla—"

"Where?" I asked, hardly able to breathe.

My own injuries would have to wait. These were more important. Awkwardly holding my phone to my ear, I was shrugging on my jacket as I heard where they were with my daughter.

Without asking any questions, Mick tossed cash on the bar, then took my hand.

I wasn't sure how he did what he was doing. How he could sense what I was going through, the emotions tumbling around inside me, but his gentle grasp on my fingers told me he did. Without asking, he led me outside toward the valet, and of course, his car was sitting right out front.

As the valet tossed him the keys, I told Mick, "Mass General. Now."

With a nod, he opened my passenger door and then hurried around the front of the car. Once he'd dropped into the driver's seat, he blew out a long breath while tapping at the GPS, searching for the quickest way to our destination without saying a word. As he pulled the car out into traffic, he finally spoke.

"You bought yourself a day or two, Margo, but this has to end."

I wasn't sure which he meant—us, or my other relationship, or both—but

I didn't ask. I simply sat twisting my hands, worried desperately about my daughter while at the same time wondering how I'd ended up in this nightmare of twisted feelings and bad choices.

one

m a r g a r e t
One month earlier

"We need half-and-half." Tommy fumed as he tried to slam the door on our Sub-Zero fridge, but the hydraulics wouldn't permit it. The door let out a slow whoosh as it refused to comply with his demand, softly closing instead.

I wished I could do the same.

With my hair still in a messy bun and dressed in rumpled pajamas, I nodded at my husband's angry statement without looking up from my laptop. My editor wanted to meet around eleven. Mentally, I went over potential assignments she might have for me, and how quickly I could make Priscilla's lunch and sneak in a workout before heading out the door.

"Margaret, did you hear me? We're out of half-and-half. Now I'm going to have to stop for coffee on my way to work. It's a huge waste of my time."

I don't know why I didn't look up and just tell him I was sorry. Maybe I was channeling the Sub-Zero, but I was so damn sick of the weak version of myself.

"Use some of Prissy's milk," I said without thinking. "It's just as creamy, and I'll grab some fresh half-and-half today."

I knew it wasn't a satisfactory answer, but for two seconds I was caught up in myself and my career rather than my husband. Distracted, I wondered if *maybe, just maybe* I would get to cover Fashion Week this year.

"It's two percent. That's hardly creamy," he said in an ominous voice.

One part of my mind noted my mistake, but I was still wrapped up in my thoughts. It had been a goal of mine to cover a few of the new gender-free fashion designers and the way they were using Instagram to market their clothes since I'd seen a documentary on the topic.

It really must have been an off morning for me, because I didn't sense Tommy approach until his hand clamped painfully around my wrist. He gripped it hard, pain radiating all the way to the bone, and any career dreams vanished.

"I'm sorry," I said quickly, knowing better than to flinch or say *ouch*. Revealing any pain or discomfort only fueled Tommy's rage, and I wanted to finish this episode and get to my workout this morning.

"It's not creamy. Say it for me, Margaret," Tommy said low, squeezing my wrist harder.

I froze, not daring to move for fear my slight bones would crack, which would only please Tommy more. "It's not." I swallowed hard, knowing it would do me no good to argue.

Tommy's eyes narrowed, and a vein pulsed in his forehead. "Not what?"

"Not creamy," I whispered.

"Tell me something. Who pays for that chair you're sitting in? The roof over your head? That expensive all-girls private school for your daughter?"

Tommy's words cut through the pain.

My daughter? Actually, she was his daughter too, but I didn't bother to get into semantics.

"You do, you do." The words flew from my mouth on repeat and out of habit.

It didn't take long for me to slip into the headspace where I gave Tommy what he wanted or expected, praying he would let go of my arm before Priscilla came into the kitchen.

"That's right, and don't you forget it."

Tommy glared at me, tightening his grip around my wrist for a beat longer, and I held my breath. If experience held true, I'd bruise and have to wear long-sleeved shirts for a couple of weeks despite the August kind of heat we were having now in September.

Trying to ignore the pain, I glanced at the window. It was barely dawn outside, and I was already having a shitty day.

You made your bed, so lie in it. That was the sentiment my mom had given me with a shrug when I'd gone to her for advice. I hadn't spoken with her since.

"Get the half-and-half today, you hear me?" Tommy released my wrist with a shove and grabbed his keys from the junk drawer.

"I will," I barely croaked out in an effort to get rid of him.

Without another word, Tommy stalked toward the garage and was gone.

The air flew from my lungs before I gasped for fresh air. I pulled up the sleeve of my pajamas, wincing at how my arm was already bruising. It needed ice, but I heard Priscilla padding down the hall.

"Hi, Mom."

She walked into the kitchen, rubbing her eyes. When she finally looked at me, I was so grateful her eyes were bright blue like mine. Her hair wasn't quite as blond as mine, but her headful of curls came from my side.

Priscilla was all mine, and I was trying to do what I had to in order to protect her. If I broke up our home, Tommy would have money and power on his side. A ruthless combination, as my mother said.

"Hey, baby girl," I said, and got a major side-eye.

"Mom, I'm in seventh grade. Please, I'm twelve."

"You'll always be my baby." I stood and pulled her skinny frame in for a hug.

"Okay, okay," she said, slipping from my hold before heading to the cabinet.

Opening the fridge, I asked, "Turkey sandwich?"

She nodded, and I gathered the ingredients to make her lunch. Priscilla was perfectly capable of doing it herself at her age, but it was something I enjoyed doing for her.

"Mustard instead of mayo," she said, pouring granola in a bowl before opening a yogurt to add to it.

As I refreshed my coffee using my nondominant wrist, the one Tommy didn't hurt, I noticed her watching. She frowned at me, with her phone in one hand and shoveling her breakfast into her mouth with the other.

"For an assignment," I said lightly. "Using my opposite hand for daily tasks."

Priscilla shrugged, not interested in reading my work. If it wasn't on TikTok, it meant nothing to her, so I was safe.

Scrolling through her messages, she said, "Mom!"

I shouldn't be surprised. Her phone was practically attached to her hand these days.

"Penny asked me to sleep over tomorrow night after soccer practice. Please? We'll do our homework and go to bed. I promise."

"Tomorrow is a school night," I said out of habit, knowing I'd allow it anyway. My baby deserved as much happiness as she could get, and Lord only knew, I tried at home but failed often.

"You wouldn't even have to pick me up after practice," she said excitedly. "I'll pack my stuff in the morning and go home with Penny."

Faced with her huge smile, I gave in. "Of course you can go. But remember to call me when you get there."

"I always do," she said, already responding to the text, her thumbs flying over her phone. "But you'll tell me again tomorrow."

I finished making her lunch, trying to figure out how I could have some fun too.

Later, as I walked out of the coffee shop on Newbury where I met with my editor, Jane, my phone dinged.

Did you get the half-and-half?

Sighing, I didn't have a chance to reply before Tommy rapid-fired another text.

Working late. Remember, I'm going to Vermont tomorrow for a deposition . . . after I drink my coffee with half-and-half. I'll be home the following day.

After moving my wrist back and forth, trying to shake out the soreness, I texted back, keeping my response short.

I got the half-and-half.

I'd stopped earlier at the store and ran the container home before traveling downtown, rushing so I wasn't late to my meeting. But there was no reason to explain that or say anything more to Tommy. It would only come back to bite me later.

Stopping on the sidewalk, I let out a deep sigh of relief over Tommy's upcoming absence, and then remembered Priscilla would be out tomorrow night too.

Wow, I'd have a night to myself . . . a rare opportunity to either sulk in my predicament or truly be happy for a few hours. I could watch a movie with a big glass of wine and forget my woes for a few minutes.

A deep breath filled my lungs, and I smiled. The sun was shining, and I was going to cover the fashion preview for *Adweek*. As a freelancer, that was a big deal, but Jane knew I stood behind my work. She didn't know I'd remained stagnant all these years because Tommy demanded it. "My hobby," as he referred to my career, was always on the back burner behind his.

My phone dinged again, this time with a text from Priscilla, pulling me out of my self-pity.

Soccer pickup is at 5:30. We have to watch a safety video after practice.

Checking the time, I realized I had ninety minutes until I had to pick her up, rather than thirty.

That's when I noticed I was standing outside an old favorite of mine, Stephanie's on Newbury. Was there any harm in grabbing a quick adult beverage before I picked up my daughter? Some might say yes, but they hadn't walked a minute in my shoes, so I went ahead and pushed through the door.

"Welcome to Stephanie's. Can I help you?" The hostess greeted me with a smile, and my shoulders relaxed for the first time all day.

"I'll just have a seat at the bar," I said quickly, my nerves kicking up a notch. This was the most scandalous thing I'd done in years, having a day drink by myself.

"Of course." The hostess waved in the direction of the lacquered wood bar, lined with high-back wicker stools.

Noticing a few others partaking in a day drink, I felt a little better as I made my way over. *See? I can do this.*

Finding a seat toward the end, I slid in, almost tugging up my sleeves before I remembered my new bruises.

"Hi." A cheerful redhead with pigtails, a permanent smile, and a nametag marked Bella, popped up in front of me. "Can I get you a menu?"

"Sure. Drink menu?" My words came out like a question, and Bella picked up on it.

"No judgment here. You can drink any time of day that we're open, and I'm happy to serve you."

"It's five o'clock somewhere," I said lamely. Embarrassed, I snapped my mouth shut and scanned the menu. I chose a glass of wine, thinking that was the most appropriate day drink. "I'll have a glass of cabernet."

"Right on it," Bella said, and she was back in a hot minute with a healthy pour of my favorite wine.

My eyes fluttered closed as I took my first sip, reveling in the exact moment my body felt truly relaxed in days. This was bliss, sitting by myself, enjoying a glass of wine in a restaurant. All by myself. Did I mention that already?

I was busy cataloguing all my feelings when someone said, "Is this seat taken?"

Granted, the line was about as cliché as anyone could use, but hadn't I used one only moments before? I almost didn't look up, but the raspy voice behind the trite words forced me to turn my head slightly.

Leaving my phone on the bar right side up, I met a pair of dark brown, almost onyx eyes, framed by a head of tousled coal-black hair. Just my luck, masculinity radiated off the verbal offender, catching me in a weak moment, forcing me to pardon his bad taste in pickup lines and offer the seat to him.

I tried to think of a reason to say no. I was married and a mother, and the chair wasn't mine to offer. But he asked me, and so I obliged.

"It's all yours—free of charge," I said with a touch of humor. I was already nervous enough with this unfamiliar midday tension, and now sex and lust radiated from this guy, drawing all the oxygen from the air around me.

"Thanks." He pulled out the high-back stool next to me and slid onto it.

His shirt was untucked and hung over his European-cut suit pants. I couldn't help it; I had to take a second look. I imagined his tie was wherever he'd left his jacket, thrown over a chair somewhere. *No doubt, a bedroom—maybe not even his—or an office nearby.*

My heart hoped for the latter. My married but miserable heart.

Back to sipping my cabernet, I scrolled through the emails on my phone, shoving the mystery man to the back of my mind, despite his scent invading all my senses. Masculine, with a hint of cologne and shampoo from earlier in the day, heavy on the tea tree oil.

My preference would have been to push him all the way out of my head, but beggars can't be choosers. I forced myself back to the present and the competitive knot twisted in my belly over my earlier meeting. Finally, I had the chance to write about something I wanted. I needed to do my best, and then I could generate more work and be rid of Tommy—if he'd allow it. I knew he'd fight it, which was another good reason why I wasn't sitting at the bar trying to meet men.

Opening my calendar app, I made a note to message a few of the designers tomorrow and introduce myself.

"Can I get you another?"

This time the man's voice was raspier, pure gravel traveling through his vocal cords as even more cliché nonsense came from his mouth. He was now comfortably settled next to me, drinking a bourbon, impervious to the wedding band on my hand.

"If I want one, I can get my own," I told him matter-of-factly. The independence felt as comforting as my robe on a rainy Sunday morning. I never got my own anything anymore.

I could get my own anytime I want, a little voice inside me said.

He raised his hands in surrender. This was when I noted the absence of a wedding band. I'm not sure why I cared. I'd said vows, and it was my nightmare to live in now.

"Honestly, I swear I was only trying to be a kind neighbor," he said with a grin.

He had the straightest teeth, bright white and perfectly aligned, and laugh lines in the corners of his eyes. A little gel remained in his hair, which had to have been styled at one point this morning, and a gorgeous, come-fuck-me five o'clock shadow lined his jaw. It was the stubble that I focused on, allowing my imagination to wander a beat or two. My brain was in such a tizzy, I didn't notice him signal the bartender to bring me another glass of wine.

"Cheers," he said to me, and a tiny hint of New York came out in his tone.

"Thank you." I lifted my fresh wine and raised it in a toast. Running my free hand over my hair, I smoothed it, both making sure the routine bun I wore was still tightly packed, and trying to settle the butterflies in my stomach.

"Long day?" he asked.

Of course he did. This wasn't some being-a-nice-neighbor bullshit. It was a come-on. That's what happened when you tried to sneak in a day drink. At least, that's what I was trying to tell myself.

Regardless, I nodded because the eye candy in front of me won over my runaway thoughts.

"Mine's been shit. Not that you asked, but it has," he said before taking another gulp of his drink. He raked his fingers through his hair, mesmerizing me, waking up my libido. Those were not working man's hands.

"You're right. I didn't ask," I said. "I'm sorry it's been a rough one, nonetheless. If it's any consolation, mine hasn't been great either."

Not sure why I'd been brutally honest with this stranger, I took comfort in my second glass of wine—one I should have declined.

"I'm Mick, a proud but apologetic transplant from Brooklyn," he said, holding out his hand.

We sat there a beat or two, Mick's hand hovering near mine, sending a chill up my spine.

"Margaret." I extended my own hand. "I'm sorry. I forgot my manners for a moment."

"Nice to meet you, Margo."

He shortened my name and smirked at me again, signaling he'd won this round. He'd met me, gotten my name, and gave me his. For some reason, I couldn't find a reason to correct him on my name. No one had called me Margo since college.

"So, your bad day, tell me about it, Mick." Scanning the bar, I wondered why I was still engaging with him, before pressing my finger on the home button of my phone so I could check the time.

Forty-five minutes until I needed to pick up Priscilla. *My daughter with another man, my husband.*

"My day . . . it's sliding off me as we speak, but I had to let a few people go today. Actually, more than a few." Mick stared into his nearly empty glass, bringing us back to the moment without any comments about my phone checking or weird behavior.

"That doesn't sound very fun," I said, realizing his rumpled appearance made sense now. I could no longer blame it on a tumble between the sheets.

Mick shrugged. "Part of the territory."

"And that is?" I couldn't help but be interested. A writer at heart, I could never get enough information.

"This is the part I hate saying," he said, "but I buy broken companies and fix them, keep them, or sell them. I know, I know . . . it sounds like I made it up or heard about it in the movies. But that's what I do. Anyway, today was awful." He took a long slug of his drink, finishing it while the ice clinked against the sides of the glass.

Bella noticed it was empty and brought another without being asked.

I couldn't help let out a small giggle. "Definitely doesn't sound fake. Maybe a little *Pretty Woman*, but not fake."

"That damn movie. Pretty sure everyone thinks about it when it comes to me and what I do for a living."

"Oh yeah, everyone?" I crossed my skinny-jean-covered legs and eyed up this stranger, wanting to be different from his movie counterpart. I wanted to be a confident, self-assured, independent woman.

"Yep, everyone."

His gaze landed on me, and I'm not going to lie, I softened. Mentally, I took back the bad assumptions I'd made about this guy, reconciling myself with being able to enjoy some small talk and bar chatter.

"One sec." He held up a finger and tapped away at his phone, which had been lighting up furiously on the bar. Setting it facedown, he said, "Now, tell me about you, Margo."

Phones forgotten, I told him as much as I felt comfortable. I quickly deduced that was my prerogative as a woman. "Writer. I'm a writer."

He nodded, waiting for more.

"*Adweek*, some fluff filler for them, and at other times I write pieces that intersect on lifestyle and business."

Pretty sure I'd just told Mick more about my work than I'd told anyone in a decade. I didn't have many close friends or confidants. Isolation was my cloak, giving me a chance at survival.

"Got it. Wrangler of words."

The smile spreading across my face couldn't be helped. It was true—I loved words.

After finishing my wine, I checked the time again on my phone. Of course, Mick asked me if I wanted another wine, and I declined. Two was more than my limit.

"Early morning exercise class," I lied to him.

Opting not to have another drink either, he paid the bill. Giving me a hopeful glance as he slid his wallet back in his pocket, he said, "I live close by, but I don't think that's what you're into."

"I wish I could say it was, but I have to pick up my daughter." I let him off easy, not wanting to mention my marriage, or the shell of one.

Standing, I followed him out of the bar. He held the door open for me, and I stepped out first.

Turning to say good-bye, I said, "Thanks, this was fun." It felt a bit like something a young girl would say, but I had never quite felt that way in all my life. Or at least, in a very long time.

"It was," he said and leaned in to give me a quick kiss on the cheek.

I let him, and why not? Okay, there were a million reasons why I shouldn't—or at least two, as in Tommy and Priscilla. But in that moment, none of them mattered compared to the ego boost I was getting. It was unprecedented and exhilarating.

He stepped back, and as I was turning to go, grabbed my wrist and said, "Here."

I yelped, "Ouch," and glanced down to see he was holding a card in his other hand.

"I'm sorry. I didn't mean to hurt you." His face was stricken with worry. This was a man who toppled businesses with a metaphorical wrecking ball, but would never hurt a human being.

"It's nothing. Injury from exercise," I said quickly when he frowned at the fingerprint bruising around my slight wrist.

His grip gentled, still lingering around the cuff of my shirt, which had now risen up my arm, but he didn't say a word. Concerned, he looked into my eyes, and for the first time in my life, I felt not only seen, but seen *through*. It was an unfamiliar yet strangely welcome feeling.

I didn't even know what it all meant, but my soul felt both whole and halved at the same time, if that makes sense. Christ, I was a writer, and I couldn't even string together a few words about how I was feeling. Hollow and filled up. Bursting with happiness and lonely as hell.

"I really have to go get my daughter." Ducking my head, I swallowed my rioting feelings and cleared my head of the wine and of Mick.

He gently placed the card in my hand. "Take this. Please. Call me if you ever need . . . put back together," he said before turning and walking away.

"I . . ." I didn't know what I was going to say, but I let it go and started to walk away, turning the card over and over in my hand until a rush of guilt and apprehension burst through my veins and I spun around.

"Mick!" I called out, walked quickly toward him. "Wait up!"

God, I'm making a spectacle of myself.

He stopped and turned, then took a step or two forward to meet me.

I stared down at the card, noting his name. *Mick Grantham.* Committing the sexy name to memory, I decided to think about this day fondly. It was a few minutes' reprieve of the nothingness I typically dwelled in.

"I, uh, I don't do this often," I stammered. "Or ever."

Mick raised an eyebrow at me, then glanced down at my wedding band. His dark hair fell in front of his eyes, and he brushed it back, keeping his gaze on me. "Oh, that. That's not what I meant. I was talking about day drinking, but that too. I don't do that either."

The undercurrent between us was torrid. Did he know what I meant? Did I have to spell out that I wanted him?

Feeling the need to explain, I said, "What I mean is this isn't really me. Making waves."

"I know," he said.

Fishing his card out of my pocket, I waved it at him. "I can't take this."

Mick stood there, thinking for a moment as time ticked away. If I didn't leave quickly, I'd be late picking up Priscilla.

"I get it," he finally said. "Tell you what. Why don't you put your number on the back, and if I ever need a listening ear over a day drink, I'll call you."

"Um . . . okay."

I grabbed a pen from my purse before I could change my mind, and without thinking about it, scribbled my full name, Margaret Long, on the back of his card. I guessed I really wanted to be found—by Mick.

Taking the card back, he said, "See you around, Margo."

The nickname he gave me struck a chord with me, leaving me with a warm, gooey feeling inside. I had no idea I needed something like that, but I sure lapped it up.

We both turned and walked away with no promise of anything in the future, but I knew that wouldn't be the last I saw of Mick Grantham. The feeling swept over me like an out-of-control wave at the beach, knocking me over with its strength and conviction.

Giving me hope.

two

margaret

Tommy poured a heavy splash of half-and-half into his coffee, sealed his travel mug, and walked over to me. "I'll be home in time for dinner tomorrow," he said curtly, tugging me close with his free hand.

Luckily, it was his left, meaning my good wrist didn't get jarred any more than it already had been. His lips brushed my cheek before stopping to bite my earlobe. Some would have thought it sensual or promising, except it wasn't a gentle nibble. His teeth sank painfully into my ear before releasing and scratching a trail to my mouth, taking hold of my bottom lip.

"Behave while I'm gone," Tommy murmured. Using his left hand again, he cupped my jaw and held me in place for a kiss.

Deciding to give in, I went through the motions, my lips moving with his. I didn't know what he meant by behave while he was gone, and a surge of panic rolled up my spine. Did he know about my day drink and who I met?

"I mean it, Margaret, don't go touching yourself. Save it for me. Tomorrow night."

Oh. That.

I breathed a quiet sigh of relief. Tommy had this thing with my orgasms being his. Little did he know, they were fake. I hadn't climaxed in years, and even back when I did have orgasms with him, they were few and far between.

"I won't." My promise came out in a whisper, but it was enough for Tommy.

With a hard squeeze on my hip, he said, "See ya."

As soon as he was gone, I pulled in my first easy breath of the day. Pouring myself a coffee and adding a splash of milk and sugar, I let out a loud sigh, something I wouldn't dare do in front of Tommy.

Free for a day, I thought as Priscilla rounded the corner, a small duffel bag in hand.

"Hi, baby," I said, and she rolled her eyes but didn't insist that I not call her that.

"Hi, Mom." She rifled through the fridge and grabbed a yogurt while I started packing her a lunch.

"What will you eat tomorrow?" I asked.

"Oh, it's grilled cheese and tomato soup day. I was going to ask you if I could buy my lunch anyway."

I paused for a moment, taking her in, with her hair twisted into a braid and the pink lip gloss on her mouth. It astounded me how quickly Priscilla was growing into a young woman. And an organized one at that.

"No problem." Something unfamiliar started to beat in my chest. Priscilla growing up meant she wouldn't be here forever . . . and I could be free. Did I have to wait?

My brain rapid-fired questions while we prepared for the day in quiet contentment.

"Dad still here?"

"No, sweetie. You need him for something?" I asked. It was almost as unusual for Priscilla to ask after him as it was for him to care about her.

"No, I like when it's just us. That's it."

I thanked God and Buddha and Allah that I wasn't cutting her sandwich in half at the moment, or I might have sliced my hand in two instead.

"I like it too," I said softly, then gave her a grin. "Girl power."

"Yeah," Priscilla said with a small smile.

With that, we continued to work quietly until we settled in the car and I dropped her at school, her overnight bag tucked slung over her shoulder, and my heart in my throat.

Back at home, I reveled in the quiet, making myself a second coffee and settling in to finish a piece on the best ads on Instagram. I lost myself in the tap-tapping of my keyboard, and before long, it was two o'clock. I submitted a fully edited piece to Jane and slapped my laptop closed to the rumble of my stomach and the ringing of my phone.

It wasn't a number I recognized, and I immediately panicked it might be the school calling about Priscilla. "Hello?"

"Margo!"

The sound of my name spoken in Mick's low, gravelly voice sent a zing down south, a feeling I hadn't had in a long, long time.

"I'm sorry, who is this?" I said, not sure why I was playing dumb.

"Is it okay that I'm calling?" He lowered his voice, probably because it dawned on him that he was calling a married woman.

"Yes," I said, ignoring my original plan to play coy.

"Forgive me for calling, but I wanted to make sure you're okay."

Sitting back in the kitchen chair where I'd been working, I looked out the window and saw the sun shining and thought about going for a walk.

"I'm fine, definitely," I said. "I wasn't even hungover. Wait, that came out wrong. I was heading off to pick up my daughter, so I didn't even drink enough to have to worry about a hangover."

Nervous, I ran my hand under my hair, over my nape where goose bumps were popping up.

"No judgment from me. By the way, it's Mick, in case you still wondered who was calling."

This made me laugh.

"I'd recognize your morning-after voice anywhere," I said, noting it had a hint of flirtation to it.

"So, that's what they're calling it these days?"

"Honestly, I wouldn't know." I felt myself smiling and wondered what the heck I was doing.

"I wasn't asking about your hangover, though," Mick said abruptly. "I meant your wrist. Seemed like you were in a lot of pain, and I wanted to check in. I am a fixer, after all."

"Oh, that. It's fine." I pulled up my sleeve, still able to make out Tommy's fingerprints. Moving it around, I was relieved that it did feel a bit better.

"Good. You know if you need a fixer, I'm your man, right?" he said, and this made me laugh even harder. "Okay, okay, I realize that was cheesy. I was concerned, that's all, and I liked our time together. I'd like to do it again."

"Day drink?" I said, trying to make light of it.

"Day, night, whenever you'd like."

"Oh." I pulled in a breath, unable to say more. Even wordsmiths got tongue-tied at times.

"What are you doing now?" Mick asked.

"Um, I just sent off a piece and was going to think about some lunch."

"Forgive me if this seems too forward, but want to meet up?"

"Uh, are you free?" My mind was such a jumbled mess, I could barely get my tongue to move.

"Actually, I am."

"Okay," I said slowly.

"Okay, you want to meet? Or okay, you're saying good-bye?"

"The first," I said before I changed my mind.

"I'm on the Back Bay. Where are you?"

"Brookline."

"Great. How about the Paula in about forty-five minutes?"

"Okay," I said again. I was so flustered at Mick's call, it seemed to be the only word I could make out.

"See you soon," Mick said, hanging up before I could change my mind.

Taking a sip of my lukewarm coffee, I wondered what I'd just done. Then I was reminded of Tommy and his half-and-half, and decided I was doing what was good for me.

Outside my parked car, I paced left and then right, my ankle boots clomping on the pavement. I should get back in my car and drive away. Walking to the left again, I thought, Why should I leave?

I liked the Paula. The last time I'd been at that restaurant was for a girls-only lunch with some of the other moms. I'd been so happy to be out and included that I'd gone home smiling and nearly floated through the remainder of the day. If I remembered correctly, I even sloughed off Tommy not eating the pasta primavera I'd made him that evening. Instead, he demanded a tuna steak, and I made it without a protest.

I was going to the Paula for a late lunch. How wrong could that be?

It was a bad idea, but like a bowling ball heading down the lane, there was no stopping now.

Beeping the locks on my car, I walked toward the Paula, its bricked-in door frame and shiny glass front beckoning me. The wind swept under my hair, chilling the beads of sweat forming there, and cooling jumbles of hormones I didn't know I had.

"Hi!" For the second time in two days, a perky hostess greeted me.

"Hi," I heard myself saying warmly.

Usually when Tommy and I ate out, he gruffly demanded a quiet table for two or three, his perma-scowl frightening the hostess and eventually the server. It was a delicious freedom to be myself, happy, light, cheery . . . whatever you wanted to label it.

"I'm meeting someone," I told the curvy blonde wearing all black.

"No problem. Did you want to wait at a table or out here?"

As I soaked in the welcoming ambience with Ed Sheeran crooning in the background, I ran my palm over my neck, feeling my pulse throbbing. I tried to speak, but a tremor made its way up my throat, tightening my vocal cords. Swallowing hard, I tried to push aside my anxiety and excitement in equal measure.

"Margo."

Mick's rough voice tickled all my senses before I could answer the hostess. Turning almost too quickly, I was overcome with a bout of lightheadedness.

"Whoa," I whispered, but of course he heard me, taking hold of my elbow.

"You okay?" Mick asked, not releasing me.

When the pads of his fingers singed my skin in a way Tommy's didn't, I instantly realized the difference between pain and burning need.

Closing my eyes for a beat, I reopened them and whispered, "Mick."

He raised an eyebrow and leaned in to speak softly. "Margo, you good?"

Never mind that this whole scene was playing out in the entrance to the Paula. A man who wasn't my husband had his hand on me, which felt absolutely decadent, and I was a second away from fainting in his arms.

"Yes," I said softly, gathering myself, trying to clear the fog in my head and the frog who'd set up residence in my throat. "Sorry about that. I just, I guess I didn't think this through. We're close to my home, and we could see someone I know." With each new word, my voice tightened with increased panic, my initial excitement overtaken by nerves.

Mick nodded. "If anyone asks, I'm a person you're interviewing for . . . what are you writing now?" He slowly released me, making sure I was steady on my feet before backing away a step.

"Fashion Week."

This got me another eyebrow raise. Taking a deep breath for the first time in minutes, I wondered what the hostess was thinking.

"Great. For Fashion Week. I look fashionable, right?"

Standing mere inches from him, I took in his pale blue shirt tucked into suit pants, his sleeves casually rolled up, as well as his designer belt and Ferragamo loafers.

Mick wasn't the epitome of gender-neutral fashion like the story I was covering, but he was delectable and tasteful. But I didn't say either of those things.

Instead, I said, "You'll do."

This time, I got a laugh before he flagged the hostess. "Two, in the back," he said authoritatively.

"Of course." She grabbed two menus and an iPad, then walked us toward the back.

I'd always loved this restaurant. It wasn't anything fancy, a neighborhood watering hole kind of place. A gastropub, they called themselves. Tommy—God, I had to stop thinking about him—thought it was too trendy for him. He preferred old-school Italian or a steakhouse.

"Is this okay?" The hostess directed her question to Mick.

He nodded, signaling for me to sit on the bench along the exposed brick wall. I slid in, watching him take a seat across from me, and wondered for the eighty-ninth time today what I was doing.

Mick Grantham was beyond handsome with dark hair and even darker eyes, a smattering of hair up his muscular forearms. An alpha in gentleman's clothing, or maybe I was a lamb with rose-colored glasses. After all, my decision-making hadn't put me in the best place thus far.

"I assume you've been here?" Mick asked once he was seated.

"I have," I mumbled.

"It's been a favorite of mine since I came to Boston. Gotta admit, any excuse to get over here, I do."

Not sure what to say, I nodded again.

"I moved here about twenty years ago for my first job out of grad school.

Consulting, of course. That's what we all did," he said. "Tired of it pretty quickly, then struck out on my own."

"Where did you do grad school?" I asked. I couldn't believe how easy all of this was feeling, other than the giant elephant sitting in the middle of the table and how heavy my wedding band felt on my finger.

"Wharton," he said like it was nothing.

"Oh."

"Okay, let's do this," Mick said when the server appeared.

"Hi, I'm Zeus. Welcome to the Paula."

"I take it your parents were into mythology?" Mick asked the server, making me smile.

"Greek mythology professors. Believe me, when I was little, I wanted to be Max or Sam, but now it's a real conversation starter, so I don't mind."

"I hear you. My name's McKenzie. My mom thought they were being creative using a last name as a first name. It was too much of a conversation starter in middle school, so I shortened it to Mick."

I smiled during their exchange, pretending like I knew my lunch date's real name was McKenzie when I knew nothing more than he went to Wharton and bought broken companies like the hero in *Pretty Woman*. At least, that's what he claimed to do.

Zeus chuckled, then asked if we wanted any drinks or appetizers while we looked at the menus.

"Drink?" Mick asked me as if day drinking were a regular thing for me or us.

"Uh, Pellegrino?" I said, and Zeus nodded.

"Something stronger when we eat?" Mick asked me.

"Perhaps."

"Pellegrino for the lady, and a Scotch neat for me."

When Zeus hurried off, Mick focused back on me.

"Now, back to what I was saying. Why don't we get the hard talk out of the way, and then go back to the small talk where you tell me where you went to school or grew up. But first, tell me what really happened to your wrist, and why sparks flew when we first sat down next to each other yesterday."

Surprised, I blinked at him. "You're asking a lot."

Mick ran his thumb across his chin, and I bit my lower lip.

"Margo, the tension is running thick between us. I had to call you today, and I'm hoping it wasn't dumb luck you wanted to see me too."

A knot of conflicted feelings and emotions settled in my belly, and I glanced around for Zeus, wanting my sparkling water to help settle it. He was nowhere to be seen, so I turned back to Mick, forced to acknowledge his question.

"Honestly, it was a bit of dumb luck. He's . . . I mean, my husband's out of town for the evening and my daughter is sleeping at a friend's house, which is an unusual opportunity for me to be all alone."

Mick's impossibly dark eyes darkened even further. "Your husband's the one responsible for the wrist."

"Cut right to the chase, don't you?" This time I raised an eyebrow. Annoyed, I shoved my hair behind my neck, my curls frizzing more by the minute.

"I don't think it was your daughter—"

"Priscilla? No, never. She's a doll," I said quickly as Zeus returned with our drinks. When he sat my Pellegrino before me in a glass, I gulped a big sip and wondered why I didn't go for some liquid courage. Noticing Mick waiting patiently, I simply said, "My husband isn't a kind man."

Mick placed his tumbler back on the table and leaned forward. "No, he's not. Look, you tell me as much or as little as you want for now. We can't deny there was something there when we met, and I know better than anyone that you need to get out of the mess you're in . . . the sooner the better."

"You're certainly a wise one?" I ended my statement with my voice tilted up, making it more like a question, but he wasn't wrong. The problem was, I didn't know how to extricate myself from my husband. It was an impossible situation.

Mick took a sip of his Scotch, closing his eyes for a second before meeting my gaze again. "My mom, she had a tough life. Tiny apartment in Brooklyn, worked all day to support my freeloading father. Instead of rubbing her feet when she came home from working retail, he broke bones or gave her bruises."

"Oh, I'm sorry."

"I took care of him in the end. As soon as my testosterone kicked in, I met him outside the apartment as he was coming home one day. I had a friend's dad who was a cop waiting on the corner. Told him if he didn't leave and promise to never come back, I was bringing the policeman home for dinner and to speak with Mom. The day before my dad had given her a pretty bad shiner, and she'd spent half the morning putting makeup over it. There was no way a cop wouldn't recognize it for what it was."

"That's awful . . . terrible. I'm glad your mom had you to stick up for her."

"That's my sob story. Haven't been able to stomach a weak man ever since."

A stinging formed behind my eyes, and I had to . . . needed to . . . change the subject. After taking another sip of my water, I said, "I'm actually from Marlboro, New Jersey. Went to Temple for school. I'd always hoped to work for the *Times*, but it never happened."

"You've got time to do whatever you want, Margo," Mick said firmly, his dark eyes sparking a glimmer of hope in me that I hadn't known in years.

Picking up my menu, I decided to choose something to eat rather than fill myself on false promises.

Not giving up, Mick said, "You can," but I brushed it off.

"Honestly, I feel lucky to do what I do. I have a good relationship with my editor, I've carved out this little niche for myself, and I have time for Priss. Priscilla. She's twelve, and obviously is the reason I don't want to upset my home."

Somewhat ironic words considering I was sitting across from Mick, a situation that had considerable potential to upset my home.

"It's only lunch," he said, seemingly reading my mind.

I nodded. "I know, and I appreciate your . . ." I searched my scattered brain for the right word. *Interest? No. Flattery? No again.* "Concern."

"I told you my story. You can share more when you want, but until then, let's enjoy each other's company. Now, what are you having?"

He eyed the menu in my hand, my fingers tingling where I was gripping the flimsy thing too hard.

"I love the arugula salad, but I also like the fries. Maybe love them more," I said truthfully. I didn't think there was any point in hiding anything since Mick appeared to be able to read my thoughts.

Zeus returned to take our orders, and Mick asked for an order of fries along with his turkey BLT and my arugula salad.

"Thank you," I told him.

"Hey, if fries are your thing, no reason to deny yourself."

We chatted a little more about his time at Wharton, how proud his mom would have been if she were alive. She'd passed away when he was in his last year of undergraduate at Fordham. Breast cancer.

"Those guys were so pretentious," he said about his classmates, "attending school on their daddy's money. Then there was me, hungry as hell. My applications for internships were always the first ones in, while my classmates were off skiing or whatever the fuck they did."

"I get it. When I was at Temple, there were a bunch of kids who couldn't get in anywhere else. They spent their parents' money and had a good time with not much to show for it at the end of four years. That's how I met Tommy," I said without thinking, and nearly bit my tongue on saying his name.

"Don't be afraid to share," Mick said. "I know what the score is. He's got you. You have a family with him." He tried to school his tone, but the disdain leaked through his words.

"We met at a study session. An English Lit class. It was part of my major, and he was taking it as a gen ed credit. We rolled our eyes at the general lack of respect most of the students had. The rest is history. Our first date turned into dating, and then living together while he went to law school. We got married the summer of his first job, and Priscilla came pretty soon after that."

Mick gave me a nod, not only listening with his ears but his eyes too. He seemed to absorb all of me. After more than a decade of being ignored, it was incredibly validating.

"Tell me, when were you going to mention your real name is McKenzie?" I asked, trying to lighten the mood.

"I was saving that for a later time, but Zeus made that hard to do."

Our food arrived, and Mick and I ate over shared laughs and the smell of salty fries, our fingers brushing when we went to take one and dip into the ketchup.

"What are we doing?" I asked, not really wanting to know. I'd been looking for a life preserver and felt like I'd found a raft with a hole in it.

"We're having lunch," Mick said simply. "I'm not going to deny something clicked between the two of us, but you have your commitments, and I'm not going to push you."

Another round of nodding on my part and we were back to small talk.

"So, tell me why you have so much time to goof around and day drink these days?" I asked, wondering if what he told me about his business endeavor was really true.

"I just signed paperwork on a company. Right now, their current leadership finishes up tasks and helps me clean house, so I have some time to myself before the messy part really begins."

"Oh. That's a far cry from me sitting at home in my kitchen on my laptop."

"Never," he said somewhat forcefully. "You create something from the ground up with your words, and I rebuild something that someone else already envisioned."

Desperate to argue the point, I wanted to contradict what he was saying, but was also inclined to drink up the compliment. My well of compliments had long since run dry, leaving me parched and dehydrated.

Sensing my inner debate, Mick said, "Don't try to argue with me. I'll win this round. You're the creator, and I'm the re-doer."

"That's very nice of you, but—"

"No buts. Now that you ate, how about that drink?"

"I don't know," I said honestly.

"No pressure, but you did say you have an evening to yourself—"

"You know what? I'd like a glass of wine. Here. What I mean is with company, not home by myself." A little rattled, I grabbed the drink menu without looking at Mick.

Sensing my apprehension, or perhaps his own, Mick turned and looked for Zeus, waving him over.

"Do you know what you would like?" Mick turned to me, and I pointed to the house sauvignon blanc for Zeus.

Mick said, "Make it two," without looking at my choice, and Zeus was off again.

Smoothing my sweaty palms across the napkin in my lap, I looked up from my empty plate, the salt from the fries still tingling in my mouth. "Two days in a row day drinking. I'm going to be transparent because I don't want you to think I'm morally bankrupt."

"Hardly," Mick said. "I'm the one who should be ashamed. When sparks obviously flowed between us yesterday, I told myself to ignore it. Hell, there are plenty of fish in the sea, right? Ones who aren't married."

"There it is. The word we've been avoiding. Married."

"For the record, I decided to let you move on, until the wrist thing. It bugged me all night because I knew . . . I knew where that came from and where it was going."

"Not necessarily," I said, sitting up straighter.

Mick didn't get a chance for his rebuttal because Zeus showed up with our wines. Once I had the stem in my hand and almost a sip on my lips, Mick raised his glass.

"To a better ending for you."

I guessed that was his rebuttal, and a large part of me wanted to believe it was possible. Despite my arguments, he was right. My marriage wasn't going somewhere good.

"Well, between the day drinking and being a mom and the marriage thing, I still want you to know I have a moral compass. Drinking isn't something I do regularly. Yes, I like to be included in the occasional girls' night out, and when my sorority sister Tammy comes to town, we go out. But the other—meeting men and spending time with them—I've never done that."

"Margo, I don't think you're morally bankrupt. First, I think you're gorgeous. Seriously stunning. Of course, attraction always catches the eye. But five minutes into talking with you, and I knew you have a better soul than most. You try to tamp it down, but you can't avoid it shining through."

My heart pounded harder with every word. Tommy never told me I was pretty, let alone stunning, but that wasn't it. It was the way Mick saw through my facade, clear through my shell and straight to my soul.

He leaned a little closer across the table so his words would wind their way to only me. "Then there's your passion for your writing, and it's clear you love your daughter more than I could comprehend. I'm thinking that's only the beginning of where your beauty begins."

"Mick," I said softly, his name a shallow whisper. "I can't. This is too much."

"It's just lunch." He turned the tables on me, easily shifting the mood and not expecting compliments in return.

"A good lunch," I said, and it was.

"One of the best I've ever had."

I took another sip of wine, then tilted my head. "As a side note, where did you get the Margo from?"

Leaning back in his chair, Mick smiled. "That's not your nickname? I could've sworn you're more Margo than Margaret."

I sat down my glass, not meeting his eyes. "It was . . . a long time ago."

"I'll tell you why it suits you." He paused until I met his gaze. "Because when you smile, it's way too bright and energetic for Margaret. You're a Margo, lighting up a room, plain and simple. But for the record, I don't think there's anything plain and simple about you."

I quickly downed my wine, leaving only a few sips. I wasn't sure how much longer I could linger at this lunch without my heart bursting and my mind going to mush. Spending time with Mick's compliments pouring like lava from a volcano was surely a way to get burned.

"So, your daughter. Does she look like you?" he asked, changing the direction again, keeping me off-kilter.

"She does. Although not quite as fair. She's such a sweetie and smart. I know Priscilla seems like an uppity name, but she's named for my grandmother."

Mick ran a hand through his hair, and for a moment, I allowed myself to pretend it was my hand. Still justifying to myself I wasn't doing anything wrong by having lunch and chatting about my daughter—and accepting overblown compliments—I forgave myself for the fantasy.

"Must be such an honor. I can tell you loved your grandma from your smile."

I swallowed. This wasn't where I wanted the conversation to go.

"I was closer to her than my with my own mom. Our relationship is . . . difficult."

When I didn't continue, Mick deftly smoothed out my discomfort. "She must have been amazing. Priscilla, that is."

Oh, Mick, Mick, Mick. Where were you fifteen years ago?

He was probably having fun like most twenty-somethings. Only I shacked up with my college sweetheart and then got married.

"How old are you?" I blurted, then my cheeks flamed. "Oh God, that was so rude."

Laughing, Mick shook his head. "Hey, we're beyond that. We've already traded all kinds of secrets. I'm forty."

"Oh," popped out of my mouth.

"Young to be where I am," he said, "but not without sacrifice, which is why I'm single. There's nothing wrong with me . . . I just focused on making money. Sounds kind of selfish, but when you grow up like I did . . ."

"It's not. That's not what I was getting at. Seriously, I wasn't insinuating that," I said, stumbling over my words. I'd made Mick feel less than, and no one knew better than me what less than felt like.

"Hey, don't go overthinking it. I know you didn't mean anything. I wanted to put it out there, that's all."

"Thirty-seven," I blurted.

"You didn't have to return the favor," Mick said with a wink.

"It was only fair."

"If you didn't claim to have a twelve-year-old daughter, I wouldn't have guessed it."

This made me giggle like a schoolgirl, or maybe it was the wine. My brain told me to get the hell out of there quickly, but instead, I just grinned at him.

As I finished the last dregs of my wine, Mick asked, "Another?"

I shook my head. "It does sound fun, but I have an evening of TV waiting for me."

Finally, my mouth and my brain intersected.

"Got it," Mick said, and looked for Zeus.

After the bill was settled, I stood, and Mick waited for me to walk out first. I felt his gaze on my ass as I made my way out of the restaurant. Normally, that would have made me uncomfortable. Probably because Tommy would have noticed, and I would have paid for it later.

"Walk you to your car?" Mick asked, interrupting my crazy train of thought.

I nodded, afraid of what would come out of my mouth.

"Lead the way," he said, and I did, around the corner to the side street where I'd parked for free.

"Here I am," I said in front of my Volvo SUV. Of course, only the safest car on the road was good enough for Tommy's wife. Ironic, considering the least safe place I ever went was home.

"This was fun. No pressure, but I'm here if you need me, Margo."

Mick's voice was low, his dark eyes drawing me in. I had to force myself not to step closer.

"It was, but . . ."

Mick reached for me. "Leave the buts for another time. I get it."

Leaning in, he brushed his lips across my cheek. Sparks lit up over my skin and back again as his mouth pressed light kisses there.

"Leave the buts," he whispered again before giving my shoulder a light squeeze. "Get in the car."

Stunned, I choked out, "Thanks," and then scooted in.

With Mick's warm gaze still on me, I closed the door, trying to convince myself that it was not only closing on the car, but on whatever this was between us.

three

margaret

Priscilla was all smiles when I picked her up from soccer the afternoon after her sleepover.

"We made s'mores in their firepit. It was so much fun!" she said excitedly. "We should get one. You just flip a switch and voilà, fire. I could use it myself, and then I could have everyone over."

I smiled, loving it when Priscilla rambled happily. Apparently, the sleepover was a huge success, and now all the girls wanted to make s'mores at home. I yearned for the days when such a simple pleasure resulted in so much satisfaction.

"I'll look into it," I said, glancing over my shoulder before pulling my SUV into traffic.

"How was your night? Were you lonely?" she asked, her mood turning somber as she stared at my profile from the passenger seat.

"No," I said a bit too quickly. "I had some wine and watched TV. I'm all caught up on my Netflix show."

"Oh, good, now you can watch something with me."

I didn't deserve her giant heart, for sure.

"No vampires," I said, glancing at her.

"Mom, seriously, vampire shows are the best kind of TV."

This made me laugh. "I'll take your word on that."

"I should've checked to see if Dad was going to be gone, and then I wouldn't have left," Priscilla said, retying her hair in a messy bun.

"It's okay, sweetie, really. I was fine."

"Oh." She jumped a little in her seat, making her bun bounce. "Mrs. Alexander said they're going to the Paula next week, on Tuesday for some meeting . . . you should be there. Six thirty, okay?"

"Parents' association. Probably about the holiday fundraiser."

"That's right. She said for you to call her if you need any more information."

I nodded and made a mental note. Typically, I was hit or miss on participating in these things, but after the small taste of a good time I had yesterday, I wanted to go out again. Anywhere was fine.

"What's for dinner?" Priscilla asked, cutting into my inner monologue.

"Chicken tortilla soup," I said, knowing this would get a reaction.

"My favorite. Yes!" She squealed, pumping her fist into the air, and went back to her phone.

A few minutes later, she looked up. "Did you make something else for Dad? He doesn't like the soup."

"Yep." I tried to push Priscilla's observation out of my mind, but it was hard. "Steak. I picked up a few steaks to grill too."

"Oh, good."

When we got home, she went to study for a test, and I finished up a few paragraphs in an upcoming article on makeup influencers.

My laptop closed, I chopped some veggies for a salad and roasted a few potatoes to go with Tommy's steak. He'd be home early around six for us to eat dinner as a family. His secretary had texted me the details.

Swallowing my pride, I tried to think about how that must have made Mallory feel. I mean, she basically was tasked with texting me to jump, and she must know I immediately went into "how high" mode.

The oven beeped, bringing me back to the task at hand.

I popped in the potatoes and veggies and stirred the soup in the Crock-Pot, enjoying the scent of the fresh tomatoes and cilantro. The soup was damn good, but the one time I'd dared to serve it to Tommy, he got up from the table and went to the bar at Morton's.

Checking the fridge, I noted the sour cream on the top shelf for Priscilla, and grated a little extra Monterey Jack for on top of mine. Slipping my grated cheese back in the fridge, I thought about a glass of wine but then reconsidered. It was best to have all my faculties when Tommy was home.

"Ouch," I said under my breath as I clipped my hip on the back door as I went out to the deck to light the grill. I already had enough bumps and bruises; there was no need to add more.

Standing outside, I looked around and thought about how seldom Priscilla had friends over, and how much she loved going to her friends' houses. Maybe I hadn't protected her as much as I thought I had.

She poked her head outside the back door. "Mom?"

"Yes, my beautiful angel?" My heart ached as I answered.

"What was the first article you ever wrote?"

"Why?"

"I'm writing a paper on you, why else?"

"Me?"

"Yes, Mom, you. Now, what was the first article?" She stood poised with her phone, ready to tap in Notes. Long gone were the days of actually taking notes in a notebook.

"Walk with me while I get Dad's steak," I said, knowing we could get lost in conversation, which I also knew would be bad for me. "It was a total fluff-meets-history piece, but I was so proud of it."

I couldn't help the laugh that escaped me.

"Your dad and I were still living in Philadelphia, and I got a gig writing for the *Philly Mag*. It was mostly fancy pics of restaurants and shops, movie reviews, and sights to see around town. My first article was on the little shops of Rittenhouse Square and their legacies."

"Oh, so did you interview people or visit the stores?"

I walked back toward the yard and grill, spraying some non-stick spray on the grates and slapping the steaks down. Glancing at my watch, I breathed a sigh of relief. I was on time.

"I did visit a number of stores and interviewed some of the apartment dwellers around there, asking where they shopped. I also noted if they mentioned if it had changed over the years."

"Did you like it? Did you know right away you were happy?" Priscilla leaned into the back door, waiting for me to answer.

"I loved stringing words together and the connections I made. I'd hoped to write more news or current events, but as time went on and I started writing about lifestyle and different marketing tactics, I realized it was a sweet spot for me. Who knew all this social media would really hit, and I would be in the right niche?"

"So cool."

"I don't know about that, but things happen for a reason. I'm lucky to do what I like and have a chance to keep doing it."

"Thanks." She tapped away at her phone, presumably entering my quotes.

I flipped the steaks. "Go wash up. We're going to eat in a few."

As I ran in to check on everything else, I wondered what dinnertime was like at the other houses Priscilla visited. Was it calm? Easy? Fun?

I was in the middle of tossing a small salad and was about to drizzle some olive oil over asparagus when the front door opened.

"Hey, I'm home." Tommy greeted me in the kitchen, expecting me to look up at the sound of his commanding voice.

"Successful trip?" I asked out of habit.

"Very. I think I'll have a cigar later to celebrate."

"Nice," I said evenly, but inside I shuddered. Cigar meant booze, and booze always resulted in increased anger.

There wasn't time to dwell on it, though, because Priscilla walked in.

"I'm starving," she said before noticing Tommy. "Hi, Dad," she said, and then started setting the table.

"It's all ready." I forced a smile as I grabbed the tongs. "I'll go get your steak while you clean up."

"I'm not a little boy." Tommy side-eyed me before glancing at Priscilla. "Did you wash your hands before doing that?"

"Of course," she said, and for the first time in forever, I worried for her safety. A curt answer that could be misconstrued as flippant would never fly with Tommy.

"Let's all sit down and eat," I said quickly, trying to smooth things over before slipping out to the grill, mourning the firepit we'd never have and the friends who would never come over to enjoy it with us.

With his steak and sides in front of him, Tommy focused on eating while saying very little. When he did speak, it was mostly bragging about his deposition skills. He did take a moment to ask Priscilla if she was starting in her upcoming soccer game. She was, and he said he would think about coming.

"I love this soup," Priscilla told me, wearing a smile just for me, and at the moment it felt like enough. Then she cleared her plates and went to her room to FaceTime friends and do whatever middle-school girls do.

"Work is really picking up, which is a good thing," Tommy said, clipping his cigar and after pouring himself a Dewar's. "We have some major expenses at the firm, and of course, Priscilla's tuition and all the mandatory donations that come along with it."

Finished cleaning up, I set aside the kitchen towel and wrung my idle hands.

Tommy came close, his alcohol-laden breath ghosting my cheek when he whispered in my ear, "Don't look stunned, Margaret. This fancy little stay-at-home writer thing doesn't come for free."

"I work," I managed to croak out.

"You don't really work. You type out some drivel, and they fill space with it."

Leaning back into the quartz counter, ignoring its bite into my back, I felt the need to stick up for myself. "I wanted to do more. I could do more."

Tommy pulled back a little, narrowing his beady eyes on me. "You will not. Not my wife. I allow you this hobby, but that's it."

Of course, I wanted to argue more, but there was no point. How could I win an argument with a lawyer? Although he considered my writing a hobby, I thought of it as my lifeline.

"Don't think too hard." Tommy gripped my shoulder, his fingers digging painfully into my skin. "I pay for you to do this. Period. Make me look good. Got it?"

He leaned close and his teeth scraped my neck, making their way to my nape. There, he bit down just hard enough to cause pain but not hard enough to break the skin.

It was a sign of dominance he'd done before. The first time, I'd mistaken it for a sexual move until he explained he was letting me know who was boss.

As if I could forget.

four

margaret

The Paula now held a special place in my heart, so I couldn't help the smile spreading across my face as I walked inside to meet Sheila Alexander and the rest of the barracudas. Even the impending craziness couldn't dampen my spirit.

I hadn't reached out to Mick, and he hadn't either, but one lunch was enough of a good time to keep my heart beating.

As for the Spring Hill Parents' Association, it was one of those members-only clubs where you were either in or out. It was no accident I was in. Tommy was a well-established attorney with his name on billboards, and a wood-paneled office downtown. He might have told me he didn't like the private school, but he donated money and liked seeing his name on the wall of fame.

His name, not mine. My name was only on the list of parent volunteers who made everything happen.

Since Sheila had taken over, what happened at parent meetings, stayed at parent meetings. Prior to it becoming the Sin City of parents' associations, there were a lot of information leaks and rumors, which always ended up sabotaging the gossips. I knew what happened inside the four walls of the Paula tonight was top secret. Strangely enough, I had practice in this from my home life and their beloved benefactor Tommy.

Noting I was a little early, I chalked it up to being excited to get out, and shrugged off any other reason—like avoiding Tommy. I'd conveniently sent him a text stating I had a school meeting and would be late. He replied all too eagerly that he would grab a steak and cocktail downtown with another partner.

With time and newfound freedom on my side, I decided to grab an appetizer and a glass of wine at the bar. Settled in with my provisions, I reviewed some notes on my phone for the fashion piece. There was an Israeli designer by the name Rinat Brodach that I wanted to reach out to.

"It must be my lucky night."

Mick's husky voice surprised me, hitting all the right switches and buttons that, quite frankly, I didn't know existed. Of course, there was no reason to look up and see who it was. I knew immediately who was looming over my chardonnay and me.

"There you go again with your effortless pick-up lines. Maybe you should come up with some better material on your own?" I served up a sarcastic reply, raising my head slowly to meet his dark eyes.

Mick's hair was as unkempt as the first time I saw him, his five o'clock shadow a touch darker and his brow a tiny bit creased. But all of it had an even more profound effect on my heart rate.

"You may be right," he said, sliding in next to me. "But, remember, it's been a hard week for me. Give a guy a break, yeah?"

His New York roots seeped through in how he pronounced *hard*, bringing out the warm fuzzies I hadn't known lived inside me. The last complication I needed in my life was a side relationship, yet I welcomed every distraction this man brought with him.

"Tell you what," I said instead of backing off. "Let me get you a drink tonight. How's that for some empathy?"

"It's a nice offer, but I'll get the drinks, if you don't mind."

Mick's hair was a wilder mess than usual tonight, and my fingers twitched to comb through it. Trying to control myself, I ran them through my own loose locks. The blown-out waves fell loosely around my face, providing a bit of a veil for the emotions I couldn't hide.

"We have an old-fashioned gentleman in the house, folks," I said in a hushed tone, but with a nip of humor and raised eyebrows. I already had that make and model, and I wasn't impressed with it.

"My momma raised me right, so pipe down, Margo."

There he went again with the nickname he'd given me within minutes of our first meeting. No one had ever done that for me—ever.

He motioned to the bartender and ordered a Scotch neat, then asked me if I wanted another.

"No, thanks," I whispered.

"Give me the tab," he told the bartender.

"Do I have any say in the matter?" I asked.

"No," he said matter-of-factly as his drink arrived.

I took a sip of my wine. "So, back at the Paula?"

Mick nodded. "I am. Got tired of the country club scene. Golf is boring as shit, and so is sitting around in those damn polo shirts. I had a tournament over the weekend, and by the end, I lost on purpose to get it over with. And you? Why are you back so soon?"

Studying him for a moment, I couldn't figure out if he was here to just be here, or if he was looking for me.

"A little of both," he said.

"Wait? Did I say that aloud?"

"No, but you're easy to read. I was reminded how much I love it here the other day, and I was also trying to be good, not reaching out. But if I ran into you . . . that's a different story."

"Let's see, equal parts liking the food and stalking? Am I right?"

When I noticed my armpits tingling with sweat, I tried not to wince. I'd never flirted like this.

"Oh shit." This time, my thoughts floated from my mouth as I saw Sheila walk in.

"Everything okay?" Mick was half turned in his seat, looking at me.

"Turn away, face the bar." I'm not sure what made me say it. Instinct, probably. When Mick did as I asked, I muttered, "Thanks."

After a sip of wine, I whispered, "I'm here for a parents' meeting. You know, socialite moms with big mouths?"

He nodded as if he did, but I didn't believe him.

"I'm going to slip away," I said, grabbing my purse as I slid from my seat. "Thanks for the wine."

Mick spoke low enough so one else could hear, his gaze still on the bar. "Have a good meeting. I'll be right here when you're done, and the socialites leave."

"I—"

"Go," he said, interrupting my protest, and I did.

"Thanks for coming tonight. We'll see everyone in two weeks, and please bring your list of potential donors," Sheila said as the meeting adjourned.

Sadly, I couldn't remember a word she'd said between the time I sat down and now. My brain pounded with Mick's looming presence radiating from the back of the restaurant.

Both too fearful and smart to turn around, I let the heat of him being there, breathing there, existing there, scald my back, but I remained still, focusing on Sheila. As I stood from my seat, she walked my way.

"Margaret, thanks for coming tonight. Priscilla said she would deliver the message." Sheila pulled me into a hug, air kissing both my cheeks as if she were European, and hopefully missed my wince as she gripped my left rib cage a little too tight.

Pulling back, she went on. "She's such a sweetie and so well-mannered, almost afraid to act her age. I wish I could get more of that out of Penny."

"It's an only-child thing," I said, brushing off any hint of what might be happening at my house.

Sheila took my elbow and leaned in. "Listen . . ."

I really wished she would stop touching me. It wasn't welcome—now or ever. I'd endured enough being touched without my permission for a lifetime.

Smiling, she said, "I was hoping you could talk to your magazine about a big sponsorship."

A shudder ran through me. I stayed in my lane when it came to my work, especially with how it set Tommy off. Keeping my head low, I pitched and wrote articles and kept my peace of mind in life. I didn't like to owe anyone any favors, or more than what I already did for keeping me on as I was. If I ended up getting a donation, Tommy would claim his manhood was threatened and potentially threaten my sanity.

"I'd thought Tommy's firm's donation counted for both of us?"

"Of course, of course it does." Smiling smugly in her perfectly snug sweater dress, with her poker-straight red hair and green eyes outlined in chocolate brown, Sheila was the consummate parent representative. "I was hoping for a little more from both of you this year. You know, I really wanted this year to be the best?"

I nodded. "I'm freelance, but I guess I can ask." I don't know why I said it, probably because I wanted to get rid of her, and mostly because Mick was silently beckoning me from the bar area.

"Perfect!" She clapped her hands together and dismissed me.

Unsure what to do, I made my way to the ladies' room, spending some time freshening up and hoping all the ladies were gone by the time I came out.

Pulling in a deep breath, I debated leaving. Priscilla was home alone, a newfound freedom she adored. She made me promise not to rush home, so she could watch the whole movie online while cyber-chatting with Penny. Sheila was probably heading home to be the perfect mom. Tommy had to stay late, dining on steak and smoking cigars with his mentor group. Why shouldn't I enjoy myself?

Drawing in another big breath, I felt a small twinge of pain in my ribs and decided to stay. If I couldn't get out of my shitty life, I should at least have fun for an hour.

"Hey," I whispered softly when I made it back to the bar.

"You survived the moms?" Mick said low, keeping his head facing forward.

"Barely."

"Can I look at you?" he asked, a smile twitching at the corner of his mouth.

"Yes."

Turning toward me, his dark gaze caught me, crinkles in the corners of his eyes that made me want to dive in and feel what he'd felt, live the good times he'd lived.

"That's much better," he said. "Have a seat. If anyone asks, we just met while sitting here."

"Right. I'm an independent woman who can have a drink—"

"So, what will you have?"

"I had a sparkling water at the meeting, so another wine. Two's my limit."

Palms up on the bar, he said, "I'm not judging."

I felt myself smile.

"Chardonnay for the lady," he told the bartender.

I noticed Mick's Scotch was refilled, but he was nursing it.

Once my wine was placed in front of me, Mick raised his glass. "Cheers."

"Back at you," I said.

"Parents' meeting, huh? Fascinating stuff, I'll bet," he said, side-eyeing me.

"Titillating, for sure." I rolled my eyes. "Private school, so it's necessary for my daughter. We're planning the holiday gala."

"Ah, now I understand. A far cry from my little corner school in Brooklyn, but when I was young, I remember all the kids walking around Central Park in uniforms. I'd be there for the zoo, and they were rushing to hockey or something fancy."

"It's a bit off base—okay, far off from the real world—but she's happy and challenged. I want Priss to learn from my mistakes. Be an independent person and have a career, family, all of it. Not broken like me."

I focused on my glass, not having a clue as to why I was opening up like this. In a bar with basically a stranger, a man who wasn't my husband, someone who was quickly becoming a close friend.

Mick nodded, his brow furrowed and eyes squinted as he thought over what I'd said. "You know, I've only known you a short while, but I repair broken things, and I don't think you're broken."

"Maybe at one point I wasn't, but since then . . . whenever that was, I've started to crack."

"Forgive me for saying, but you need to walk away from the defeatist attitude. I see you as a game changer, Margo." He looked deep into my eyes when he said my name, as if he were making sure I truly heard what he'd said.

Sipping my wine, I searched for added courage in the perfectly blown glass. "You know those bookmarks and coffee mugs with inspirational slogans like dream big? Maybe you don't get to Target often, but you get the picture. Aisles of tchotchkes with this slogan on them. Anyway, I was passing through Target one day, getting toilet paper, and I passed a section of all this stuff. Stickers, tumblers, stationery, you name it . . . all marked with dream big, and I thought, why not me? Why can't I dream myself out of this existence?"

Mick nodded but didn't interrupt.

"Then I got home and put away the TP and placed a spare deodorant in the closet for my husband, tossed a box of tampons in my drawer, and placed a little notepad that said dream big on my husband's desk."

Mick opened his mouth to say something, but I held up a hand to stop him.

"For some stupid reason, I thought sharing the sentiment with him would make him understand how I was feeling. That I had dreams and aspirations too, and together we could both have a good life. A big life. How silly of me to think a notepad would help him move forward with me, but it didn't. All it got me was a bruised ass and a broken heart."

Although my last confession was barely a whisper, I still glanced around to make sure no one heard other than Mick. Maybe I was a little hopeful he didn't hear.

He took a long gulp of his Scotch and swallowed. Running a hand through his hair, he turned to face me, a raging fire in his eyes. For a second, I thought the intense emotion was directed at me.

"For the record," he said, "I know what I'm about to say is overstepping, but I don't give a shit. I should also say if we weren't here at this bar, I'd pull you into my arms and hold you tight while I told you that you're worth something better. Not only something or someone more decent than what you landed, but someone who would light a fire under you. I can tell you after knowing you for five minutes that your passion is meant to be big. You were put here to do something huge. The drive burns right through you. It radiates through your whole being."

Drinking in his heartfelt inspiring words, I could feel my own heart beating a furious accompaniment to them. "Mick . . ."

"Don't ruin this," he said curtly. "Finish your wine and go home. Be safe and dream big. Always. Do it for me. Do it for you. Just do it."

He turned and finished his Scotch, then tugged a black Amex card out of his wallet and tossed it on the bar.

Apparently, the conversation was over before it started, and I found myself furious. This was my escape. My turn to be in charge. How dare he shut down the conversation just like that?

Fuming, I stood, yanked my purse strap over my shoulder, and turned to go without a word.

It was only when I got to my car that the tears came. I took my time going home to be sure they were good and gone before I walked into my reality—the opposite of anything Dream Big.

five

margaret

The house was quiet when I got home that night after the meeting. Padding down the hall, allowing my fuming mood to cool, I decided it was for the best. Mick didn't need to be saddled with my broken life. He already put broken businesses back together.

Seeing the light on underneath Priscilla's door, I decided to put my own life together.

"Hi," I said, peeking inside Priscilla's lavender-painted room, boy-band posters lining the wall opposite the bed, and a poster of the Eiffel Tower above her.

I'd always thought staying with Tommy was more important than my mental and physical health. If I left him, we'd probably have to move, and Priscilla would have to sacrifice this room, this bright and airy space. But maybe not. Maybe Priscilla would be happier where she could have friends come over.

Tucked into bed with a book, Priscilla looked up. "Hey, how was the meeting? Boring?"

I laughed a little. I couldn't admit to her that I couldn't recall a second of the meeting, and I certainly couldn't tell her what I was really up to. Despite the

44

way the evening ended, I had fun.

"It was actually nice. Good to see people and be a part of something," I said, trying to describe how I was really feeling as close as I could.

"Oh," she said with a grin. "That's good."

"How was the movie? What are you up to now?" I asked, taking in her rosy cheeks and braided hair.

"It was great. No vampires. Reading something for school," she said, responding in typical teen fragments. Then frowning, she looked away. "Mom . . ."

"Yes?" I motioned toward the edge of the bed, asking with my eyes if I could sit.

"I had to go into your room. Dad wasn't home, so I thought it would be okay. I know he doesn't like me to snoop."

"Oh, what happened, sweetie?"

"Nothing, really." She sat her book down next to her. "I got my period."

My heart nearly exploded. My daughter got her first period, and I was out flirting with a strange man? If I could call myself a heartless bitch, I would.

"Mom, seriously, it's okay. I know all about them. It's all Melody Roberts talks about, and we had a class at school."

"Oh. But did you know how to—"

"Yes. Melody actually demonstrated to all of us."

I couldn't help my nose scrunching up. I felt it wrinkle, and immediately tried to school it.

"Not like that." Priscilla sat up straight. "She used her hand in a weird way."

"Gotcha," I said, stroking her blanket-covered leg. "We used to teach each other how to take our bra off without taking our shirt off. Things have come a long way."

Priscilla laughed. "Anyway, if you saw anything out of place, I was under your sink taking some tampons, but I'll need some of my own."

A chill ran down my spine, all the way to my ankles. "Sweetie, I don't get upset over messes. It doesn't matter to me." I hesitated to say what I was thinking, but then let it fly. "I'm not Dad."

"I know," she said, her jaw firm.

"I'll stop tomorrow and pick up some supplies for your bathroom. Do you have any questions for me? Do you want me to go over how to use the tampon again?"

She shook her head. "I know how. I'm a woman, like you always told me when we went to the bathroom together when I was little. I'd ask what you were doing, and you'd say when I was a woman, I'd know. Also, like I said, we have class at school with Mrs. Roth."

I smiled, but my chest burned with a healthy dose of love and admiration for this human being I helped to create and mold.

She is a golden cloud among all the dark ones in the sky.

"Mom, don't cry." Priscilla leaned forward and hugged me.

I hadn't even realized I was tearing up.

"Okay, baby, okay," I murmured into her beautiful head of curls, silently promising to put myself back together for her.

"Love you," she said, and I knew I was being dismissed.

"Love you more," I whispered back into her hair.

Shutting her door softly, I floated toward my room, knowing Tommy wasn't home yet. I couldn't even pretend to be upset he wasn't here for the period moment. It certainly wasn't something he would understand or be compassionate about.

Heading to the bathroom, I checked for any messes Priscilla might have left. Of course, nothing was out of place except for our combined mental status.

My daughter shouldn't be afraid to grab a tampon in her own home, I thought as I stepped into the shower. Scrubbing off the day and the bad residue Mick left on my mood, I made a firm decision for the sake of my daughter.

I needed to see what was out there other than my Tommy-ruled world.

"Hi, Sheila, it's Margaret," I said to her when she picked up the phone much later the following day.

"Hi, Margaret, everything okay? Penny mentioned something this morning about the girls planning another sleepover this coming weekend. I'm happy to host, as usual."

Running my hand through my loose hair, I leaned back, allowing the sun to hit my face. I'd been sitting in the yard, making some notes for an upcoming piece.

"No, nothing like that. Although, I'm happy to host. In fact, Tommy is going to Miami on Saturday for a lawyers' convention, but that's not why I'm calling. I spoke to my editor this morning, and the magazine is happy to be a partner for the gala. In fact, they want to send magazines for all the attendees, in addition to making a donation."

"Really? That's fabulous," Sheila said, and I could practically hear her brain working over the line. "Magazines, hmm. We could do an awards-style grab bag with a few items. I wonder if you would like to secure some items? Off the top of my head, things like candles, cupcakes, maybe a little throw pillow . . . you know, like they give at the Grammys. This is simply perfect with the theme being Hollywood Holidays."

She asked how much the magazine was donating, and when I told her, she sounded impressed. Next thing I knew, she told me she was putting the magazine's name on the banner. What she didn't know was I told Jane, my editor, how the marketing mogul Ezra Paul was a parent at the school, and they decided to jump through every hoop possible to get to him. Jane even pulled some rank in expediting approval.

"You know what? Let's grab coffee. How's Monday? Then we can flush out this grab bag idea. Sound good?"

"Sure," I said, knowing the coffee would be an approved outing for me.

"How about that little place over by the school? The one with the gluten-free muffins? Right after drop-off?"

"The Bean Stop?"

"That's it."

"I'll be there. Talk later," I said, ending the call before I backed out. Branching out and living life was on my to-do list. If working with Sheila was how I started, then that's how it would be.

Closing my eyes, I let the sunshine pour over on me, warming me and making me feel alive before Tommy came home and black clouds filled the house.

I wasn't sure how long I'd been sitting like that when my phone rang. Without looking at caller ID, I slid my finger across the screen. "Hello?"

"Margo—"

As soon as I heard his voice, I wanted to hit disconnect. "Mick—"

"No, please don't say anything. I owe you an apology. Is this okay, my calling?"

Inhaling harshly, I said, "If you mean to ask if I'm alone, I am. If you mean because you were rude last night, then no. I'm not sure what I did, but I didn't deserve that from you."

"So, she's got a little bite to go along with her bark. I knew I liked you, Margo."

"Mick, seriously. What do you want? I appreciate the compliments, but I hardly think a few drinks and a lunch warrant this amount of introspection."

I spoke my mind to Mick in a way I never would have dreamed of talking to Tommy. Okay, maybe I did once or twice when we were dating, but we'd quickly fallen into the routine of him demanding and me acquiescing.

Mick chuckled. "I'm just kidding about the bite, but I do like it. You should never let anyone make you feel bad about yourself, which is why I'm calling. I did a bang-up job last night of mucking things up."

Standing, I paced, holding the phone to my ear. "Listen, I'm going to be brutally honest since you seem to be familiar with the type of domestic situation I'm in. I don't do this. Extracurricular relationships, I mean. I take care of my daughter and keep my head down, but that's changing. I'm going to start taking care of me. I apologize if I used you to figure that out—"

"Don't ever apologize for saying you're going to put yourself first. I'm fucking ecstatic to hear it, and I want to see it."

"That's the thing. I'm not sure that's a good idea."

"I know. That's why I'm calling to apologize and say I won't do anything like that again. I like you, Margo, and I'm going to wait for you to straighten things out."

Swallowing some unidentified emotion, I fumbled over my words. "Mick . . . that's not what you should do. Or what you deserve."

"Tell me, when is the next time you can escape for a cocktail or coffee? Casual. No expectations."

I wanted to shout *Saturday*, but instead, I said, "I'll have to see."

"Fair enough. Do you want to text me when you know?"

"Okay," I said, giving in without much argument.

I'd never been apologized to before. Fifteen years with Tommy, and he'd never said he was sorry. He'd often said *it's a new day* and *we'll figure it out*, but never *I'm sorry*.

"I'll be waiting," Mick said, drawing me out of the dark and into the light. "One more thing. If we can find a quiet corner, I'd like to lean in and whisper how stunning you are into your ear while nibbling on your earlobe. They would be words just for you, and you would tumble into me, running your lips along my neck until our mouths met."

Such simple words, nothing special or out of the ordinary. A PG fantasy, likely stolen from a made-for-TV movie.

Yet, I could almost feel Mick leaning close and whispering words to me I'd never heard before. Shivers ran down my spine and gooseflesh broke out under my silk blouse. I imagined how his lips might feel, tickling my earlobe.

To say my few minutes of resolve were wrecked would be putting it lightly. It had been a while since I'd had companionship, let alone affection.

"You know the ears and the nape of the neck are both sensitive areas with hundreds of sensory receptors, right?" Mick asked.

"I can imagine," I said.

"But I'm guessing you don't know firsthand?"

"How did the conversation end up here?" I plopped back down in the chair, trying to control my breathing.

If we were in a boxing ring, I'd throw in the towel.

"Wouldn't you like to know? Because I can't stop thinking about you," Mick told me.

I'd never admit to falling down this rabbit hole to him, but I was a complete Alice in this situation.

Speechless, I could only say, "Oh."

"I'd like to try," he said matter-of-factly, and sweat beaded at the nape of my neck.

Not quick enough with a comeback, I took a deep gulp of air and hoped for a rapid change of subject. It was obvious my big-ass she-boss attitude was a farce.

Seeming to sense I was freaking out, Mick said, "Don't worry, I'm going to wait for you to tell me you're ready."

"Let's stick with coffee, so you don't over-flatter yourself," I shot back, swiping my hair to one side, hoping my neck would cool. My cheeks were probably flushed and red.

"Believe me, this little chat is nothing. When you really come undone with me, Margo, you'll finally be free of all the dead weight you carry around with you. I'll take coffee. To start. But—and this is a big but—rest assured that I plan to take you apart and put you back together again."

Closing my eyes for a second, I swallowed, almost feeling his gaze on me despite him being on the phone. I bit my lip and quickly stopped fantasizing.

"Let me know," Mick said, and the line went dead as if we hadn't just lit the phone and my backyard on fire with our words.

"Sure," I said softly to myself.

As I stared out into space, my alarm went off, alerting me to pick up Priscilla. It was a very welcome diversion from the strange combo of guilt and giddiness filling my heart.

six

mick

Sitting astride my Peloton bike, pedaling toward a personal record, I alternated between looking at the instructor on the screen and glancing at the view of the Back Bay.

Of course, I lived in the largest unit in my building—the penthouse with the best views—because that's what little boys who grew up in shitty row houses did. We strived to live better, to make more money, to provide even more to those we loved, and to throw all that shit back in everyone's faces.

Problem was, I'd worked too damn hard and had too little time over the years for personal connections. Or maybe I hadn't found the right woman to enjoy life with by my side?

Lately, I'd been spending an inordinate amount of time thinking about my past, present, and future. I'd worked my ass to the bone, building my reputation and my company. When businesses were in trouble, they came to me.

So what if my mom had watched *Pretty Woman* so many freaking times that I identified with Richard Gere's character? Although, I'd never admit that to anyone.

"Ten, nine, eight, seven, six, five, four, three, two, one, and we are in a descending recovery," my adorably peppy, non-sweating instructor shouted at me.

I turned the resistance down and saw I'd come in twenty points higher than usual. Better I take my tension out on the bike than out in the world. Not that I'd ever be violent. I'd seen enough of that to make my stomach turn while growing up.

Of course, this led me to think about Margo as I unclipped and swung my leg behind me, forcing my other foot to unclip.

Wiping my face with a towel, I wondered why I was so hung up on her. She was married, for fuck's sake. I certainly didn't need that headache. I had enough women who would be happy to warm my bed.

I padded toward the fridge and pulled out a premade shake, downing it before heading to the shower. My body was refusing to cool down, and it had nothing to do with the bike and everything to do with my newfound rage for Margo's husband.

Married Margo, who I had zero business pursuing. The same woman who said she didn't do this sort of thing, whatever this was, and who looked like a beaten dog when I gave her the brush-off at the Paula.

I'd been down this path once before, although not as severe. Jaime was only dating a bastard who beat her when we met and got involved. I helped her with leaving and kept her warm during the breakup. When she was ready to fly, I said good-bye.

But this infatuation I had with Margo would never be that easy to navigate away from.

After putting myself through a cool shower, I got out to my phone buzzing with a text.

Hey, I know it's Saturday and you probably have plans later, but turns out I'm free.

That's all it read, but it oozed with hesitation and reluctance. I also noted Margo didn't use her name anywhere. Maybe she wanted to keep communication impersonal?

Can I call? I sent back, and she answered, *Yes.*

Knotting the towel around my waist, I grabbed the phone and pressed send while walking into my closet. Setting the phone down on speaker, I listened to it ring twice and then a third time before she picked up.

"Hi," she said, and I could hear birds chirping in the background.

"Hanging outside?" I wanted to act casual, but it was unclear who I was trying to calm. Her or me?

"I'm just back from a run and cooling off in my yard. Priscilla's inside, working on a school project."

"Got it." Margo was being discreet, but it wasn't because of him. Protecting her daughter, I could get behind.

"She's going to another sleepover tonight, and I'm solo. I was going to stay in, but a drink sounds kind of nice, I think?"

Margo's nerves and hesitation seeped through the phone the way the sweat had poured out of me moments earlier. She made a statement sound like a question, but I wasn't the person to answer that.

"Let's do it," I said lightly. If I gave her a moment to overthink it, the prospect of us meeting would be over. Although, that would probably be for the best.

"Okay," she said.

I figured it was better than a flat-out no, although I wasn't sure why I was working so hard for this hookup. It was unlike me, but that first day, her worst really touched something inside me.

"How about I send an Uber to pick you up and bring you into town? I'm in the Back Bay. We can go somewhere around Copley. Are you comfortable with that?"

"Under normal circumstances, I would say as long as it's not a steakhouse, I'm cool with it." Her voice lowered on the last part, and then she added, "That's where . . . *he* likes to go. A steakhouse."

"Not my scene anyway," I said quickly. "I'm more of a wood-paneled bar or an Italian place on the North Shore kind of guy."

"Oh," she said softly.

Immediately, I felt as if I should apologize. "I didn't mean to compare us. That was wrong."

"No offense. It actually made me smile. I'm not a steak-place kind of gal."

Of course she wasn't. Margo was the type of woman you sat in a quiet corner with, lingering over cocktails and antipasto for hours, never wanting it to end.

"But I have to say, it's kind of strange for a guy named Mick, short for McKenzie, to be an Italian guy."

I couldn't stop the laugh erupting from my chest. "You got me. My mom was a nice Irish lass named Peggy, but I had a coach in high school, an Italian guy, Frankie Pappa, and he introduced me to real Italian food."

For a moment, I thought about Frankie and how he'd taught me to be a man. He showed me right from wrong, and I'm sure he would think what I was doing right now was a mix of both. Wrong to pursue a married woman, but right to want better for her.

"I can come to town," she said softly. "It's not far."

I could feel the heaviness hanging on each of her whispered words.

"Should I send an Uber to your house?" Honestly, I didn't go around picking up married women. I wasn't sure how this worked, but I felt like Margo needed someone to take charge.

"Um, okay. Maybe next door?"

"Sounds good to me. Do you want to text me the address?"

"I can do that."

Our conversation was feeling a bit tense, each statement blander and blander. Granted, she was sneaking a call in her backyard, away from her kid, but I didn't like the way this felt.

"Margo," I said, and her *yes* was breathy. "I want you to know I would never hurt you. In any way. If this is too much—"

"No," she said, not allowing me to finish. "It's not too much. Just new, okay?"

"Okay. I'm looking forward to seeing you," I told her, and I was.

"I have to go. I'll text you the address."

"Sounds good. How's the Oak Bar at the Fairmont?"

"Never been," she said, and I knew it would be perfect. "Bye," she whispered before ending the call.

After I sent the Uber later, I put on dark jeans with a white shirt, and rolled up the sleeves. I ran some shit through my hair that my fucking hairdresser insisted I use if I continued to insist to wear my hair longer. Deciding against loafers, I slipped my feet into my Adidas Boosts and headed toward my parking garage.

I didn't plan to drink much, and figured I could valet at the hotel where the bar was. In case Margo wanted me to drive her home? I wasn't sure.

Leaving the keys to my Cayenne in the center console, I told the valet, "Maybe two hours, tops," and slipped inside the Oak from the street entrance.

There was a grander entrance through the hotel, but this was the one I preferred. The street-side door was for locals.

The place was pretty packed, but my usual corner was empty. Sliding into a high-back stool, I pulled up my Uber app. Since I'd sent the car, I wanted to make sure the driver wasn't doing anything weird.

That car showed to be in front of the attached hotel, and I decided a drink was needed. As I tossed my card on the bar, my favorite bartender appeared.

"What can I get you?" Wes asked.

"Lagavulin, neat, and keep the card. A friend is joining me."

Wes nodded, and he was off.

I propped my shoe on the footrest of the empty chair next to me and looked around the place. Heavy chandeliers, wooden accents, and a marble bar, it was an alchemy of different materials. Like my life.

"Lagavulin, neat," Wes said, interrupting my thoughts as he slid my drink in front of me. "Water?"

"Large, sparkling, and two glasses," I said just as Margo entered the room. I could feel her presence as she gazed around the large space, looking for me.

Her eyes met mine, and I felt that down below. Crass, I know, but the truth.

I stood when she arrived at my quiet corner. "Margo . . . hello."

"This is great," she said, looking around the room. "Perfect little corner too."

I nodded. "Sit," I said, watching her slip out of her leather jacket and hang it on the back of her chair. She wore a black silk blouse that tied around her neck into a knot or a bow. It was tucked into dark jeans like mine.

"Is this okay?" She'd caught me staring.

"I can't help myself . . . it's more than okay. You look gorgeous." My words part whisper and half growl, I kept them low enough for her only.

When she was seated, Wes came back and poured us each a sparkling water.

"Something stronger?" I asked Margo while the kid lingered.

"Do you have a wine list?" The moment she asked, he produced one and said he'd be back.

"Are you in a white or red mood?" I couldn't help but babble while she read the list. If I didn't, I'd probably cage her against the bar and put my mouth on hers, but I didn't think that was a good idea for a variety of reasons.

"It's actually a little chilly out . . . gah, I can't stand weather conversation," she said while smiling, her eyes creasing the tiniest bit in the corners. "Anyway,

I'm thinking red."

I waved for Wes to come back, and she ordered a glass of cabernet before turning her attention to me. "Everything good with the ride, and at home?"

Before answering, she ran her fingers through her hair. It was wavy tonight, wild like her spirit, and my fingers itched to join in on the fun.

"Yes, the ride was great. Thanks. Home was fine too," she said while wringing her hands on the bar.

"Don't be nervous," I told her. I wasn't sure she should believe me, but I wanted her to.

"He's away," she said quietly. "Business trip. He won't even ask me what I did while he was gone as long as everything is just so when he gets back."

I nodded. I understood manipulation and abuse. My mom had endured it for years. It was the only form of communication I'd witnessed during my childhood, so I'd taught myself to be different.

"Priscilla is at a friend's house. She prefers to go to her friends' places. I didn't quite understand it until recently, but our house is different. It's tense. Anyway, I'm going to try to push on and get out. That's not something I really wanted to do until I met you," Margo said sheepishly, looking down at her hands.

Her wine arrived, and I waved Wes away after he set it down.

"To pushing on," I said, tipping my glass toward hers.

"Whatever that means," she said before taking a sip. When she set her glass down again, her cheeks were pink. "I know it's odd that you could motivate me like that. I mean, I just met you . . . I'm sure you think I'm a nut."

"I don't. Flattered, maybe, but I don't think you're a nut."

She tilted toward me, her layers of hair cascading to one side. I couldn't help myself, but my hand traveled to her bare shoulder and skimmed her hair behind her. Goose bumps flitted across her skin, yet my palm felt on fire.

"It's just you made me think about a better space for me . . . and my daughter. Hearing your story, I could see how the situation still affects you. I don't want that type of story for Priscilla. This may sound bad, but I want to be her hero, not the other way around."

Swallowing, I took in Margo's made-up face, and I wanted to wash off all the makeup and get to know who she really was underneath. "No offense taken. I commend you."

"Good. I just wanted to get that out of the way. This is such new territory to me."

"Another toast, to new territories."

We clinked our glasses together and then drank.

Margo leaned an elbow on the bar and faced me, looking more relaxed. "So, tell me about your day. It must've been more exciting than mine."

"I don't know about that. I usually work a bit on the weekends. Today, I ran over numbers, seeing how many employees we can keep on. That's the shitty part about what I do. Letting people go. Whether they're good at their job or not, they're still people."

"I didn't think about that," she said, then sipped her wine. Her lips curved over the glass, leaving a red stain from her lipstick behind. "My dad lost his job when I was young, then my mom kicked him out. Eventually, he got a new job and she let him come back. It's been a rough road for him, and my mom is the least sympathetic person I know, so she didn't have any regrets about kicking him to the curb. She's not one to understand much or help others."

I could tell Margo's mind was wandering toward something else, but I didn't push.

"We don't talk all that much anyway," she said with a small shrug.

"Sounds like you and your mom are pretty different."

"We are." Her smile widened. "I try to be a different type of woman and mom. At least, when I'm not with him. It must be something learned inside of me . . . to take that type of . . . whatever it is."

She let it hang there open-ended. When her smile faded, I gently touched her chin, tipping it toward me. Despite the electricity running between us from the tiniest bit of skin-to-skin contact, I kept my cool.

"Hey, don't do that. You said you're pushing forward. Think about that, not anything else. Hear me?"

Margo shook her head. "Let's change subjects. We came here for a good time, not for you to shrink me." She laughed at her own joke and took a big gulp of wine.

"Fair enough. Tell me about your day. Busy with your daughter? Writing anything interesting?"

That's when Margo really came alive, telling me about making lunch with Priscilla and then sitting down to write her latest piece. With her eyes sparkling from excitement, her hair bouncing all around her face, and her smile expanding by the minute, I knew I had to be careful when it came to this woman.

Margo could sweep me up into her arms, and I wouldn't want to untangle myself. I hadn't felt that way in a long time.

seven

margaret

"Ugh, I'm sorry for rambling on and on," I said to Mick. "It's just I'm so excited over this piece. I've been watching this trend for a while, gender-neutral clothing, and I was so excited they asked me to write about it. I don't get to talk about work a lot, so thank you for humoring me. Or at least, tolerating me."

Finished with my monologue, I went to take a sip of my wine and noticed the glass was empty. "Shit," I murmured.

I was seriously screwing this up. Whatever this was, which was nothing.

"Don't be like that. I like it. I'm a business guy, intrigued by all things happening out there. I never even heard of this trend. I'm not really into fashion," he said, gesturing to his attire. "Don't tell anyone, but my assistant orders most of my stuff online for me."

"Your secret is safe with me," I said before pretending to zip my mouth shut.

"Now, how about another round?" Mick asked. "And some food. So I can hear more."

Who was this guy? He wanted to hear more from me. And he wanted to eat at the bar, with no one waiting on him hand and foot, attending to his every need.

"Uh, yes. Let's. I don't have to drive, and I am kind of hungry."

"Good," he said before waving the bartender back. "Wes, we're going to sit here and have some food. Okay?"

"Of course. What can I get you?"

"Anything look good to you?" Mick asked me.

"The mushroom flatbread?"

"Great. We'll take a flatbread and a shrimp cocktail."

"And another round?" Wes asked.

"Absolutely," Mick said before shooing him away.

"Do you come here a lot?" I asked, despite my brain telling me not to.

"If I have a business meeting, I'll usually bring them here for drinks, but then we'll get a table. Sometimes I like to pop in for a drink by myself, and I aim for this corner."

"I didn't mean to pry. Ugh, now I went and admitted what I was thinking. I can't seem to keep it on the surface with you."

This made Mick laugh. "That's pretty damn good. I don't want BS, and for the record, I can hardly see straight when I'm with you." He leaned in as he said it and ran his nose across my cheek. "This okay?" he asked when he got to my ear.

My heart was pounding in my ears and my stomach was in my toes. This was risky, but it felt decadent. I took a beat to answer, and he leaned back.

"I didn't mean to get close in public," he said as if reading my mind.

"Don't apologize. I liked it. A little too much. It's just . . ."

"I get the *it's just*, and just know if we weren't in a public space, I wouldn't have moved. As long as it was okay with you."

If my heart had pounded before, now it was punching the lining of my chest, straining for and wanting a type of affection it had never received.

Wes arrived with our drinks, and suddenly I wanted nothing more than to toss mine back, cancel the order for the food, and go somewhere private with Mick. Deep in thought, I was running through depraved ideas when Mick spoke again.

"Later. Now, tell me more about the clothing and how you found out about it."

"Really?" I asked, feeling like a fool.

"Really." Mick picked up his Scotch and took a sip, never taking his eyes off me as he waited for me to respond.

Sadness swept through me, filling the emptiness inside. This was what it was supposed to be like when a man cared about a woman.

After taking a sip of my own liquid courage, I answered his question. "I was watching a fashion reality show with Priss. You know, everyone would have two days to complete a certain collection, and then the judges vote someone off. There was one designer who was making all these cool gender-neutral designs. Both Priss and I loved them. Of course, Tommy . . ." I stopped midsentence, realizing I'd messed up.

"Go on, no judgment here," Mick said, catching my slipup.

"Anyway, he didn't care for the designs when Priss showed him. I know better, but she keeps trying with him."

Mick nodded, his eyes warm pools of understanding, making me believe his original toast to push forward.

Wes appeared again with our apps. "Chef sent out this crab dip on the house. It's new, and we're giving it a try."

"Thanks," Mick said, turning his attention back to me.

It was all too much . . . the high ceilings filled with my overabundance of emotions, and the murmur of small groups gathered around parts of the bar hummed in the background. The intimacy of Mick's corner, up against a mirrored wall, felt like a cocoon rather than an all-too-open place where I was exposed. Then there was this man who wanted to know more about me.

"The real question is," he asked, "did the designer win the show?"

I shook my head. "Sadly, no. She should have, but they went a more traditional route. Female and male looks. Don't get me wrong, they were gorgeous, but something about this other designer's looks intrigued me."

"I hear you. I can see you're a cutting-edge person. Look how you found social media before everyone else did."

I was dipping a shrimp in cocktail sauce when he said this, and I almost dropped the expensive piece of shellfish. "I can't believe you remember that." My response came out breathless. Thank God, I stopped myself before explaining that even Tommy didn't understand that part of my career.

"I remember everything," Mick said quietly, his hand ghosting my wrist. It wasn't sore anymore, and his touch lit up my whole body rather than make me cringe.

"I like an underdog. Someone who is trying something new and different," I said, trying to explain myself, and then decided it was better to pop a shrimp in my mouth and shut up.

Mick hadn't eaten anything yet. He kept his gaze on me, bringing his thumb up to wipe a drop of cocktail sauce from the corner of my mouth.

Like in the movies, my body went *kaboom* as if fireworks were exploding in my belly. I felt like a college girl in love at first sight, attempting to extinguish them. Instead, I took a healthy slug of wine, hoping it would douse the fire starting to burn inside me.

"Looks like we have something in common. That's why I love what I do. I take failing enterprises no one else believes in and make them work."

I nodded, thinking how proud and earnest Mick was about his work. It wasn't a power trip or a tool to overpower those less successful than him.

"As a writer, we're always trying to show something nobody believes in, except us."

"I can see that," he said, taking a shrimp.

From that moment, I lost track of how long we sat in that corner. Long enough, I started to think about it as ours.

"I like this," Mick said, pulling me from my thoughts.

"It's nice. Easy."

"Good. Good times should be easy."

"I've never had something like this."

"How about we don't talk about that, but how you'll have a lot more of this."

When we left, it didn't take much more than Mick saying, "Want to go back to my place for a drink?" to get a yes out of me.

For the first time . . . ever . . . I'm living my life for me.

At that thought, guilt skittered up my spine.

I knew it was wrong, but I also knew the way Tommy treated me was wrong. Rather than believing two wrongs don't make a right, I convinced myself they canceled each other out.

Much later, the noises coming from me were absolutely shocking and unlike any sounds I'd ever made before in my life.

"Mick, oh God," I whispered on a moan as he took my foot in his hand

and gently brushed his fingers over the sole. His palm stopped on a pressure point and pressed hard, and I couldn't help what came out of my mouth. "I may orgasm, seriously."

I sat up and stared into his eyes, feeling equally uncertain and safe. I should have left then, but I lay back and enjoyed the foot rub Mick was giving me.

"Only you," he said, smirking.

I pushed up again so I could take all of him in. The crinkles around his eyes, the tiny furrow in his brow, and his messy hair. Mick teased me like he'd known me for years.

Continuing to take his time with my foot, he said, "It kills me when you call me Mick. I don't know why, but for the first time in my life, I want to be called McKenzie. By you. It could be just for us. You may be the only person I've ever wanted to call me by my formal name."

His voice caused a rash of shivers to run up and down my spine, while his hands worked some secret voodoo on my feet.

"Ah, this feels so good. Please don't stop, McKenzie," I said, giving Mick what he wanted.

We were lying in front of the fireplace in his penthouse, sprawled on the couch. Mostly naked, we lay with our heads at opposite ends, my feet in his gentle hands. It was an intimate moment, much like between two people who had lived together for a decade. Yet here we were, one week after meeting in a bar, committing the worst transgression a woman and man could commit.

Adultery.

After the best evening I'd had in a long time, I'd gone home with Mick against my better judgment, breaking my own rules about not doing that sort of thing. I could say it just happened or he forced me or make some excuse for our behavior, but the real reason was that we both wanted to. It was a dangerous combination of need and want.

As soon as we arrived at his plush condo, lust seemed to fill the room, making it impossible for us to get farther than the large wooden door. We'd clawed at each other's clothing as my legs went up around his waist. We didn't talk about it or analyze it, we only acted on whatever crush of feelings was bearing down on us.

In my mind, it would be a one-and-done type of thing. I would get this urge, this itch, out of my system, and then would go back to my sad existence with a great memory to look back on when the sadness got too heavy.

Except, now Mick was asking me to have special names for him. For me to be the only one to call him by his given name.

After we'd had the hottest quickie known to man against the wall in the hallway, my bra still on and the rest of our clothes scattered all over the foyer, Mick carried me to the couch and laid me down. He tossed a blanket over me before walking to the kitchen, his ass on full display, and grabbed a bottle of red and two glasses.

He didn't mention the fading bruises on my thighs and back. He ran his hand gently over a scar on my hip, and after the fact, I realized he hadn't gripped that hip when he thrust into me against the wall. Our wineglasses sat half full on the ivory lacquered sofa table behind the plush navy velour couch, their high quality leading me to guess that Mick had an interior designer.

"Come here," he grumbled with authority, and I flipped over, sliding up his body until our mouths met. It was an intimate move usually perfected over time.

He nipped at my bottom lip, and I moaned with abandon like we were a well-oiled sex machine. My desire for him rose again, and I started to convince myself this needed to be the one-and-done arrangement I'd expected it to be.

Then Mick's palms ran down my back, causing a greater stirring in my belly and goose bumps to break out all over my skin. It was a level of closeness I wasn't sure I'd ever achieve again, and I wasn't ready to toss it away.

"Goddamn, Margo, this ass," he said, squeezing the subject at hand. "You know I'm into all parts of you, but when you walked away from me that first day, I couldn't take my eyes off your ass."

Smiling, I closed my eyes and savored Mick's gentle touch.

"I'm hard again. Like a goddamn teenager," he said into my ear, his voice raspy while his breath feathered over my earlobe, wreaking havoc on my nerves.

Crawling out of my skin with need, I said, "Take me."

That's all it took before he rolled me to my back and crawled down in front of me, his mouth meeting my core. Between the scraping of his teeth and his skilled tongue, I went off in a matter of minutes.

I should have been embarrassed, but I couldn't stop reveling in the moment.

Before I could return the favor, Mick was inside me, pushing deep, filling all of me. Somehow, he'd managed to wrestle on a condom while I was coming down from orgasm heaven, and now it felt downright decadent again.

I hadn't meant for us to get to this place, this position, this anything without setting some ground rules. Yet here we were, and I couldn't bring myself to care.

"You feel so good," he told me, sliding in and out at a snail's pace, making sure I felt every thrust.

I babbled some nonsense about ecstasy, and then said something vaguely like, "Harder, please."

Mick didn't need to be persuaded, and immediately did what I asked or begged for.

After a few harder thrusts, we were both hitting our moment in unison again like a well-rehearsed pair. We rode it out together until we were sated. I kept waiting for awkwardness to set in, but it didn't.

Sipping our wine after the second time, Mick mentioned he was off to Chicago for a meeting next week. "Wish I was staying in Boston, then we could continue this," he said matter-of-factly, like there was a *this*.

"It's probably for the best," I said quietly.

"You say that like you're going to poof out of my life at any second," he said, calling me out on my shitty answer.

Standing up and snatching my clothes from the floor, I started to get dressed. "Unfortunately, I am. This can't happen again. I don't know what I was thinking."

This time, the guilt and shame were no longer tiny tingles but full-on lightning rods, lighting up my every vein. My feelings were as heavy and stark as the stainless kitchen behind me. I was a bad person. Period.

"I need to go. Can you call an Uber?" I was almost fully dressed. Rumpled, but dressed.

"I can ride with you—"

"No worries," I said, finger-combing my hair into a low ponytail. I'd freshen my makeup in the Uber. Not that anyone would be home to notice, but still.

Mick tapped at his phone, mumbling, "Just a few minutes away."

When I didn't respond, he looked up.

"Did I do something? I need to be sure I didn't hurt you, or say something that hurt you." He stood but didn't approach. "Margo, I thought we had some sort of understanding. I would've never—"

"Nothing like that." I found my bag and slung it over my shoulder. "I had fun. That's what this was . . . right? Fun. Letting off some steam." I acted as if I did this all the time, when in fact, I felt like a soldier dropped into enemy territory.

Running his hand through his already messy hair, Mick frowned. "I don't know. I was hoping it wouldn't end this abruptly, but okay. I would never go against your wishes, you know that?"

Heading toward the door of his condo, I said, "See you around, Mick the fixer. Thanks for a great night."

He padded over and pulled me close, brushing his lips over my cheek. "It's been a pleasure, Margaret."

His using my full name burned, but it had been my idea to get up and walk out in the middle of a glass of wine. I was having fun, no one was waiting for me, and when they were, it ended in pain.

I was leaving, though.

"'Bye," I said quickly, and then got the hell out of there.

If I knew anything at all about myself, it was that I wasn't capable of this type of thing. Wishing the elevator would make a speedy approach, I scolded myself for even meeting Mick tonight.

"You know better," I whispered under my breath as the doors opened and I hurried to the ground floor to catch my Uber.

eight

mick

"Now boarding Platinum members and the first-class cabin," the woman behind the podium said into the microphone.

With my briefcase tucked under my arm, I scanned my boarding pass and walked down the jetway. Exhaustion hit about twenty minutes ago. Rather than grabbing a coffee, I had a few fingers of Scotch at the airport bar. I'd worry tomorrow if it was a bad decision, but right now I wanted to catch some z's on the plane and get home to catch up on my latest business interest.

Seated in first class, I closed my eyes until the airline attendant walked by, offering, "Water? Coffee? Champagne?"

Opening an eye, I asked for water, and she asked, "Still or sparkling?"

Instead of answering like the grown-up I was, I was transported to the night at the bar with Margo. Our bottle of sparkling water had sat there mostly untouched while we drank the real stuff and had even realer conversation. She was the first woman I'd connected with in a long while, and she was taken.

"Still or sparkling?" the attendant asked again, still waiting for my answer.

"Still, please."

The flight attendant hustled off to attend to my needs, and I laughed to myself.

She couldn't fulfill my needs if she tried. The caveman in me wanted the wild-haired blonde who breathed life into me with her love of writing and all things mysterious to me.

This version of me wanted to take Margaret up against a wall again, maybe a little slower. Then again, harder. The decent man in me wanted to rescue the broken woman and put her back together, maybe making her mine along the way. Neither was a good idea, but I couldn't stop thinking about her.

"Here you go," the slight brunette said, handing me my water. She stood there a moment longer, batting her eyes at me.

I pretended not to notice. I drank my water and closed my eyes, hoping for some rest.

The Chicago project was mostly wrapped up. I'd bought a flailing app, a high-tech rating system for schools, and turned it around fairly quickly. It provided rankings for every school in the country, elementary through college, and offered a fee-for-service feature for those who wanted actual reviews on a school.

It was a fun project, but not a company I wanted to hold on to. Tech-type companies were best sold to techies who wanted to advance them. I repaired their corporate staffing and brought in a new designer, and that helped tremendously. It started seeing profits pretty quickly, and now I had a buyer, from Boston too.

Thank God, going over the paperwork in my head brought sleep easily. I dozed for the rest of the flight, waking up when we touched down in Boston.

"Plans for tonight?" the brunette asked as we taxied to the gate.

"Just home." My answer was curt, but I wasn't in the mood to lead her on.

"Oh, you're from here? I thought I heard New York when you said water earlier."

"Originally, but now I call Boston home."

She nodded, trying not to look hurt. "Any restaurant recommendations, then?" she asked, obviously trying to save face.

"Anywhere in the North Shore has good food and drinks." I was certain she did this route often, and I wasn't sure why she needed me to tell her where to go.

"I'm staying in the Back Bay," she said, "at the Copley."

Our conversation was getting stranger by the minute, especially since that was where the Oak was. And now my thoughts were straight back to Margo.

"It's not far," I said just as the captain gave us the obligatory two dings and we were safe to stand, which I did immediately.

At almost a foot taller than the attendant, I barely had to reach up for my briefcase. When I got it down, I told her to have fun and got the hell out of there. With luggage in hand, I went straight to my SUV and headed home.

Opening the door to my place, I thought I could still smell Margo. All honeysuckle and innocence, trying to keep my hand from wandering over past bruises. I hoped she was safe.

After calling for takeout, I sat down at the kitchen bar to review a staffing report for my latest venture. I would have to lay off forty-five percent of the current staff, which always pained me.

Lost in thought over the families who would be without a job over the holidays, my phone buzzed. The door buzzer downstairs was connected with my phone, and I assumed it was because my food had arrived.

But when I said, "Hello," into the phone without looking, it wasn't the delivery person downstairs.

"Mick?" Her voice was soft and questioning.

Just at the sound of my name, I felt like an absolute dick. I hadn't called or texted Margo since I left town, but with the way she ran out on me, I felt it was best left alone.

With all the worst-case scenarios running through my head, I asked, "Margo, you okay?"

"Yes . . . yes, I'm fine. I didn't mean to worry you or bother you."

"Don't be silly," I said, pacing. If the food came, they could give it to someone else. I wasn't hungry anymore.

"I didn't know if you were in Chicago still, but I wanted to call and say I'm sorry for the way I ran out on you."

I imagined Margo sitting huddled up somewhere to make this call, her hair falling around her face.

"That's not necessary. I get it. You're not mine to have. I will say, I liked our time together. All of it." I wanted to let her off the hook, but I didn't want her to think I took our time together lightly.

"Honestly, I do. I just didn't feel good about myself after we . . . but then again, I don't feel great about myself ever. In our actual time together, I felt amazing. And so I didn't want you to think I was mad at you or that I don't think you're amazing. You are."

I could have sworn I heard her sniff back tears, and I was done for.

"Margo, what's going on?" I asked, leaning back against the wall.

"Oh, nothing. I put the half-and-half on the top shelf of the fridge, and it froze," she said distractedly.

"So? It will defrost if you leave it out, I'm sure."

"We didn't have time for that this morning," she bleated out.

All of a sudden, I understood. "Let me guess. He takes half-and-half in his coffee?"

"Yes," came the weak response across the line.

"Are you hurt?" I asked, but she didn't say anything. "Can you talk?"

Still nothing.

"Margo?"

"I'm fine. A little bruised. The thing is, Priscilla heard us. She stepped in and told him to stop, and now he's gone."

I blew out a breath, both relieved and worried even more.

"This is exactly what I didn't want to happen, and now she's involved. My daughter."

"She'll be okay," I said, like I really knew anything about kids.

"What if he hurts her?"

If I weren't paying extreme attention, I would have missed this. "Do you think he's coming back tonight?" I asked, forcing myself not to say I was on my way.

"I don't know. He's never done this before. And Priscilla is locked in her room, all into TikTok like nothing happened."

"It's a defense mechanism, babe."

The endearment slipped from my mouth, but I was caught up in some alternate universe. I knew all about that defense mechanism—knew it all too well.

"Let her be. She'll come out and talk when she's ready. Listen, I want you to relax. I know it's hard," I said, trying to speak calmly. "Hopefully, he's gone for the night. Do you want me to come check on you?"

Why the fuck did I say that?

"No, no, that's a bad idea," Margo said, and her next words came out rushed. "Thanks for listening. I've got to go."

Then, as quickly as she'd called me, she hung up.

I wanted to call back, but I didn't. The phone rang again, giving me false hope, but this time it actually was my food arriving. When I finally sat down, my appetite fully gone, I sent Margo a text.

I'm here for you.

It was wrong and a bad idea, but I couldn't stop my finger from tapping out the words.

After a mostly restless night's sleep, I left whatever tension that remained on my Peloton bike and dressed for work. Looping the knot in my tie, aggravated I had to wear one, I made a firm decision to leave Margo in my rearview. Maybe I'd check on her, but this was a situation I didn't need. It wasn't my problem.

I drove to my office where the lawyers were waiting to begin the paperwork on the sale. We spent most of the morning going over clauses and addendums. When lunchtime rolled around, my assistant reminded me he'd made a reservation at Capital Grille for us. Lawyers liked that type of treatment, so I rolled down my sleeves, hit the head, and walked around the block with a bunch of tight-asses from both sides of the deal.

"Grantham. My assistant called ahead," I told the host with a smile.

"Oh, sure, we have your round table ready. Is the back corner okay? Your assistant said you may like some privacy."

"That's perfect."

Jeffrey got a little crazy at times with the requests on my behalf. It was only lunch . . . not a Senate hearing. But he was a good assistant and put up with me.

As we walked through the restaurant, we passed the table diagonal from us, another round one that held a big group of loud talkers. I sat with my back to them, but their conversation still reached me.

"She does this shitty writing for a magazine and rides my coattails with the parents' association. You'd think it would be enough. Now she's got her boss, and I use that term loosely, involved with the school event, making her look like some big shot."

Something about what he was saying pricked my mind, but I couldn't place it. Besides, wasn't this a business lunch? Why was he discussing his personal life?

"What's next, big guy?" a lawyer from the other team asked me.

"If I told you, I'd have to kill you, Craig."

He guffawed, but I knew this guy. He'd represented another tech company I looked into buying, and he was always digging for an inside tip.

"Come on," he whined.

I shook my head. "Let's get this deal done first."

My lawyer then took over, mentioning the sale of a recent baby-product company they had all worked on. It was based in Pittsburgh but growing pretty big, and now was being sued for a patent infringement.

"Don't worry, though, she won't be acting like such a big shot anymore. I told her to tell the committee her boss changed her mind. There will be no donation from her, making it look like she's in power. I'm the man, and all she does is write fluff shit."

The words floated from behind me, and again, something in my spine tingled.

"I don't doubt it, Long. We all know you wear the pants in your house."

Tuning out the patent talk at my table, I was all ears. Our server showed up, and I told her to take everyone else's order first.

"But I gotta say, I can't see Margaret trying to assert herself. She's always so meek at our events."

"The way she should be. Quiet and in the corner."

"Wish I had a setup like you."

"It's not bad, having a wife who puts up or shuts up, and a side piece who does what I want."

My blood raged through my veins. I could feel the vein throbbing in my temple, and my earlier resolve to leave Margo alone quickly dissipated.

I couldn't listen anymore. To think, the asshole was cheating. Margo's choices probably haunted her day and night, and this ass was right at home with all of his behavior. He deserved everything coming to him.

"And you?" the young server asked, eyeing me like she'd like to order me.

Maybe a month ago, but now I was full-blown stuck in a love triangle, with a side of abuse to go with it.

"Steak salad. Medium. Iced tea," I mumbled and went back to eavesdropping. My lawyer could catch me up later.

nine

margaret

I sat in the little coffee shop near the Paula, checking a few emails, my mind wandering.

I'd spent the morning interviewing two fashion designers over Zoom while sitting in the same seat at the window bar. With earbuds in, shutting out the world, my coat underneath my butt and my bag on the hook by my knees, I could almost forget the night before.

Paisley, the second designer, couldn't believe that I didn't have an intern or assistant after being a writer/journalist for well over a decade. It was kind of funny . . . she was almost interviewing me.

Apparently, her parents had wanted her to be a writer, but she'd chosen fashion over a lackluster career. Her words, not mine. They told her fashion was a pipe dream and destined to be a dead end, especially the gender-neutral line. Of course, Paisley now had her very own young, hip clothing line and an intern, who she actually paid in addition to signing off on credit for her design program.

The interview left me with a ton of notes that required organization, for which I was grateful, and a newfound love of my own career. I might not have an intern or a full-time gig, but I had something to call my own, which I'd scraped and clawed to have . . . and to keep.

After two hours of Q&A on the ins and outs of being an up-and-coming fashion designer, I still craved something more to take my mind off the true task at hand. Writing was not only my passion but my escape from reality.

I jotted down a few notes.

The field Paisley's parents wanted her to get into is as important as the one she ended up choosing, although polar opposites. One involves creating something new and edgy, and the other is an age-old profession. Writing can be edgy too, but stepping outside the expected norms is risky. I guess the same can be said for fashion, but Paisley always had her sights set on clothing free from gender roles.

Damn, if I didn't know that. I often wrote about the mundane, but my situation was unique. Held back by the man I was married to . . . which brought to mind the task at hand.

Without thinking, I picked up the phone and dialed Sheila when I should have been calling Jane, my editor. Sometime in the middle of the night, I'd concocted a plan.

Sheila answered, sounding chirpy as usual. "Margaret, how are you?"

I imagined her sitting there, her red hair straightened to perfection, her lips painted on, and not a wrinkle from her head to her Prada heels. It was hard not to be jealous. Sheila seemingly had it all.

Pushing any thoughts of my messy self out of my head, I said, "I'm well, thanks," turning on my manners before asking for a favor. It was a tactic I'd learned in college. Sadly, it didn't work on Tommy.

"Have you found a dress yet for the gala?" she asked.

I rolled my eyes. Tucking my wavy hair behind my ear, I cleared my throat.

"Not yet, but it's on my list. About the gala, I spoke a bit further with my editor, and she wants the donation to be anonymous. If the magazine does this donation for us, there will be so many others asking."

The idea came to me around three o'clock in the morning, after I got up and smeared a little arnica lotion on my butt for the bruising and took an Advil for the pain.

The magazine rarely checked up on these things, and this was the only solution I could come up with. Sheila still got her donation, and I saved face with work. If I was going to leave Tommy, I'd need my work to provide not only an income, but an outlet for me. I'd also need Sheila as a friend, to help control the rumor mill so it didn't affect my daughter.

"Money is money," Sheila said. "I know they hoped to make connections, but it's not my problem."

I breathed out a silent sigh of relief. "Great. Let me know when the program is finished if you want some proofreading. Obviously, I would be thrilled to do it."

"Another great idea," Sheila said delightedly, and I couldn't help the sense of satisfaction flooding me.

"Thanks, talk soon." I decided to end the call before it went south like everything else in my shitty life.

Except for my wonderful Priscilla, who wore a bra and got her period. She was growing and blooming. It was time I woman-ed up.

I stood from my seat, suppressing a squeak from pain.

Last night was the wrong time for me to have told Tommy about my magazine's donation to the gala. He was already two drinks in and angry over another firm wooing away a client.

I don't know what had come over me. I was increasingly sassier and more carefree with my words. It was almost like I was egging him on, but I hadn't meant for Priscilla to hear our arguing. I'd begged Tommy to be quiet, and that only angered him more. He'd shut our door, thrown me on the bed, and began to hurt me.

Good news was he didn't take my pants off. Bad news was this wasn't anything like BDSM, where I'd be provided after-care.

After Tommy had left and I made the mistake of calling Mick, I checked on Priscilla and then went to soak in the tub. I made sure to soak extra-long, allowing my mind to go to a blank space.

Now, walking out to my car, my bag loaded with my laptop and my coffee refilled to go, I didn't know why I trusted Mick or leaned on him. He was just a fling. An indiscretion. A mistake . . . or not? I didn't know, but I also didn't totally trust my judgment when it came to men.

Tommy wasn't always like this, was he?

Seated in my Volvo, I thought back to when we were much younger, and I was incredibly naive.

I hadn't even unpacked or taken my dirty clothes out of my luggage when I got home from the bus station. I'd gone to see my parents and missed Tommy terribly. They kept asking why he didn't come home to New Jersey with me. I didn't have an answer. He had studying and was busy, I kept telling them.

Like an eager and desperate woman, I pictured him making special plans for me when I came back. Now, as I lay down on the cool surface of my hardwood floor, I didn't know what I was thinking. Like an idiot, I'd been dreaming of a romantic bus-station gesture from him—flowers, jewelry, the possibilities were endless—only to be greeted with a welcome back *sign and a limp tulip.*

My expectations had been way off base.

Now, as tears dripped down my face, I only had myself to blame. I reminded myself that he'd made a sign and plucked a flower, obviously a thoughtful soul with school on his mind. A good guy.

I wasn't the stupid girl wanting to get married to the bad boy. Tommy was a decent guy.

Hot and fiery embarrassment, sadness, and a loss of pride washed over me completely. In minutes, I managed to convince myself that I was the one in the wrong.

Taking a look at the clock on the dash brought me out of my walk down memory lane. I shook my head, cursing at myself. Way back then, I'd mistaken Tommy's manipulation for niceties. He'd played me.

I knew many women didn't have supportive husbands, but I also knew they weren't all physically and emotionally abusive to them. As I pulled out of my parking spot, it was hard not to mentally beat myself up.

I should have seen the signs.

I didn't know better, but now I did. For my daughter's sake and my own, it was time to do right. Or try to do one right thing—get out—while doing something wrong?

Because I couldn't get sweet, handsome, emotionally generous Mick out of my mind.

A few days later, Tommy left early for Vermont again.

This time he'd be away for two nights, and I planned to breathe free. Him being the sole counsel for a large granite quarry was like a Christmas present that kept on giving. At the moment, they were being sued for some faulty product, and I hoped the case went on for a long while.

Sitting on the toilet gingerly, I looked down and noticed the tiniest of rolls had formed in my lower abdomen. "Forget it," I said aloud, and when I forced myself to sit up straight, the roll disappeared.

Closer to forty than thirty, I had to give up any vestige of body loathing left from my earlier years. I did my best at taking good care of myself. Mick thought so, but Tommy, not so much.

I peed, wiped, and pulled up my leggings, dropping the entire train of thought. Staring in the mirror while I washed my hands, I berated myself. I had zero business thinking about Mick. I had a day to myself, and I should be grateful.

With my butt finally feeling better, I decided to do yoga. I set up my mat under the window so I could enjoy the afternoon sun streaming inside, and found a class on my iPad. Closing my eyes, I allowed the music and the instructor's soothing voice to calm my nerves.

Pearl Jam's "Breathe" played in the background as we did a series of sun salutations. With every movement, my mind felt lighter and my body stronger. I bent over in downward dog and took a long inhale, followed by an even longer exhale.

That morning, when I'd dropped off Priscilla at school, I'd promised her a girls' night out tonight. She asked to go to Newbury Street and look at clothes. As I twisted myself into crow, I smiled at the floor, thinking about spending some time with her.

It could have been my imagination, but she seemed relieved Tommy was leaving as he called out, "'Bye, Priscilla," the entire extent of his good-bye to his daughter.

I would have been upset by his lack of emotion, but not Priscilla. Maybe that's why I was still stuck in the gerbil wheel of trying to fix Tommy instead of bettering myself.

ten

mick

I'd held off as long as I could. There was only so much distracting I could do, and then my overactive brain took over. My need to fix problems was a blessing and a curse.

As I trekked up Newbury Street to meet an old friend at his hotel for a drink, I thought about texting Margo.

The need I felt to check in with her was persistent. Why? I didn't fucking know. I was a perfectly settled bachelor. Sex came my way when I wanted; financially, I was set for three lifetimes; and I didn't have any strings, which was how I wanted it.

Yet here I was daydreaming about a married woman.

Pulling open the door to Nike, I shelved thoughts of Margo and reminded myself what I needed. A new pair of running shoes for travel. I could have sent Jeffrey, my assistant, to get them, but he had gone home for the day, and I was leaving in the morning.

Heading toward the running shoes, I paused for a second, thinking my mind was playing a trick on me. I could have sworn I saw Margo standing the middle of the women's clothing section, holding about a dozen pairs of shorts.

Squeezing my eyes shut, I decided a vacation was in order. Clearly, I was working too hard.

"Priss, these are all too short. I don't think the school would allow you to wear them, even if I did," she said to her daughter.

"But, Mom . . . please?"

They went back and forth, bickering like I assumed mothers and teenage daughters did, while I took in Margo. She was wearing black leggings, ankle boots, a long gray sweater falling off her shoulder, her hair tied back at the nape of her neck, and glasses I'd never seen her wear before, but were definitely sexy.

"I don't think your dad will be happy," Margo said with a frown.

"Seriously? He spends about three minutes per week with me, Mom," Priscilla said before her gaze landed on me, standing there and staring at her.

It took me half a second to realize Priscilla had no idea who I was, and this situation was about to head into stranger-danger mode.

She cocked her head at me and gave me the side-eye while whispering, "Mom . . ."

Clearing my throat, I decided to go for it. "Hi, Margaret," I said, using her formal name. This wasn't a time for familiarities.

"Mick?" Margo took me in. "What are you doing here?"

"Buying shoes."

I decided not to say much more. This was a wrinkle I hadn't expected, and I didn't want to divulge more than Margo wanted me to.

"Priscilla, this is Mr. Grantham. I interviewed him recently for an article," she said, using my fabricated excuse from when we met at the Paula.

I held out my hand to Priscilla. "Nice to meet you, but just Mick is fine." Then out of the fucking blue, I said, "Mr. Grantham was my dad, and he wasn't a good guy, so I prefer Mick."

Margo's eyes widened and Priscilla's narrowed, trying to decide if I was reading her thoughts.

"I'm going to New York tomorrow," I said, turning toward Margo. "Can't go and not run the High Line, and my shoes are on their last breath."

She nodded, and I could tell she was becoming increasingly uncomfortable.

"You two enjoy yourselves," I said, knowing it was time to say my good-byes.

"Nice meeting you, Mick," Priscilla said politely.

"Same here," I told her.

I gave Margo a nod good-bye and she waved, and that was it.

Well, at least I had my check-in on Margo. I saw her breathing, living, and spending time with her daughter. In front of the sample of the shoe I wore, I waited for the clerk to get my size, and told myself to text a New York friend for drinks. A female friend.

Instead, I texted Margo.

I didn't mean to make things awkward. Your daughter is a miniature version of you. It was nice to meet her. Enjoy your time with her.

I looked toward the women's section, but they were long gone, and I assumed Margo gave in to the short shorts in an effort to get her daughter and herself out of the store. I only tried one shoe on, then told the clerk to wrap them up and was out of there.

Brian, my buddy from Wharton, texted to say he was at the hotel bar, and I let him know I was on my way. It had been about six months since I last saw him in Miami, where he lived with his wife and new baby. He'd gone into the commercial real estate business, and where better than in a place full of sunshine and dreams?

"How are you, tough guy?" I slapped Brian on the back as I grabbed the seat next to him.

He'd played football in undergrad, and earned the nickname Tough Guy because when he got drunk, he always thought he could beat up anyone in the room.

Brian scowled at me. "Are you ever going to stop calling me that? I keep myself to the two-drink-limit rule these days."

"Scotch on the rocks, Lagavulin," I said to the bartender, and then turned toward Brian. "That's because your beautiful Amanda told me to remind you. Often."

His head fell back in laughter. "Damn straight. I do what my woman says. Speaking of which, you ever gonna get yourself a good woman?"

I shook my head. "Not meant for it." It had been my standard line since our last year of school. The guys knew my background, and they never pushed.

"It's time you put what happened with your pops behind you. You're not that guy," Brian told me as the bartender slid my drink in front of me.

"To not being that guy," I said and tipped my drink toward his. "It's not for me, though," I added, despite the niggling in my chest over Margo.

"I know, I know. Your businesses are your babies and all that."

"That they are, my friend. And you know what? When I'm done growing them, I set them free with zero thoughts or worries about them."

"Tell me what the latest deal is."

I took a sip of my drink and felt myself unwind for the first time in days. With Brian, I didn't need to worry about discussing details. We weren't in competition, and we often called each other for advice. I told him about the Chicago deal being done, and my latest acquisition.

"Tomorrow, I'm checking out a struggling New York restaurant chain. I don't really want to get into that business, but Jamie . . . remember him? He was a year ahead of us . . . he called me to look at it. He's a business broker in Manhattan."

"I do. He was the guy with the pet pig?"

"That's him. Now he has a husband and a set of twins."

"Can't see that dude raising kids. You, yes. Him, no."

That's pretty much how the evening went. Business talk coupled with jabs at me.

I don't know what kept me from telling him about Margo. Maybe her being married? Whatever this longing feeling I had for her was . . . I needed to keep it to myself for the moment.

eleven

*L*ater that evening, I poured myself a small glass of red wine and sat on the edge of the tub as it filled with warm water.

When your husband uses your body as a moving target, Epsom salt baths become your good friend. Although I tried to soak in them when Tommy wasn't home. If he saw me, he'd take it as a further sign of weakness or submission.

Priscilla and I had a fun dinner at Stephanie's before picking up cupcakes to go from a bakery and heading home. It wasn't until we were in the last five minutes of our drive, she asked, "What did you think that Mick guy meant by his dad wasn't a good guy?"

It shouldn't have caught me off guard, but it did.

"I, um, I'm not sure," I stammered.

"You know, I think he meant like Dad." Priscilla said it matter-of-factly while staring straight out the windshield.

Of course, I couldn't find the right words.

"He's not nice," she said. "I mean, sometimes he's nice to me, but never nice to you. You think I don't notice, but I do. I don't like it, you know?"

"Priscilla—"

"I don't tell anyone, if that's what you're worried about. That's why I don't have my friends around a lot. It's not really any of their business, and I don't want you to be embarrassed."

She sneaked a peek at me, and I wished I weren't driving. Then I realized that's why my smart daughter had waited to have this conversation until we were in the car.

"That's not what I meant, sweetie." I cleared my throat before continuing. "I meant, I'm sorry you have to know about this. That you have to see this at home. I blame myself because I've tried to hide it."

Emotions flooded my body—shame, guilt, and anger—all directed at myself. The very thing I'd tried to avoid had happened, and I never expected to have this conversation with my preteen daughter.

"No, Mom, don't. This is on Dad, not you. I know that."

I didn't know when Priscilla became so worldly . . . or why she was smarter than me. My mouth opened and closed like a fish, the right words—the wrong ones too—stuck in my throat.

"Maybe we can be like that Mick guy? He seems to have gotten rid of his dad . . . and now he's happy," my daughter said.

Needing to be the parent, I glanced at her as I struggled to find the right thing to say. "You know, I don't know what that was all about, but you may be right. Mick seems to have left whatever hurtful things in his past. Maybe we will too. It could be a motivator."

"I hope," she said before we turned into the driveway. As soon as the car was parked, she raced upstairs to her room with her new purchases and cell phone in hand, presumably to show all her friends what I bought for her.

"I hope so too," I muttered before walking straight toward the kitchen for a much-needed glass of wine.

Wineglass in hand, I leaned against the counter at my bathroom sink with the shower running, hiding the sound of my crying. Tears rolled down my cheeks as I stifled my sobs.

I had to do something, but I didn't know what. I thought about asking my mom for help again, but quickly pushed that thought away.

Pulling my shirt over my head, I sniffed back the last of my tears and picked up my wine for another sip. I didn't have any proof of Tommy's abuse. I'd never gone to a doctor or hospital with my injuries, and had never called anyone for help. It was his word against mine. One thing I knew for sure was I didn't want to involve Priscilla in this.

As I was undressing, my phone lit up on the bathroom counter, and I couldn't help but look.

Hope you had a fun time with your girl. She's sweet, like you.

I didn't need to glance at the contact to know who it was. Mick—my biggest mistake, and also the man I wanted the most. I whipped out a quick response before undressing and getting in the shower.

We did. Thanks for being cool.

As the water washed over me, I thought it through and decided to let it rinse away my transgression. Tonight's conversation with Priscilla was a call to action.

My spirit renewed, I wrapped myself in my robe, grabbed my wine, and sat down on the bed only to find my willpower gone.

Getting away from Tommy was going to be hard. He would hold everything over my head until I was powerless. I knew that as well as I knew I was righthanded and my second toe was longer than my first. He just would.

Being with Mick made me feel alive and, quite frankly, powerful, so when he texted back, I decided to respond.

I wasn't sure how to play it, so I thought simple was best.

BTW, you looked and smelled amazing.

It took me a while to digest those simple words. They weren't deep or flirty, but just right. Especially for someone who hadn't heard a compliment in over a decade.

I must have taken too long to answer, because another text came in.

Shit. Is it okay to text?

I scrambled to tap out a response.

Sorry. Yes, it's fine. Thank you. You didn't look so bad yourself.

As quickly as the resolve rained over me in the shower, it had dissipated.

Why, thanks. I'm off to New York in the morning, but I'd like to see you when I get back. I know you said we shouldn't, but I think we should.

There it was—a straight-up ask. Why would Mick do it any differently? He was a successful businessman who couldn't have gotten to where he was without being straightforward and persistent.

I don't know. Obviously, I'm not sure it's the right move.

I wanted to see him as much as I needed to draw my next breath. Even my daughter was taken with Mick.

Can I call?

There it was, his gentleness mixed with a touch of compassion, and maybe, just maybe, a tinge of his own insecurity. Probably not, but I could tell myself that.

Yes.

It was only a matter of seconds before my phone rang.

Looking up, I confirmed my door was closed and answered on a whisper. "Hello?" Standing in my robe, I picked up my glass and tipped the last dregs of wine into my mouth.

"Margo," he said on a soft breath, and I smiled. "I don't want to keep you long. I met a friend . . . a work buddy . . . for a drink, and I couldn't stop thinking about you."

My smile widened. "Oh."

"That's right, and now I have to go to New York."

"Poor you," I said while setting my empty glass down.

"Ha! Well, if I'm being honest, I'd rather see you. But I'm going to check out a company, and then I'll be back."

"It's tricky," I mumbled.

"On your terms," he said quickly. "Always."

When I nodded, forgetting he couldn't see me, he asked, "You there?"

"Yes, I zoned out. Sorry."

"Hey, listen, I didn't mean that quip in front of your daughter. About my dad. I've said it so many times, it just comes out."

Sitting gingerly on my bed, I glanced around the room, panicked for a minute that Tommy might walk in. What the hell was I doing?

Taking my power back.

"It's okay. Well . . . actually, it gave her an idea. On the way home, she mentioned to me that she knows more than I believed she did. She knows I'm not treated very nicely, and mentioned I should stop that." Swallowing my pride, I went on, pouring my heart out to a guy I barely knew, but the first person I'd trusted. "I'm not sure if she meant physical or just the general way he treats me, but I decided she's right."

"Good. Good, Margo," Mick said firmly. "You should get out. And like I said, when it comes to me, it's on your terms."

"Okay."

"I'll be back in two days and call?"

"Okay."

"Night, Margo."

"Night."

I put aside my phone before crawling under the covers, forgoing brushing my teeth. The bed was cold, but I welcomed it. Chilly meant I was alone, that the heat of Tommy's menace wasn't next to me.

As I curled up into the cocoon of my robe, I lost myself in the chill.

twelve

margaret

A week had passed since the awkward run-in with Mick, and the even more unsettling phone call that followed.

Currently, I was lost in my thoughts as I walked the aisles of Wegman's, tossing things in my cart, thinking about the following night when I was supposed to meet Mick for sushi. As I placed two containers of half-and-half in the cart, I heard, "I can't live without the stuff."

It was a male's voice, deep and baritone, and immediately brought to mind a different man's rumbly voice. Mick had called the day before.

"Sorry, I didn't mean to startle you," the voice said.

This time, I looked up and met a pair of brown eyes I somewhat recognized.

"Dale. Dale Shuckey," he said, introducing himself with a smile. "We're on the gala committee for the school. My daughter, Annabeth, plays soccer with Priscilla."

Smiling, I nodded. "Of course."

"I should've led with that." He laughed, shaking the container of half-and-half in his hand. "It's good stuff."

"I wouldn't know. I'm more of an almond-milk gal." I picked up a quart of almond milk from my cart and used my best Vanna White hand interpretation in front of it.

"Annabeth mentioned wanting to try almond milk. You like that brand?"

"Um, yes, I do." Rolling my shoulders, relieving the strain from my crossbody bag, I stood there waiting for Dale to say something else, unsure of what to do.

"Oh, good. If she hears Priscilla's mom recommends it, then it's way better than if I do. You know, I'm learning this teen-girl thing on the fly," he said with a small chuckle, yet I noticed a sadness in his eyes.

Jogging my memory for any details of Annabeth, I remembered she was Priscilla's teammate who lost her mom back in kindergarten.

"Ugh, I'm sorry. I'm being rude. Caught up in my mind with all the things I have to do. This is a good brand."

Dale's smile faltered a little as understanding dawned on him. He'd realized I'd just remembered about his late wife.

"Hey, don't. It's cool. I'm doing the best I can."

"You know what? I'm learning how to deal with teenage girls as I go too. It seems like every night I'm racking my brain to understand some new phenomenon or temper tantrum."

He rolled his eyes. "And the social media. My Lord. My business uses all the apps, but I find myself calling our marketing person more and more to explain Tik this and Snap that."

I tried to recall what Dale did for a living, but I couldn't remember, but thought it was nice that he had the flexibility to buy his own half-and-half. For a moment, I wondered if when his wife was alive, he physically hurt her over half-and-half.

Pushing my hair behind my ear, I decided to stand in the dairy aisle and chat some more. It felt nice to do something pseudo-normal. Freeing. Like getting a drink with Mick.

Oh, Mick . . . And just like that, my thoughts returned to his handsome face and longish hair and his gentle hands.

Dragging my mind out of the bedroom, I told Dale, "Social media is my jam. That I have covered, much to Priscilla's dismay, I'm sure."

"You do?"

"The whole topic sort of fell into my lap, literally. My first writing assignment was on social media, and I've been covering apps and such since then. For

Adweek."

Dale leaned a little closer to whisper, "You're my hero."

I was so caught up in this new me, I wasn't sure if he was hitting on me or being serious. I caught him glance down at my hand, and his gaze skimmed over my wedding band. He leaned back but didn't make any excuses for his behavior.

Look, every lady likes when a charming man leans in, right? Or maybe it's only the ones who live with monsters like I do?

"I don't know about hero status," I said, "but I keep a tiny side-eye on my budding social medialite. If you ever have any questions, let me know." For someone who hadn't been forthright in a very long time, I was certainly putting myself out there.

Dale stepped closer and ran his palm down my arm. I couldn't help leaning into the soft touch when I should have pulled back.

"Really?" he asked. "You know, it would be great to have a sounding board. Someone who isn't from work. Someone who really knows what they're saying when it comes to tween girls."

I couldn't believe this was me, standing in the grocery store, making friends with a guy. Okay, the dad of a friend of Priscilla's, but a friend no less.

"Sure. It would be nice too. I actually don't talk to many of the other moms . . . or dads."

"Great," he said, stepping back. "Here." He pulled a card out of his wallet and handed it to me. "That's my cell. Why don't you text me your info?"

The card, the promises of texts, were too much. *Mick. Mick. Mick* was all I could think.

Somehow, I pulled myself together, and said, "Perfect," taking the card with a smile. "Don't forget the almond milk."

He grabbed a quart and said, "Talk to you soon," and we parted ways.

As I went down the next aisle, looking for avocado oil, I kept looking over my shoulder. I was giving *Girls Gone Wild* a new meaning, picking up guys in bars and meeting dads in the grocery store. Luckily, no one saw us—I hoped.

One good thing was Tommy did nothing for the house or Priscilla or me. Errands, school meetings, volunteer committees, all that was beneath him. Another bonus was he'd been called back up to Vermont for an overnighter tomorrow.

As I strode to my car, I mentally repeated my latest mantra. *Ignore, ignore,*

ignore.

This one word was the chalice I drank strength from. For the last week, every time I was alone in a room with Tommy, I'd whisper the word *ignore* in my head on repeat. I was determined not to fall into his trap or allow him to hurt me again.

Making a new friend gave me added hope of a new life, a new home for my heart to grow.

The next night, I sat with Priscilla as she ate pizza and told me about soccer practice.

"... and Annabeth got the goal, but she slid really hard on her hip and she was limping."

"Oh no. I just saw her dad yesterday in Wegman's. He asked me about almond milk."

"She's always talking about how her dad tries too hard. Her mom died, you know?" While I nodded, Priscilla took a bite of her pizza. "Mmm, this is so good. Take a bite."

She held her slice of white pizza with fresh tomatoes toward me. I couldn't resist and took a nibble, hoping the grease didn't drip down my chin.

Wiping her own face, she said, "Yeah, poor Annabeth. Can you imagine?"

"No," I said, shaking my head.

"She said her dad goes overboard with everything. She's okay now, she said. Of course, she misses her mom, but this is her life."

"You should have her over."

"Maybe," Priscilla said, grabbing her crust.

"We could do a girls' night with her, you know? It could be fun."

"Mom, seriously, we are not going to hang with you."

"I know. Really, I do," I said, more for my own breaking heart than for her. "So, a lot of homework tonight? You need a good shower—"

"Duh, and always a lot of work."

"I won't be late."

"Where are you going again?" she asked, taking a sip of her LaCroix.

It wasn't like I never ventured out. Sometimes, I went to a work thing or school committee meeting. On a few occasions, I met another mom, so this wasn't so out of the ordinary. But my lying about where I was going was.

"Quick work meeting and a get-together with a few writers."

"Sounds good. You should have a good time, Mom." With her hands in her lap, Priscilla stared at me, seeing all the way to my soul. My brave, smart girl, a ray of sunshine clearing away the dark skies.

"I will, baby girl," I said, reaching over to smooth a strand of hair out of her face.

"Go," she said with a smile, digging through her backpack before setting a big history book on the table. Then she picked up her last slice of pizza from the to-go box.

"Love you," I said, guilt heavy on my shoulders. But I deserved a moment's happiness, and the end game was to get out for myself and my daughter.

"Love you too, Mom."

I snagged my keys from the counter and blew Priscilla a kiss.

thirteen

m i c k

For our next get-together, I chose an exclusive sushi place near my condo. Not because I wanted to be showy, but I felt like the exclusivity would offer us some privacy. I knew Margo was leaving her daughter home alone to meet me, and this would likely be a dinner-only deal, but I wasn't deterred by that.

In fact, I was pretty sure things had rolled around too fast for us. I'd had enough time to think about it in New York, and then when I returned, I got caught up with work, and Margo explained she couldn't get a night off.

I waited outside the restaurant rather than heading in for our table, and exactly one minute after seven, Margo pulled up at the valet in her Volvo. She handed the keys to the attendant and looked up with a smile only for me. At least, that's what I told myself before mentally berating myself over falling for a married woman.

Margo smiled shyly as she walked toward me. "Hi."

"Hey," I said back with a wink.

We were careful not to hug or embrace like I wanted to before we walked into the restaurant side-by-side.

"Grantham," I told the host, and he nodded.

"It's so pretty in here," Margo said, taking in the navy walls and dimmed chandeliers with wide eyes.

"Sushi is good too," I said before hip checking her.

I couldn't help it—I needed a tiny bit of physical contact. Something else I'd berated myself for days over. I mean, if I was going to hook up with a taken woman, why pick one with a whole host of issues? My therapist wasn't far off when she told me I had rescue fantasies.

"It's been a while since I've had great sushi. I'm excited."

And that's why I couldn't stay away from this fair-haired beauty. Margo's need to experience life was infectious.

Seated at a table in the back, Margo in the booth looking out and myself in a chair directly across, I noticed her eyes were all made up, her lids sparkly, and her hair was in gentle waves.

"You look beautiful," I whispered. "Wish I could be next to you, pull you close to me, and breathe you in."

With her gaze downcast, she breathed out my name. "Mick."

"I know. I'll behave."

She looked up and gave me one of those smiles just for me.

"Tell me, everything okay getting here?"

She nodded. "I sat with Priss while she ate and made sure she was getting started on homework."

"You're a good mom," I told her.

"If I can get her out of this situation," she said.

"You will. My mom worried about it too. I know because she told me after the fact, but she always felt bad she didn't have the guts to do it earlier."

"I hope I have the guts," Margo said softly.

"Oh, you do." I wasn't entirely sure, but I was going to encourage her.

The server interrupted our moment, and I asked Margo what she was up for.

"One glass of red," she said.

I ordered a bottle, intending to leave the rest for the server. I decided to go with a Sapporo for myself, and asked for some edamame and dumplings, sending the server on his way.

Margo and I made small talk about my trip, seeing my friend from Wharton, and where Priscilla liked to get her pizza from, Village Pizza.

With our drinks poured, we clinked glasses, and I said, "To slowing it down a little. To getting out and finding new happiness."

"Really?" Margo raised her brows at my words.

"Really," I said before downing a sip of my beer. "We hit the ground running, and while I enjoyed every second of it—immensely—it was too rushed."

She nodded. "It was a little fast."

"It was. Look, we know the chemistry is there," I said, and this made her blush. The smallest hint of pink bloomed in her cheeks. When I teased, "And that was only the very tip of things to come," the pink turned to red.

"Mick . . ."

"Is that a warning or promise?"

"Both," she said.

"Fuck," I said and leaned in. "You look hot in that blouse."

Margo was wearing a black blouse, the buttons stopping right above her cleavage.

"But I'm getting distracted. What I want you to know is there's no rushing on my part. Of course, I don't want to see situations like with your wrist again, so time is somewhat imperative. But when it comes to you and me . . . I'm here."

Like a class A idiot, I laid it all on the line, a mistake I didn't make when it came to business. But when it came to my personal life, apparently all rules flew out the window.

"Tell me about your week," I said, changing the subject.

"Oh." She picked up her wine and took a sip. "Mostly the same. I'm writing a quickie piece, filler, on the power of reels when it comes to makeup."

"Wait, that sounded like a foreign language to me."

"Right. Reels on Instagram are quick, quirky video clips. Makeup influencers are using them for brief tutorials, and they attract a lot of eyeballs."

I nodded. "I have a lot to learn."

"You sound like one of the dads from Priscilla's class."

"Do I now?" Jealousy bubbled up inside me, which was ironic considering Margo was a married woman.

"Ha." She chuckled. "He's a widower, nothing to be worried about, other than he has no clue what to do with a tween girl."

"That makes two of us," I joked, and Margo's smile vanished.

"Yeah, I know," she said. "But Priss is my world."

"As she should be. I don't ever want to take that away from you. Not ever."

Her smile reappeared, and she talked a little more about this Dale character needing help with TikTok. I tried to follow along, but truthfully, other than LinkedIn, I didn't do much social media.

Our server arrived with some food, and Margo looked confused.

"I ordered us the tasting menu," I told her. "So we could talk more and worry less about what we were eating. Is that okay?"

Suddenly, I felt like an oaf. Margo didn't need someone making decisions for her.

"Sounds great," she said, rolling with it.

"It's basically a little of everything on the menu," the server said and left us to eat.

Margo reached across the table to pick up an edamame, looking happy with the selection so far. "You know, Priscilla was very taken with you. She commented that we could be happy like you." Keeping her gaze on the table, she seemed ashamed to admit how much this pained her.

"I don't know much about teen girls, but I do know about the situation Priscilla's in, and I'm sure she knows more than she's let on. She's going to be okay."

"I hope."

For the rest of the evening, we didn't discuss heavy stuff. We laughed and lingered over a lot of sushi. I learned a shrimp tempura roll was a weakness for Margo, and we ordered an extra roll.

She stuck to her one glass of wine, opting for a Pellegrino afterward, and I didn't pressure her. It wasn't an act. Despite falling for a married woman, I was a good guy.

At a few minutes after nine, Margo said she had to head home.

"Of course," I told her, handing my Amex to the server.

After I settled the bill, we stood, and I couldn't help my hand grazing her lower back as we walked out of the restaurant. I wanted to touch her a lot more.

Outside, waiting for her car to be brought around, it couldn't be helped when I leaned in and whispered, "Fuck, I want to kiss you."

It was the slightest gesture, but Margo leaned into me, whispering back, "Next time," as her Volvo appeared.

I rushed to hold the door for her myself. After tipping the valet, I told her, "Text me when you're home safely."

Margo nodded. "Thank you. This was a lot of fun. A perfect night."

Then she drove off to her house she shared with her abusive husband and daughter, and I wondered what the hell I was getting involved in.

fourteen

mick

I wasn't expecting to hear from Margo after sushi.

Although I'd laid it out there, I expected her feelings would continue to shrivel and close in on themselves. She was a scared bird sharing a house with an angry fox.

But none of this meant my near constant thinking about her came to a stop. The day afterward, I texted her.

That was fun. Thank you.

She didn't respond for a few hours, which didn't bother me like it would a younger guy. I was knee deep in the restaurant negotiation. I'd fallen for the broken-down Italian chain Jamie sold me on, or maybe it was his stories of his twins and the pig that won me over. I didn't know much anymore.

"Listen, they're wasting money on rent and shitty buildout," I said on speaker phone to one of the guys who worked for me. "I need you to go to New York and put pressure on the landlord. Either get us out of the lease or renegotiate, the latter being better. It's a good location, but we need a better interior and ventilation. Then we need a great manager. Yes, it's all about the chef, but he's not a business manager, and he's running it into the ground."

"Sounds good," Bradley said, tapping away at his laptop in the background. He was probably already pulling up reviews of managers we could hire away.

"Hole up at the Soho Club," I told him. "I'm sure you'll hear your fair share of trade gossip while you're there. Call me when you have some solid leads."

Bottom line, I couldn't say no to Jamie, but I also didn't have time to mess with this right now. I was busy assembling new management in my latest acquisition, and thinking about taking an outdoor strip mall for a steal . . . in Florida.

My phone dinged as I walked along the windows in my office, and my assistant walked in with a garment bag.

"For tomorrow. You have the awards dinner at the Fairmont. Cocktails at seven. Dinner at eight."

I nodded, dismissing him. I wanted to go as much as I'd like to go for a dental cleaning. I hated social events.

Looking at my phone, I saw Margo's text response.

You beat me to the thanks. It was really fun and THANK YOU.

I quickly responded.

All caps. You must've had a really good time.

Done with texting, I picked up the phone like the no-nonsense man I was . . . a self-professed tough guy.

"Margo," I said on a sigh when she answered. "How are you?" I asked, noting I hadn't asked if I could call. I didn't give a fuck anymore, but I should because it could blow back on her.

"I'm good. Finishing up a coffee and making notes on ideas for upcoming articles."

"Sounds productive," I said, leaning back in my desk chair.

"I want to have some pitches ready to go, you know? So I can make some money."

"Ah, good plan," I said. She was thinking about getting out, which wasn't only good for me, but mainly for her.

"Thanks." Her tone lowered as she said it, and I could tell she was rethinking her words.

"It's great that you're thinking ahead," I said, and I meant it. It was something my mom didn't do, and I wished she had. "I'd love to see you again," I blurted, and I also meant that.

The line was quiet for a beat before Margo said, "Me too."

"I know it's a lot of negotiating, finding time and space for you to make it work."

"Maybe tomorrow? If it's not too soon . . ."

"Never," I said, not mentioning the black tie event I was scheduled for. *Fuck it.*

"I can text you."

I wasn't going to argue. "Perfect," I told her. "I'll let you go now."

"Thanks," she said before disconnecting.

I didn't know what Margo was thanking me for—the night before, the call, or letting her go. I decided it was the former two and went back to work.

Margo's text came in the next day just before three o'clock.

I'm free around 7:30.

Elbow deep in hearing about some restaurant manager I absolutely had to steal from a competitor, I told Bradley, "One sec," and picked up my phone.

Good. I have an event at the Fairmont. I can kiss some rings at 7 and then meet you in the corner of the Oak at 7:30?

I tried to sound casual, like we did this all the time.

Sounds good.

I texted her a check mark and went back to Bradley.

From then on, the day sped by. I showered at my office, changed, and arrived in time for the cocktail hour at the event. I set an alarm on my phone for five minutes before I was supposed to meet Margo, so I could scat. As soon as it rang, I made an excuse to the person I was speaking with and headed for the elevator.

Pulling my bow tie loose as I made a beeline for the back corner of the Fairmont's bar, I saw it was free. It wasn't a see-and-be-seen spot, so it was often available. Sitting on a stool, I made sure Margo wasn't somewhere else in the bar before the bartender, Wes, came and took my order. We chatted a bit before Margo showed up, wearing a beautiful ruby-red blouse and jeans.

"I'm underdressed," she said, frowning. This was why I hadn't told her about the tux.

"Nah, I'm overdressed. You're the one who looks . . ." I leaned in as she sat down to share the last part. ". . . good enough to eat." Pulling away, I asked,

"Wine?"

She raised an eyebrow. "Trying to get me drunk, Mick?"

My name coming from her lips did something to me, bringing out a caveman I didn't know existed within me.

"One glass of wine?" I asked, being more specific.

"One," she said.

When Margo leaned over to pick up the wine list, I noticed she winced as she moved in the seat.

It was easy to fill in the blanks on my own. I didn't have to ask if she was okay or what had happened. I knew she wasn't okay, and I didn't want to know what happened.

So, I grumbled, "Margo . . ." The rest of the words were stuck in my throat.

"Don't," she said quickly, giving me a warning look.

"No."

When I leaned close, she edged away from me, awakening emotions buried deep inside me.

"I'm not the one you fear, you hear me?" My pulse rioted as I made demands I had no business making. "I'm burning with the need to protect you, and I don't want you to be afraid. But I don't want you to lie to me. I want to take care of you."

She nodded. "Let's get the wine, okay? Then we can talk."

There was a slight smile on her face as she asked, so I decided to ease up on this conversation for a while.

"Fair enough," I said, bringing my hand up to smooth her hair behind her ear, paying no mind to where we were, who might see, or who might care.

But all of that went out the fucking window when Margo winced, and my inner caveman went rogue. Swallowing my anger, I had no idea what was happening to me. I'd only met this woman a short while ago, but I already considered myself her personal protector.

"White or red?" I asked Margo as if nothing was amiss.

"I'm going to go with red." She smiled wider as she pointed to a selection on the menu, and didn't appear to be faking.

I motioned for Wes and told him to bring a glass of the cabernet Margo showed me. He was gone and back quickly, and the tension seemed to drain from Margo after her first sip.

"Margo . . ."

She nodded slowly. "We had it out. It was a bit worse than usual," she said, then took another sip. "I don't want to dump this on you. I'm out, we're here, so we should enjoy."

Leaning in, and noting this time she didn't lean away, I found her hand underneath the bar, and my thumb caressed hers.

"Dump away," I told her, and she frowned. "Or let's just have a good time."

Her phone lit on the bar and she gave it a quick glance. "Oh, one sec."

After reading her phone, she said, "Priss is at Penny's. She'll be home tomorrow after school. Sorry, Penny is one of her friends. Anyway, that was a group text from Penny's mom saying they're all okay."

I smiled, thinking it was sweet how involved she was with her daughter.

"No problem," I told her and meant it. I was never going to come between her and Priscilla.

"Do you mind if I scroll through the pictures real quick?"

"Go ahead," I said, nodding toward her phone and then taking a swig of my drink.

"Okay," she said a few seconds later, putting the phone back down. "I saw proof of life, and now I can breathe better."

"To breathing," I told her, and she raised her glass.

"So, the tux?"

"I had an event upstairs. A colleague of mine was receiving an award, but he won't notice I ducked out."

Her hand landed on my knee, and I'm not going to lie. My body woke up.

"Oh no. I didn't mean to take you away from something important."

"Never. This is way more fun," I said, and I meant it.

"Well, you look pretty good." Her hand moved across my knee and back again, her palm lighting my body on fire.

"You look pretty damn good too. So good, I'd like to eat you up . . . but let's get some real food," I said with a smirk, trying to joke.

"You're making the whole take-it-slow argument very hard to accept," Margo said, then grabbed her drink to wash down her words.

"Is that so?"

She nodded.

"Well, we are taking it slow. Like it or not."

She ran a hand through her hair, and her blouse fell open at her cleavage, showing me exactly why I didn't want to take it slow.

"What do you say? Some food?" I asked instead of taking her back to my place.

"Sounds perfect."

We leaned in so close, our heads were almost touching as we read the menu together.

"Fries?" she asked with a grin. "I'm in the mood to be bad."

"If that's your kind of bad, I don't want to be good," I said.

This set her off into a fit of laughter that continued all through my calling Wes over and ordering. I added a flatbread and some shrimp.

"You know what? Bring some of those lamb meatballs too," I said, and Wes was off to do his thing. Once he was gone, I turned back to Margo. "What's up now on your writing agenda?"

"Really? You want to know?"

"Really. I want to know it all."

"I'm almost done with all the preliminary interviews on the fashion piece, and now I'm sketching out some pitches. This whole meet and greet with Dale . . ."

I couldn't help the growl that escaped my mouth. Or the laugh that followed. "You know what? I'm a grown man, successful, independent, and you bring me to my knees."

This got me an even bigger laugh from Margo, her head thrown back with abandon, exposing the expanse of her neck.

"Oh, don't do that," I whispered in her ear. "Makes me want to nip and lick my way up your neck to your mouth."

Her chin tucked down now, she stared at me and deadpanned, "Hey, Mr. I Want to Take It Slow . . . stop making lewd suggestions." Her lips tipped up, so I could tell she was joking.

"Touché, touché. Now, back to Dale and your idea."

I made a note to check this Dale guy out. Could be he'd sniffed out Margo's situation at home and was moving in for the kill. Not that I was any better, but I spotted her first.

"Well, he's so lost when it comes to social media and parenting, and it occurred to me that not everyone knows as much as I do. He'd like me to give him some tips, but I've come across a whole series of apps to help monitor kids on their phones. And get this? Most of them are developed by women. STEM moms," she said, laughing while saying the last part.

When I gave her a confused look, she explained. "You know, S-T-E-M. Science, technology, engineering, or math. It's big in schools."

I couldn't help but grin. Margo's excitement was contagious.

"Damn, you're smart. I really dig it," I said as our fries arrived.

"I don't know about that, but this is pretty cool, and I have a call in to my editor. I want to do a spread, and you know what the hook is?" She paused and grabbed a fry.

"What's the hook?" I asked, watching her chew and wanting to lick the salt off her lips.

"These apps could charge a ton for ads or sponsors. Can you imagine how big and specific an audience advertisers would be reaching? On an app developed by moms for parents?" She took a sip of her wine, then mumbled, "Shoot. I didn't mean it like that. I'm going on and on about parenting."

"Hey, it's cool. I love how enthusiastic you become when you're excited about something. It's hard not to catch the spirit . . . even if I have no idea what you're going on about."

"How about I have a few fries and some more wine and take it down a notch, and you tell me what's happening with you."

She took a fry as Wes delivered the other appetizers, and she kept chewing, nodding her thanks.

"I bought a restaurant in New York. Foolish investment. I had the money to play around with, but not the time."

"Wow. A big place? What kind of food? Tell me everything."

It was the first time I'd talked business with a date, a woman who I didn't do business with. It was strange but comforting to share the details of it with someone. I went over the risks and how the restaurant was basically falling apart.

Margo listened intently, and every so often, ran her hand over my knee.

From afar, we were two people in lust. Sexual tension radiated between us. If you came too close, though, you'd see her wedding band and my lack of one, and know someone was going to get burned.

"So, I sent Brad there to deal with it because I need to spend my time here."

"Lucky for me. Although, I should say I'm sorry for the randomness of today. When I texted yesterday, I didn't mean to make you change your plans or be so . . . formidable."

Bringing my hand to her face, I gave my thumb permission to swipe her cheek, feeling the softness of her skin and absorbing every shock wave the touch brought me.

"You can be as formidable as you'd like, and you know what? You don't ever have to apologize for your behavior to me."

Her eyes turned downward, and I took in her lashes fluttering. She looked up and stared at me before speaking again.

"When I look into your eyes, your deep, dark eyes, which should be sinister, but they're not, I believe you. I believe I shouldn't have to apologize or be hit for forgetting to pick something up at the store." Her hand came up to cover her mouth, to force her admission back inside, but it was too late.

"You know what? I'm done with slow," I said in her ear, and she peeked up at me, her eyes shadowed by her hair. "Not that kind of slow, but the kind where I can hold you and run my hand down your back and kiss you as much as I want."

Her breath caught in her throat, and she nodded. "That may be nice."

"Let's go," I said. "We have some more time tonight?"

Before she could answer, I backpedaled a little. "I don't want to pressure you."

"I have time."

Slapping my Amex on the bar, I willed Wes to hurry.

"You know," she said, "I have all these pockets of time, and I don't even know what I filled them with before. I guess being sorry for myself."

Signing my name on the bill, I looked up. "You don't have to do that, play Monday-morning quarterback. You're moving forward, so don't dwell on the past."

"Thank you," she said softly, and we stood.

"I would take your hand, but let's not give ourselves away," I said matter-of-factly.

"That's fine. Now I can stare at your ass in that tux," she whispered before falling in step behind me.

margaret

"I took an Uber here," I told Mick when we stepped outside the bar, my heart stampeding in my chest. It wasn't nerves or fear of getting caught or hurt. It was anticipation of being held, of being cared for in a way I never had before.

"You okay to ride over with me?" he asked, handing his slip to the valet. Of course, his SUV was directly out front, and it only took a few seconds for them to whip it around.

I simply nodded, and then Mick opened the passenger door for me.

The sky was a midnight blue with stars twinkling in the distance. A breeze brushed by me as the door closed, and a chill ran down my spine.

"Ready?" Mick raised an eyebrow, turning to face me as he got settled in the driver's seat.

"Ready," I said firmly.

The foreign car purred as it rolled out of the driveway and onto the street.

"Do you mind if I open the window?" I asked.

"You don't have to ask shit like that, Margo."

Cracking the window, I inhaled some much-needed fresh air and closed my eyes, thinking this was normal. And it could be, if I weren't married to someone else.

"Not for long. You need to break free," Mick said, bringing me back from what I thought were my private thoughts.

"Did I say that aloud?"

He nodded and made a sharp turn into his building. Entering from the garage, we went up the elevator, his hands on my waist and his mouth on mine as soon as the doors shut.

"I know it's wrong, but it feels so right," I mumbled.

"This isn't you, Mar, to lie or be untrue," he said, holding my hand, shortening my name even further.

I shook my head as the doors opened and we made our way into his penthouse.

"Maybe we can make it beyond the door this time," he teased, leading me toward the sofa. "Sit. Water? Wine?"

"Water," I said, my throat dry with anticipation.

"Sparkling? Still?"

"Sparkling," I said as he moved toward the open kitchen. "I take it you don't go to the grocery store yourself?"

He laughed at my accusation, raising his hands in the universal sign for surrender. "Caught. My housekeeper's name is Rochelle, and she's a queen. Shops, orders supplies from the 'Zon, waits for handymen, cleans, keeps me in line. Only thing she doesn't do is cook."

He returned to me with Pellegrino in a water goblet.

Handing me the glass, he said, "I know it makes me look terribly spoiled, but I'd rather work than mess with all that shit. I can do it all. Believe me, I did my time when I was growing up. There wasn't a thing I didn't help my mom with. And Rochelle is well compensated, including benefits for her and her son. She's a single mom."

"You don't need to defend yourself to me." I sipped my water rather than tell him I couldn't stop admiring his past passion for protecting his mom, and the way he was a white knight when it came to anyone else he met.

I wondered if I had a son like Mick, would he do the same for me? Priscilla was doing her part to encourage me to get free. Girls and women talk, but men take action, right?

"We do," Mick said.

"Ugh, talking out loud again. It's becoming a bad habit with you. There's something about you. I let my guard down, which is a big deal because I don't think I've lowered it in a decade."

"That's a great compliment."

He leaned forward and took my goblet, setting it behind us on the table. Then he used a fingertip to bring my face close to his, his lips caressing mine. Softly at first, then a little firmer until my mouth opened and his tongue entered my mouth.

We sat like that for a long time, kissing, his palm roaming my back, under my shirt, my skin on fire. When we finally broke free, my lips felt wrung out in the best way possible, and my body was hot with need.

"You need to get out, Margo," Mick said, cupping my chin lightly. "Not for me, not for us, but for you."

"I know. I'm trying to think about the best way. I called a lawyer. Did the preliminary stuff, asked questions. We're going to meet."

"Do it sooner rather than later," Mick said, his eyes black like the night, but inviting like a warm bath in the winter.

"Okay."

"Good."

We kissed a while longer, and my groin ached. My body had never felt so primed.

"Mick," I murmured.

"I know, but not now. We did that once. Rushed. Once you're free, we can take our time."

My libido was wild, making me want to crawl out of my skin.

"Am I panting?" I asked, and this got me a huge barrel laugh.

"A little." Mick smirked when he said it, and it was more cute than sinister.

I wanted to go to bed. I desperately wanted him inside me. I needed to tell him I'd made a mistake in thinking we rushed last time, but before I could, he took my hand and pulled me up.

"Believe me, I'm aching for you, but we're doing this right. You are getting out of the bad place you're in, and then we're making it good together. I'm going to call you an Uber."

I walked to the window and looked out. "I love this view."

"Me too. Especially when I'm on my exercise bike to nowhere."

This made us both chuckle as we looked toward his Peloton.

"I hope to share this view a lot more with you." Mick came up behind me, kissing my earlobe and whispering promises for our future until the Uber app pinged.

Then I was on my way back to the *bad place*, as Mick had called it.

sixteen

margaret

"Have the best time," I shouted at Priscilla as she boarded the bus for their fall class trip.

It was the second week in October, and the air already hung limp with condensation and heavy with decisions I needed to make.

Priscilla turned and waved, calling out, "Stay warm." The evenings were already chilly and the mornings chillier.

"I'm pretty sure I made Penny pack an extra five sweaters," Sheila said as she stepped next to me on the sidewalk.

"Yep, I loaded Priss down with instructions to wear layers."

Pulling my jacket tighter, I took a sip of coffee from my travel mug. Despite being sad over Priscilla leaving, I was a tad thrilled over taking my coffee away from the house. I'd poured my mug and scooted from the kitchen before Tommy came downstairs. I'd been doing my best to avoid his presence, and when I was forced to spend time with him, I nodded a lot and stuck to short responses like "you're right" or "okay."

"I'm at a loss with what I will do with two nights to myself," Dale said as he appeared on the other side of me.

"Not me," Sheila said as we waited for the bus to pull out. "While those girls are picking apples and braiding one another's hair, I'm going to make a stiff martini and attend to some serious self-care."

Dale looked in her direction and raised an eyebrow, and they exchanged a look.

Sheila snorted. "Not that kind of self-care. Jeez, Dale, get your mind out of the gutter."

I finally got the joke, but was shocked at the level of closeness Dale and Sheila apparently had.

"Bubble bath, reality TV, and a good exfoliation, if you must know," Sheila said.

Dale nodded, and I went back to my coffee, thinking I hadn't been properly caffeinated. Or maybe my own transgressions were making me suspicious of everyone else.

"Will you be at the next meeting?" Sheila asked.

"Remind me when it is?" I'd forgotten to put it in my calendar.

"Next Monday. Same place, the Paula."

Happy to have my phone to pull out and allow my messy hair to fall and shield my face, I felt a blush burn my cheeks. The Paula would forever hold a special place in my heart, since it was where I met Mick for lunch and then drinks.

We'd met for lunch once and a quick happy hour drink since our sushi dinner, now choosing more discreet locations. I wondered if he would meet me at the Paula next Monday.

"I'll be there," I finally said, looking up from my phone. Juggling my phone and my travel mug, I turned to Dale. "You coming?"

"Wouldn't miss it. It's an excused absence from parenting."

"That's the truth if I ever heard it," I said with a chuckle.

"Hey, thanks for the article you sent," Dale said to me, brushing his hair back off his forehead.

He was wearing sweatpants, a hoodie, and running shoes, and it was the first time I'd really noticed how handsome he was. He was a good one, a keeper, and he needed to find someone to cherish him. Lord knew, he'd cherish her back.

"What article?" Sheila asked, standing awfully close to Dale.

"Oh, Margaret was kind enough to pass on a TikTok tutorial," Dale said, and a blush tinged his cheeks. "We ran into each other a couple weeks ago, and I admitted that I don't know much about it. You know, these girls are going to be living on it soon."

"I'm so glad they weren't allowed to take their phones on this trip," Sheila said, moving on with her own agenda.

I nodded, although I wished I could say good night to Priscilla.

"Oh well, I have to be getting on with my day to myself. You going for a run, Dale?" Sheila asked, her expression blank but her voice a bit too high.

"Yep, a long one, and then off to the office. Signing off on a new product line today, a closet design system for Bed Bath & Beyond."

"Wow," she said.

"Lots of luck to you," I said to Dale, and "Enjoy your self-care," to Sheila. "I'm heading out to finish writing a piece and then brainstorm some new ideas."

In reality, I wanted to call Mick. It had been a week since he'd instituted his go-slow plan. Honestly, I was ready to go a bit faster, but I knew better than to push for anything more. Bad decisions only made bad choices worse.

Mick was successful in business for a reason. He worked hard. I certainly wasn't going to call him first thing in the morning, all needy and begging for sex because it had been a week since I'd seen him.

Over the past week, we'd talked on the phone a few times, and I'd sworn to him that I was working toward an endgame. In reality, I hadn't made much progress. For some reason, I was having a hard time pushing forward, dismantling the fake castle I'd built around myself.

The bus honked and started to pull away. All of us looked up and waved at the darkened windows where surely our daughters were busy gossiping and not caring about us waving.

"See you both on Monday," I said to Sheila and Dale, waving with my free hand before I turned and took a sip of my coffee on my way to my car.

Later that day, I was in the kitchen, humming and singing to myself while making a homemade flatbread and caramelizing some onions to put on top of it, when the garage door lifted.

"Alexa, turn off," I told the device playing Madonna.

"What the fuck is that?" Tommy barked at me as he came inside. No *hello* or *how was your day?*

Knowing better than to ignore his question, I said, "Flatbread. I was making a mushroom, onion, and goat cheese flatbread."

"For me? You think I want to eat that shit?"

Tommy stood before me in his suit, his hair perfectly combed and a snarl on his face. He hadn't mentioned coming home early, and I was perplexed as to why he was here but didn't dare ask.

"While you're at it, tell me what this crap is that you're wearing." His snarl turned into a menacing smirk.

"I was going to make some bacon-wrapped scallops too. And shrimp cocktail. I stopped at the market." I answered his first question, not thinking it necessary to explain my leggings and oversize T-shirt.

I'd hoped to make some small bites for myself, munching a little before he got home for his bourbon. Then I could leave him a plate and excuse myself to bed for my own self-care. Of course, this plan was all based on his working late, which apparently wasn't happening.

"Seriously? I don't want that."

When he slammed his hand on the kitchen table, I couldn't help but flinch. Rather than risk getting burned, I hurriedly turned the cooktop off. My onions wilted in the pan, the smell barely registering over my own fear wafting around me.

"You put on the calendar that Priscilla was on her class trip. I made the mistake of taking that as an invitation to get a piece of ass."

Oh.

"Shut your mouth, Margaret. Whatever is about to come out of it, bottle it. My dick is going to fall off from lack of use."

This was a fresh argument from Tommy, and I wasn't sure what to do. Mystified, I stood there, trying to figure out what was happening.

He was up for sex?

Giving me no time to move away, he grabbed my arm, spinning me around and forcing me to face the oven. I didn't know whether he saw me turn it off or not, but I didn't let him in on the secret.

With my right arm twisted behind me, he told me, "Brace yourself on the oven with your other hand."

A chill I'd never felt before ran through me. Tommy had never forced sex on me. I didn't know why I didn't think he would never try. When it came to him, pretty much everything was fair game.

So caught up in fear and worry, I didn't hear the whoosh until his hand cracked my ass. He must have cocked back in record time, because another blow hit me before I could swallow. This continued for a while, and I couldn't help but think how lucky I was that he didn't rape me when he finished. I didn't want him anywhere near me, let alone inside me.

Without anything further, he said, "I'm going for a steak and a few drinks."

Like a vampire, he disappeared before I could catch my breath and turn around.

When I finally did, my chest collapsed in a long exhale, and then a second one when the garage door opened and closed. It wasn't until I was sure he was really gone that I realized hot tears were streaming down my cheeks.

I had to get out of this situation fast. Tonight, or tomorrow before Priscilla came home.

There were good people out there. Decent men like Dale and Mick, and my daughter needed to know that.

seventeen

mick

My phone rang with an unidentified number, and I debated answering. It was around seven at night in the middle of the workweek, which was still considered to be working hours in my life.

Despite being in the middle of answering several work emails, I was trying to get in a few sets of pushups on my living room carpet. I picked up the phone because maybe it was an offer on the building I was trying to sell. I had a warehouse I'd acquired in one of my dealings that I was trying to unload.

"Hello? Grantham here," I said.

"Hi, Mr. Grantham. It's John Wiley. John, at the Oak Bar," the poor kid said, stumbling over his words. "Wesley's buddy."

"I know. What's shaking?" I said, trying to calm poor John's worries.

"You told Wes to give you a ring if we ever saw the pretty lady around town. Said she was going through a tough time. She's here."

I started pacing in front of my window, ignoring the lights twinkling in the distance as I ran through worst-case scenarios of all the possibilities of what the fuck could actually be happening.

I'd just had a drink two nights before with Paul from the office at the Oak.

Wes had asked me where my new lady was, and I'd said, "She's at home." I'd thought about saying more, but only added, "Life isn't easy for her."

An unspoken current ran between us. Without words, he let me know he'd seen her wedding band—maybe it was the tiny glint in his eye. Plus, he was a bartender, for God's sake. They saw everything in their job, and were more accurate than a therapist.

"Like I said," I'd told Wes, "things are tough for her. If you ever see her out when you're working, or even when you're out on your own, let me know."

I couldn't really identify why, but I felt like the shitstorm Margo lived in was going to blow up into an F4 tornado. She'd insisted she was making progress, but I didn't believe it.

In the end, I knew there would be some aimless seeking of relief. I remembered my mom hitting the dating scene hard, like it was a full-time job and she was gunning for an end-of-year bonus. It was as if she'd been a captive cat who'd been let loose and went wild on the town, feasting on garbage and scraps. Predictably, that's exactly the type of men she met. Scraps. And that was *not* fucking going to be the case with Margo.

Now, if I was hearing correctly, the woman I was irrationally falling for was at the same bar we'd shared two separate evenings at, and she didn't let me know she was going. Visions of what might be happening skirted across my mind, none of them good.

"She's pretty lit up, has some guy falling all over her . . ."

"What did you say, John?" I'd been so caught up in my own damn head, I had to ask him to repeat himself.

"I'm sorry. I don't mean to bug you. She's just pretty lit up, and some guy—"

"No, no. You're not bugging me. I'm on my way. Make sure she stays there and doesn't go anywhere with that prick. Christ, make sure she doesn't even go to the bathroom," I said quickly and then hung up.

Snatching my sweater from the couch, I pulled it over my head and grabbed my keys. Not bothering with the elevator, I took the stairs to the garage, trying to pound out the anger burning through me.

A rush of colder air smacked me in the face when I burst into the garage. While it had a welcome calming effect on the dark mood flooding my veins, I reminded myself I had a coat in the car, and put it on before I got in.

Why do I care? I predicted a blowout when I got to the bar that would ripple out onto the sidewalk.

I stormed into the Oak from the side door. I'd parked out front, but rather than walk through the lobby of the hotel, seething and snarling, I took the moment to walk around the outside of the building to clear my head.

As soon as Margo spotted me, she squeaked out, "Mick."

"Margaret," I said curtly.

The sad look that filled her eyes told me she noted that I didn't use her nickname. I was too mad at her to be my usual self, full of intimacies and cute greetings, but also cautiously optimistic that nothing horrible had happened.

After taking in the scene, I stared at Margo and waited for her to say something, knowing full well my feelings for her were over-the-top, and my reaction to this unwarranted.

"Pardon me," the guy hitting on her had the nerve to say.

Well, he could just shut right the fuck up.

"Pardon yourself," I spat out, throwing his words back at him.

Then I couldn't help myself. Staring him down, I asked, "You in the business of picking up taken women?" With my back to Margo, I watched him reach for his credit card and slap it on the bar.

Good boy, I thought, and then he had to go and ruin the moment.

"Dude, she said she was separated."

"First off, don't fucking *dude* me," I told him. Then I had to make something abundantly clear. "Second, I'm not her sorry excuse of a husband. Either way, if I were you, I'd get the hell out of here."

Then the slimy bastard leaned around me to ask Margo, "You okay? Want me to drop you somewhere?"

I answered for her, letting him know she was more than fine, and shooed him off.

With my focus entirely back on Margo, I asked, "What did he do?"

I didn't mean the loser prick who just exited stage right, and she knew it too.

Rather than answer, she reached for her glass.

Unable to stomach watching her drinking something another man had bought for her, I took her glass from her hand and set it aside. "Tell me what happened. I'll get you a new drink that piece of shit didn't buy you before I take you back to my place and make you forget both of them. If that's what you need. Do you need a reminder of how we work?"

"Mick, please," she begged, and my impatience reared its ugly head.

"Talk," I said firmly, my coat still on, the cold air long forgotten, my internal temperature rising.

"Same as usual," she whispered.

She typically didn't go into detail, but the bruises and scars I'd seen on her forced my imagination to work overtime.

"How did you know I was here?" she asked.

"Fucker," I said, ignoring her question. After muttering some other nonsense under my breath, I said, "You need to push forward and get out like you said you would. If not for me, then—"

I didn't have a chance to finish because her phone rang, interrupting. I wanted to tell her to do it for herself, but really, I wanted it for me.

Margo's voice started to quiver during her low phone conversation, then panic swirled around her as she stood and yanked her coat on.

Only one thing could scare her this way—her daughter.

I reached past her and tossed cash on the bar, then took her hand in mine, giving zero fucks about who saw. Margo needed someone—needed *me*—and fuck it, I was going to be there for her.

I guided her out through the lobby, toward the valet, and into my SUV.

As she slid into the passenger seat, she just said, "Mass General. Now."

I put it in the GPS, making sure we went the most direct route.

As I pulled away from the curb, I made my feelings known. "You bought yourself a day or two, Margo, but this has to end," I said, meaning her sham of a marriage to a brutal man.

I wanted us.

I needed us to see what we could become, free of shackles. I'd care for her and her daughter like they were my most precious commodities.

I wasn't even sure how I knew any of that, or how I even knew I wanted whatever this was or is. I just did.

eighteen

Before Mick could even put the car in park in front of the emergency department, I flung open the door and ran to the entrance.

"I'll park and be in," Mick called after me.

I thought about telling him not to. It wasn't his place to take care of me, but I only nodded without turning around. For years, I'd had no one to lean on—this was new to me. I assumed Mick would head to the emergency room. He hadn't asked exactly where I was going, but he was resourceful.

We'd kept the chatter to a minimum in the car as I fiddled with my phone and waited for an update from Sheila. It was my preference not to dissect my erratic behavior while Mick's words rolled around in my belly and mind.

Priscilla was in the hospital and needed me, and where the hell was I? Picking up random men, trying to sooth a collapsed heart and an aching backside.

I beat myself up on repeat for not picking up Sheila's original call. Naively, I'd thought it was about the damn parents' meeting. I'd also missed a call from an unknown number and ignored it, too busy flirting with some douche of a guy.

118

In reality, I should have been worried about getting the hell out of my abusive marriage.

"Margaret," Sheila called to me as soon as I walked through the emergency room's automatic doors.

Looking up, I saw her standing on the other side of the metal detectors. She bit her bottom lip and held her cardigan tight around her middle, looking nothing like the confident parents' association piranha I once thought her to be.

"My daughter's in there," I said to the security guy, tossing all my belongings in a bin and hurrying through the metal detector.

All I could mumble was a quick thank-you before Sheila had her arm around me, pulling me into a hug. I can't lie—after Mick saying he would be in, it was the most comforting gesture I'd experienced in years.

"She's going to be okay," Sheila whispered, her palm running up and down my back as we walked. "She fell from the bunk doing some dance routine with the girls. Penny is in a boatload of trouble with school and me because she sneaked her phone and was videotaping the whole act, but she's really a hero because she called me right away. I called the teachers, because of course, the girls were afraid to go and tell."

"You know what? Let's skip the semantics," I said, wanting to get to my daughter.

Not taking offense, Sheila nodded. "You're right."

"Where are they?" I asked as she guided me down the hall.

"After taking some x-rays and an exam, the doctor is waiting to see you. Priscilla told them to wait for her mom because she said she needs you, and—"

"Of course she did," I said quickly, interrupting. "She can't go through an accident without a parent."

"Um . . ." Sheila wrung her hands, starting to say something else, but paused when Mick barged down the hall toward us as he bellowed my name.

"Margo. Margaret!"

Sheila and I both turned, taking in the panicked yet gorgeous man calling my name.

I started to say, "My friend Mick drove me here," just as a second loud voice carried through the air.

"What the hell is this?" a booming voice bellowed in the hall.

I could have sworn I just heard Priscilla call for me from the room we were standing in front of . . . but circumstances didn't allow me to investigate.

"When you didn't pick up your cell phone, I called the house," Sheila said quickly, trying to explain, but Tommy cut her off.

"Margaret, where the hell did you go? What the hell is this?" He waved his hand at me, presumably at my outfit, but it didn't stop me from flinching. His voice became increasingly louder as he spoke. "No one could reach you. What kind of mother are you? Our daughter was injured on a damn school trip, and you're nowhere to be found."

"I was out for a bit, cooling off from the . . ." I scrounged deep in my belly for the words and the courage. "From the state you left me in," I said in a loud voice. It wasn't the time or place, but Tommy had hurt me long enough, and I'd hidden it for too long.

"The state I left you in?" he demanded, his veins popping out in his neck, sweat beading on his forehead. "My state is the one you should be worried about, after getting me all worked up for nothing. Then I try to get some work done, so I can pay your bills, and this woman is blowing up the phone."

He flung an arm toward Sheila, and all I wanted to do is take his attention away from her. She was nothing but an innocent bystander.

"Tommy, our daughter needs me," I said, trying to reason with him. "No doubt, I need to be a mother first and good to myself second, which is what tonight was. Good for me. But I never anticipated an accident like this, so if you will let me go to our daughter—"

I didn't know if it was real or not, but I swore I heard Priscilla calling me. I moved in the direction of her voice, but Tommy grabbed my arms and shook me hard in front of the only people who'd cared enough about me to come.

"Answer me. Where the hell were you?" he screamed at me, snarling.

He'd never made a scene in public before. Although, he'd never tried to force sex on me either . . . so tonight was about a lot of firsts.

Feeling my lips quiver, I sucked back impending tears. A cocktail of fear and embarrassment ran through my veins.

"Tommy, let me go see Priscilla," I said softly, trying to pull my wrist free and deescalate the spectacle. "I'm here now. I can take over, and you can go back to work. We can discuss all of this later."

I couldn't even look at Sheila, afraid to see her expression. She was probably horrified by my situation, and even more so by my docile behavior. The thought of this made me pipe up.

"Just go, because this is over. This cycle of you hurting me," I said through gritted teeth, still trying to free my wrist.

"I want an answer," Tommy growled out, tightening his grip.

"Tommy," I pleaded.

"Hey, she wants to go see her daughter," said a furious grumbly voice I'd know anywhere.

I'd been silently hoping Mick didn't get involved, and realized he'd bided his time and now was done, actually seeing me be abused.

Tommy squeezed even tighter, and I was grateful this wasn't the same wrist he'd squeezed last time. "Mind your own business. I don't even know who the hell you are," he yelled at Mick, tossing his head back, all the while not taking his hand off me.

Sheila decided to pipe up. "He drove Margaret here. He's a friend. He can be here . . ." She trailed off as she realized what she just said.

I'm guessing Sheila didn't have much personal experience in the domestic violence arena. Maybe she hadn't said where I'd been, but she'd confirmed who I was with, and by doing so, had unwittingly make things worse. She'd meant to defuse the situation, but this information lit a fire in Tommy I'd never seen before.

"*He* brought you here?" Tommy spat at me, pushing me back toward the wall.

Phantom Priscillas called to me from everywhere, and I wondered where the doctor or anyone was. Why was the hall so empty? A continuous symphony of beeps and dings played from the nearby nurses' station.

"Stay here," Tommy demanded, letting go of my wrist.

This time, I definitely heard Priscilla yell out, "Mom!" But I couldn't go to her because when Tommy released me, he punched Mick in the jaw.

"Sir, you're going to have to calm down."

Finally, someone from the hospital made an appearance. A nurse, I thought. The man was wearing scrubs and taking in Tommy's beady eyes, hopefully thinking he needed to call for backup.

Luckily, Tommy's punch barely moved Mick an inch. He stood tall, staring down my husband, a warrior coming to my defense. It couldn't have been a worse scenario, and I still hadn't seen my daughter.

"I will not calm down. My daughter is injured and hasn't been treated because she was waiting for her mom to get here," Tommy said, his voice rising with every syllable. "Her mom, who was apparently out with *this fucker.*"

"Hey, take it down a notch," Mick said, then addressed the nurse. "My friend would like to go see her daughter, but this man just got physical with her. I'm pretty sure she needs an x-ray of her own, on her wrist."

I couldn't look at Mick. Refusing to meet Tommy's menacing glare, I focused on poor Sheila. Her wide gaze bounced from me to Mick to Tommy and back again. Her mouth hung open, and red splotches had formed on her neck.

Everyone's focus turned to my wrist, which was swelling and turning redder by the second.

"Sir, please sit down over there," the nurse said to Tommy in a forceful tone, then grabbed his walkie-talkie and called for security.

"That's bullshit." Tommy turned to stalk toward the hospital exit, clearly not caring about his daughter.

"No, you don't." The nurse came over and clapped his hand on Tommy's shoulder.

Tommy stilled, clearly unsure of what to do, and sweat beaded on his forehead. This nurse was a burly man, clearly not taking any shit, and wasn't his broken wife.

Finally, Mick swung an arm around Tommy's shoulders, stopping him. "The man said to wait." To the nurse, he said, "Tell security to hurry."

Finally, Mick's attention swung to me.

"Go see Priscilla," he told me. "Sheila, right? Can you go with Margo?"

"Margo?" Tommy asked. "Who the hell is that?"

No one had a chance to answer because security arrived, and I ducked into Priscilla's room, wanting to avoid whatever happened in the hallway. I genuinely felt bad for the security staff and worried for Mick, but I needed to be with my daughter.

As soon as Priscilla saw my face, tears slid down her cheeks. "Mommy," she said through raspy tears.

I leaned close and brought her cheek to my chest, trying not to hurt her arm and shoulder, which were in some sort of makeshift sling. Over and over, I whispered, "I love you, baby girl."

Priscilla wept softly, and we sat there for a while, just leaning on each other.

Sheila hovered, trying to blend into the background. Occasionally, she walked toward the doorway to see what was happening.

A bit later, Sheila kissed my cheek and told me to call her whenever I needed her, no matter the time. She needed to go home and see what was happening with Penny on the trip. I assumed she also needed to process the events of the night.

The doctor showed up a few moments later, apologizing for the delay. A man had fallen and broken his spine, and had to be stabilized before the doctor was free to come back to Priscilla.

I learned Priscilla broke her collarbone and forearm. She'd need surgery and a cast on her arm, and would have to wear a sling for her collarbone for a while.

Priscilla told the doctor she was lucky her mom worked from home and would take good care of her. Ever the dutiful daughter, she sang my praises.

She also said, "That's my dad they called security on, and they should know he does that all the time to my mom. I want you to tell them that," she said pointedly to the doctor.

"Priss," I whispered.

"No, Mom."

The doctor nodded, explaining they would take her in a few minutes to get everything set, and we would be here for a few hours or more. He told me to get a cup of coffee and relax, that my daughter was in good hands.

A few minutes after that, Mick came in the room, and Priscilla smiled like the boy band BTS had arrived.

"They want you to press charges. Me too," he grumbled, standing next to me while I sat on the bed. "I said it's up to you."

All I could whisper was, "I'm sorry you're involved." To Priscilla, I said, "And you too, baby. I'm sorry."

"Don't do that," Mick said. "I'm not sorry I was here. It's time you did that."

"He's right, Mom," Priscilla said, sounding so much older than her years.

"I assume he wants to make some deal against my pressing charges?" I asked, because I knew how Tommy operated.

Mick nodded.

This type of thing had happened once long ago. Tommy and I had gotten into a big fight in the yard, and he threw me down on the grass. I'd had a bruise on my hip for months.

A neighbor had seen and told me to press charges.

Tommy had caught wind and talked me out of it, threatening he would take Priscilla away. Surprisingly, he'd behaved himself for a while after that. It was the only six months of peace I'd had in our marriage.

But I didn't tell Mick any of this. No point in opening old wounds.

Tommy would win this time too, so I wouldn't bother to press charges. Why? Because I'd been dumb enough to have a goddamn affair before ending things.

I couldn't dwell on all of that, though, because they came to get Priscilla for surgery. Of all people, she asked Mick to walk with her gurney on the way there.

Kids had an uncanny way of finding the sore spot and holding their finger on it.

nineteen

margaret

The next morning, I sat at my kitchen table in my robe, drinking coffee while Priscilla slept in her bedroom.

Tommy wasn't home. I didn't know where he was, and I didn't care.

I was deep in thought about everything I'd done wrong when a knock sounded from the front door. Standing, I hesitated, wondering who it was. I ruled out Tommy—he'd just bust in. Mick was a possibility, but he would call or text first.

Peeking out the window, I relaxed at the sight of Sheila standing outside in yoga pants and a puffer jacket, holding a bakery box.

"Hi," I said, opening the door.

"I didn't mean to show up unannounced," she said quickly. "I just couldn't stop thinking about you." She crossed the threshold without being invited inside.

"Excuse my appearance," I said, waving my good arm in front of my robe.

"Hey, I wouldn't even be upright if I were you," Sheila said, a tear forming in the corner of her eye.

Walking toward the kitchen, I beckoned for her to follow. "Come in."

Her curious gaze took in the open floor plan of the sprawling first floor, the cheery canary-yellow walls a direct contrast to the lives lived inside them. She walked behind me to the kitchen, bakery box in hand.

"Have a seat," I told her as she handed me the goodies.

"Scones and muffins," she said. "I thought Priscilla may like some."

I smiled. "She's asleep, but I'm sure she will."

Sheila slid onto one of the barstools at the breakfast bar, clasping her hands nervously on the counter. "Margaret . . ."

Glancing at her, I caught my breath. "Let me make another pot of coffee first. Before we do all of that."

She nodded, and I busied myself with the coffee maker.

While it was brewing, I said, "I'm sorry you had to see all that last night." I stared at the tile floor, afraid of what I'd see in her eyes.

"Margaret, I'm sorry we didn't pick up on anything. I mean, we're not close friends. At least, we weren't, although now we're becoming closer. But the girls? Priscilla never said a word, but the way she didn't want anyone to come over to your house, I just . . . I don't know. I'm smart, and I should have realized."

"Don't. Please. I didn't ask you to be a detective, and I didn't want anyone to fix anything for me. I was trying, but I made a mess in the process."

The coffee maker beeped, signaling it was done.

"How do you take it?" I asked Sheila while moving toward the Subzero.

"Half-and-half, if you have it."

I couldn't help but chuckle. "Oh, I do."

"What's that all about?" Sheila asked, cocking her head to the side.

Taking out the half-and-half, I poured some into my grandmother's cow-shaped creamer. It was one of the only family heirlooms I had left. Tommy had wanted to fill our house with all new stuff, but I'd sneaked this little relic in. This morning, its presence was giving me a boost of strength.

"It was one of the many fights Tommy and I had. He needed his half-and-half, and if I didn't make sure we were stocked, it . . . it always turned violent."

After setting a steaming mug in front of Sheila, I placed the cow next to her and then opened the fridge for my milk.

"That's . . . that's not normal, Margaret. You know that, right?"

I nodded, sitting across from Sheila, my mug in front of me. "In fact, that's how I met Mick. I was nursing my bruised self-esteem and a sore wrist over a glass of wine by myself, something I'd never done before, and he sat down next to me."

The story came out in bits and pieces as memories rushed back.

"I want you to know, meeting strange guys . . . that wasn't something I ever did before. I don't want you to think I'm that woman. The adulteress. But I guess I am."

"Shhh." Sheila reached out and took my hand. "You aren't that woman. As far as I'm concerned, Tommy broke your vows when he hurt you. You deserve happiness, and I want you to get it soon. Grab all of it."

Thinking, I stared at my coffee. "Although, Tommy gave in too easily. I don't think bullying me was his only skeleton in the closet. I'm just glad we hadn't . . . you know . . . in a long while. In fact, that's what this last fight was about, before I'd gone out and Priss got hurt. He wanted sex," I sputtered, feeling like a fool.

"It's okay," she said. "You don't owe someone intimacy who isn't kind to you."

I nodded. "You're right."

I couldn't believe the woman I used to see as a major helicopter parent and parents' association mogul was giving me comforting advice. I had no clue where her understanding and compassion were coming from, or this unusual friendship. All of it caught me off guard.

"Thank you, Sheila." Uncomfortable with the sex conversation, I changed the subject. "How is Penny? I hope she didn't get into too much trouble. They were being kids, and she was the brave one who asked for help."

"She's okay. Three days of afterschool detention, and a week of no phone after seven o'clock at night at home. Peter thinks we shouldn't punish her at all, but I needed to back up the school."

"Oh God. Peter. Your husband, right? I think I've only met him once or twice. Did you tell him?"

All of a sudden, the reality of what she'd witnessed crashed down around me. Everyone would know and look at me differently.

"I didn't go into detail. I mentioned that Tommy wasn't who he seemed to be. A little rough around the edges, and not the kind person he projected."

"Please, Sheila. I don't want the gossip hounds to have any fresh meat. It wouldn't be good for Priss."

She shook her head. "I would never. In fact, I feel so bad about it. Had I known, I wouldn't have told Tommy. I'm the reason he was there, and you got hurt."

My wrist ached, still red and swollen but not broken, although it was nothing compared to my daughter's physical and emotional injuries. She'd heard the whole battle in the hall, and then made her preferences known when she asked for Mick—a man she'd met once—over her own father.

"I'm not pressing charges," I blurted. "The police said I could, and encouraged me to. But Tommy called late last night and said he'd provide me with the house, a good-size settlement, and will continue to pay for Priscilla's schooling through college if I don't make waves. I agreed. Of course, I need a lawyer . . . to make sure everything I sign is kosher."

"Are you sure?" Sheila asked.

"Yes. I want all this to be over. I want the sun to set on this chapter and rise on the next one. Does that make sense?"

"It does, but I want to be sure you don't regret this later."

"He needs his income to pay for Priscilla. And let's be honest, I had my indiscretions."

Sheila frowned. "Those don't compare to what he did. Plus, he's giving in so easily."

"He is, and who the heck knows why. I don't even care. Plus, you can't say my indiscretion doesn't count. It does." I stared at my coffee mug, guilt eating me from the inside out. "I wasn't born to be a bad person."

"Anyone who talks to you for two seconds can tell that. Take Peter, he said you're so kind. And me . . . Jesus. I was ready to suck every bit of work you would give me on the event."

This made us both laugh.

"Oh, we needed that," I said, still chuckling.

"Tell me about Priscilla," Sheila said, turning serious again. "The girls all want to visit. I hope that's okay."

"Well, it'll be a big recovery for her. She'll be out the rest of the soccer season, but back for next. I know it. As for her heart, she seems more resilient than me. She never felt close to Tommy, and didn't even ask for him last night."

Sheila's face crumpled. "God, I never should have told him."

"It's okay, you didn't know. To be honest, I'm shocked he even showed up."

We both sipped at our coffee. Then Sheila opened the box and said, "Have one."

One look at the cranberry-orange scone, and I gave in. She didn't need to say anything more.

My phone rang as I took my first bite, and I held a finger in the air, excusing myself for a minute.

I swiped my finger over the screen to answer. "Hello?"

"Margo," Mick said, his voice soft yet rough around the edges.

"Sheila is here," I told him.

"I needed to check in. He didn't come home?"

"No. We spoke around one in the morning. Like I texted you."

Sheila took it all in, pretending to be interested in her muffin. It was probably the most carbs to pass her lips in a month.

"I'm going to call a lawyer later," I said, "and tell them what he proposed. I want to do the preliminary paperwork as soon as possible. It can't get processed or filed for a while, I think."

"I still think you should press charges."

"Like your dad, you told him the police would be back, but you didn't do anything that day. I took a page out of your book."

"Good one, Mar."

There Mick went again with the nickname for my nickname, and my resolve to be a good married woman melted. Yes, Tommy and I were separating, but I'd told myself to behave.

"I want to see you," Mick said. "When?"

"Mick . . ." It was the first time I'd said his name aloud in front of Sheila, and she raised her eyebrows. "I don't know."

"I do," he said. "It wasn't ideal how this all blew open, but it's done now. I'm coming over later, bringing dinner from the Paula. Ask Priscilla what she wants. Text me. I have to run to a work appointment . . . I'll call a little bit later."

He hung up before I could answer. Some women might have been put off by that, like he was bossing them around, but it was actually the first time someone had offered to take care of me.

"Well?" Sheila asked, reminding me she was here taking care of me too.

Somehow in this nightmare of a situation, I'd found an extended family a million times better than my biological one.

twenty

m i c k

Work was the salve I needed. It's how I overcame the torturous memories I had of my childhood.

Somehow, though, I'd put myself back in a similar scenario.

Kicking up dirt outside my car while on the phone with some chef in New York I was supposedly trying to hire, I had a random thought.

I should have shacked up with one of the women I dated over the years.

It would have been simple. I could have provided them with a good life, and they would have been a companion. But at the end of the day, there was no passion in my belly for them or a life with them. Why I found that fire with a married woman was anyone's best guess.

An injured—but not broken—married woman.

When I looked at Margo, I saw an amazing combination of grit and grace. My mom had the latter in spades but lacked the former.

Huh. Maybe that's why.

"Right, exactly. We'll deal with your exit strategy where you currently are and take care of all the legal fees, and then restructure your contract with us to compensate for whatever fees you may incur due to a buyout," I told Michael, the chef I apparently needed. It didn't matter I'd never dealt with a restaurant before. I knew how to steal an employee.

Like someone's wife . . .

I pushed the thought from my mind. Margo was long gone from that relationship, even if she was still legally tied to it. I wouldn't let any guilt eat me up over the one night we'd shared. Her asshole husband deserved what he got, and it was over. Like ripping off a Band-Aid.

"Absolutely," I told Michael. "Send all the paperwork to us, and we'll take care of it."

Hanging up, I called Margo to tell her I'd be bringing dinner over. She tried to push me away, but it wasn't happening. I'd work my ass off to make her happy.

Which was how I spent the rest of my day, finishing up the restaurant deal and also receiving two bids on the warehouse.

I'd been at my desk for a few hours when I finally received a text from Margo, telling me what to pick up at the Paula. I ordered it myself for a six o'clock pickup. Some things were best done by me, rather than by my assistant.

I finished the most pressing issues and headed out, wondering if we would eat with or without Priscilla. I knew she was pretty much bedridden for a few days, so I didn't know whether I should be in her bedroom or not.

"Hey, thanks. Here, let me take that."

Margo answered the door, clearly overcome with anxiety. When she reached for the takeout bag, I let her take control of the food.

"Follow me," she said, walking in the house.

It was one of those uppity McMansions, filled with designer furniture and zero character. In other words, not Margo.

After walking through the foyer, with a living room on the left and some type of formal dining area on the right, we reached the kitchen. This room with its pale blue tiles and gray swirled counters, large stools at an eating bar, and a plethora of kitchen appliances, felt more like Margo.

She set the food on the counter and turned to me. A long pause stretched out between us.

"How is Priscilla?" I asked, filling the void.

Margo let out a long breath. "Physically, she has a long haul, but she'll be fine. Emotionally, she insists she's good, but I don't believe it. She's dozing now. Do you mind if I let her rest a while longer before we eat?"

"Of course not. Let her sleep."

My answer came quickly. I wanted my actions to speak for themselves . . . I'd never come between Margo and her daughter.

"She's probably more resilient than you give her credit for," I started to say, then thought better of it. "Fuck. Yeah, this is going to affect her. Look at us. I fell for you at Stephanie's, and then I saw your wrist, and old habits die hard. I couldn't stay uninvolved."

"I don't want her to be scarred." Margo bit her lip and twisted her hands together.

"Come here." I reached out, my fingertips brushing hers, and she walked slowly into my arms. "Let me hold you."

Margo stood stiffly in my embrace for a moment, then relaxed. "This isn't normal. I mean, us. We met, slept together, and that should have been it. Now you're all mixed up in my life."

"Sometimes life doesn't make sense." I chuckled, and she tipped her head back to stare at me. "I know. That sounded silly coming from my mouth."

I wanted to tell her how I saw her husband that day at the restaurant, what he said, and how any man worth his weight would have punched his lights out. But I knew the wounds were too raw.

"This is all happening fast," I said, "and not the way we would have planned." Margo sighed. "I know this is probably hard for you. Being in his house."

"No." My response was firm. "Although this place doesn't feel at all like you, I don't give a shit about him. What I worry about is how he gave in so quickly . . . like he was looking for an exit strategy."

I knew what Tommy's reason was—at least, I thought I did. His girlfriend, the side piece he'd mentioned. But this wasn't the time to bring that up.

Margo licked her lips and rested her head on my chest. "I hate leaning on you like this. Literally and figuratively."

"I want you to," I whispered, and I meant it. As I held her, I wondered when I would tell her about the restaurant run-in I had with Tommy.

"He was unhappy. Obviously. Seeing you, I'm sure, was the final straw, because nothing irks him more than being showed up. The partners at his firm are the most important people in his life. He'll tell them we're divorcing because he was done with me, and I'm fine with that. I'll take the blame if it gets him out of my life. I couldn't do it on my own, so I guess I'm grateful for the scene at the hospital."

"You would have figured a way." I didn't want her to think of this as another failure, and I hated her taking the blame, but he was gone. For good, I hoped.

All of a sudden, a weak, "Mom," rang through the house.

Margo immediately pulled out of my arms. "Duty calls. I'll be right back." She padded off toward the stairs.

As I watched her retreat, I took another glance around the kitchen, liking the well-used feel and thinking about the stark contrast to the rest of the house. Under other circumstances, I would have hunted around and fixed myself a drink, but I didn't know if Margo drank around her daughter. Hell, I didn't know much of anything about how they lived.

Shaking my head, I was wondering what I'd gotten myself into, when I spotted Margo helping her daughter down the stairs. With her uninjured arm around Margo's middle, Priscilla walked slowly, holding her elaborate cast and sling awkwardly.

I hurried to the bottom of the stairs. "Can I help?"

"How about pull out a stool? This stubborn girl decided she wanted to eat in the kitchen."

"Hi," Priscilla said while I held out the stool for her.

"There you go. Slide right on," Margo said, orchestrating the steps from behind her daughter.

Priscilla did as she was told, her braced arm still in limbo.

"If I turn the stool a bit, you can lean your cast on the counter," I told her.

"Good," she said.

"You may want a pillow to put underneath," I said to Margo, and she sprang into action.

"Comfy?" I asked, and Priscilla nodded.

"Your mom told me a few things you like, and I got them all," I told her while Margo opened the bags.

"Too much," Margo grumbled, but I ignored her.

With curly fries, a grilled cheese with tomato soup, and an order of crispy Brussels sprouts with bacon in front of her, Priscilla smiled. "I love anything cheesy or buttery."

"Butter makes everything better," I said. "My mom used to say that. She loved sourdough bread smothered in warm butter." The memory made me smile.

"I think this is yours," Margo said, interrupting my reverie.

Taking in the salad with grilled steak on top, I nodded. Margo had her penne primavera in her hand and sat next to Priscilla. I wedged my stool around the corner so I could see both of them.

"Oh, shoot. I forgot drinks." Margo jumped up.

"That's usually my job," Priscilla said with a small smile.

"How about you tell me where to go, and I'll do it?" I said, but Margo was still standing. "Sit," I told her. "Start eating and just tell me."

She directed me to a cabinet. I poured two filtered waters, and Priscilla asked for a soda.

"Please, Mom?"

Margo acquiesced, and I found a Coke in the back of the fridge for her daughter.

Seated again, I took a sip of water and turned to Priscilla. "When I was fifteen, I broke my leg. Bad football injury. Not even high school football, just a bunch of us goofing around in a turkey bowl. You know what that is?"

She shook her head. "Sounds funny, though."

"It's on Thanksgiving Day when a bunch of punks get together to play pick-up football. Problem is, the ground is typically wet and it's cold out, and there are always injuries."

"Oh," Priscilla said.

We were talking a little about my injury and recovery, when Priscilla said, "Aren't punks usually music people?"

This sent both Margo and me in a fit of laughter.

"Back when I was a kid, punks were jerks," I said. "I guess they don't say that anymore."

"You know," Priscilla said, tugging out a curly fry, "my dad hardly ever talked with me about when he was a kid. I know he was adopted and didn't like the family, but he doesn't mention friends either."

"Priss," her mom warned.

"It's okay," I said. "Not everyone has good memories from being a kid. Sometimes the memories we make later are better."

This gave Priscilla pause, and then she smiled.

"See, Mom?" Turning to me, she said, "I liked you right away. Thanks for bringing my mom to me that night and protecting her. I'm not mad at you."

I was about to respond when she said, "Oh, and that's not because you brought all this food. I mean it."

"You're a good egg, Priscilla," I told her, watching Margo's gaze flick between the two of us. "By the way, that's the opposite of a punk."

The rest of the evening went by with easy conversation and laughter as we all enjoyed ice cream sundaes made by Margo. When we were done, she helped Priscilla upstairs, and then ran back down.

Giving me a sad smile, Margo said, "I'm going to help her get ready for bed, and it may be a while."

I winked, pulling her close. "One kiss, and I'll get out of your hair. Deal?"

"Deal," she said, then pressed her mouth to mine.

Our lips danced for a while, as if they'd been partners for a lifetime, yet there was still so much I had to learn about Margo.

She pulled back first, giving me a curious look. "Is it weird?"

"I don't know what you mean, but no. Maybe we should have gone slower, but we didn't. You can't second-guess it. We're here, and it looks like we have a chance at something great."

Margo didn't respond, only gave me one more quick kiss. "Thanks."

"Lock up," I said firmly, kissing the top of her head. As we walked to the door, I took her hand in mine. "Here's to a lot more times like this."

"The food?" she teased.

"The kisses," I tossed back.

"With punks."

With her final word, I was out the door.

twenty—one

onday, before the parents' meeting at the Paula, I sat in my car, steadying my hands before tackling the task I had in front of me.

Sheila had kept the parents' meeting at the Paula, insisting that normalcy would be a good thing. I wasn't sure there was anything normal about my life before, now, or ever . . . but here I was.

Penny had come over to keep Priscilla company while I was gone, to watch a movie together and get her anything she needed. It wasn't a guilt-driven decision, though. Penny missed her friend and was worried for her. I hoped Priscilla could go back to school in a day or two. The girls had assured me the other students would help her get around and would carry her backpack.

I arrived fifteen minutes early on purpose—not to have a drink like I told Sheila, but to call my parents. It was a task I didn't relish, but a necessary evil.

Imagining having to endure a chorus of *I told you so* and *you didn't try hard enough*, I dialed my mom. I wasn't even ashamed that the last I spoke with her was Mother's Day, months before. After all, she didn't even wish me the same sentiment when I called.

My mom answered stoically, as usual. "Margaret."

"Hi, Mom," I said, trying to act happy to hear her voice.

"It's been a while."

I wanted to tell her the phone worked both ways, but dropped the idea. No use in fighting today. Especially when I was about to drop the divorce bomb on my very Catholic mom.

"I know. Life's been hectic. Priscilla fell and broke her collarbone and one of the bones in her arm. She had surgery and is recuperating now."

"Oh, poor girl," Mom said, but then I remembered that Priscilla hadn't spoken to my mom since Mother's Day either.

When she didn't ask the how or when or any other details, I asked, "How's Dad?"

"He's fine. His gout's been acting up, but otherwise fine. Still working."

My dad had worked in a pharmacy the last few decades. He was in charge of non-pharmaceutical inventory and dealt with deliveries.

"That's good. Working, I mean."

"Uh-huh," my mom grumbled.

I wasn't sure how this woman was the daughter of my grandmother who I'd loved so much, or my own mother. The kindness fairy had skipped over her or something.

"Anyway, I wanted to call because I'm getting a divorce. It all just happened, but Tommy is helping to push things along. Since neither of us are contesting, it may be over soon."

I didn't mention how Tommy and I had talked on the phone late Saturday night, and he'd been willing to overlook my fault—the adultery I hadn't admitted to—for my silence on his fault. In other words, if I kept quiet on his abusive behavior, he wouldn't contest a no-fault divorce with everything I needed in the settlement. I'd agreed because I wanted out. I needed to put this sunset behind me and look forward to the sun coming up on a new day.

Mom sniffed. "Sounds like you rushed into this whole thing. You know, God is looking down at you and disappointed. I told you a vow is a vow, no matter how difficult it became."

Closing my eyes, I took a deep breath. "I know, but this is what we both want. The marriage is broken and can't be fixed. It's what's best for Priscilla."

"If you want to tell yourself that. Anyway, you know how I feel, and that's it. I'll tell your father. 'Bye, Margaret."

And just like that, my own mother hung up, dismissing me.

Sliding my phone over in my lap, I breathed deeply. I guessed shorter was better when it came to the call with my mom, and now it was over. With ten minutes to spare until the meeting started, I decided a drink was in order.

Once I had a glass of wine in hand, I texted Priscilla to check in. Her response came back quickly.

Mom, I'm fine. Promise. Xo

Her response was short and sweet, but the *xo* made my heart ache. At least I'd taught my daughter to be caring and affectionate, despite my marrying the male equivalent of my mom.

I couldn't help but laugh to myself. A therapist would have a field day with me. Lucky them, I didn't have time right now.

The meeting went well enough.

No one asked me anything personal, which meant the gossip network hadn't picked up anything yet on me. With Sheila as my guard dog and Tommy on lockdown for fear of his own reputation, I felt pretty settled in my status.

I got home in time to see Penny putting her coat on downstairs before Peter picked her up, and thanked her about twelve times.

"We watched *Mean Girls*," she told me, laughing. "It's funny for an old movie."

This made me roll my eyes.

"We love Priss," she added. "All of us. I'm sorry about what happened."

"It was an accident," I told her, and realized by the confused look on her face that wasn't what she meant.

"Oh," I said, gathering my thoughts. "I'm sorry that you girls have to know about this," I said honestly.

If I knew one thing, it was that Priscilla needed her friends, so she could feel free to confide and share her feelings with who she wanted. She'd bottled up enough as it was.

"Priss seems okay," Penny said with a shrug. "I mean, she seems like she's processing it all okay. My mom asked me to check in, so I hope you don't mind."

I leaned over and gave her a squeeze. "You know what a silver lining is, Pen?"

She nodded. "A lucky circumstance from something terrible or hard."

"Exactly. Priscilla and I didn't have many good friends before this, and finding out how lucky we are to have you and your mom is a silver lining to this tragedy."

She smiled. "I hope so."

When a quick honk came from outside, Penny said, "I'll be back on Thursday to work on a project with Priss."

"Night, Penny," I said, wondering how these girls got so wise. I was decades older than them, and clearly not as smart.

The thought stayed with me as I went upstairs and checked on Priscilla. She needed some help brushing her teeth and getting comfy in bed. I sat with her a bit before she dozed off, and then I padded back downstairs.

Debating a second glass of wine, I prepped the coffee maker for the morning and did a quick inventory of the fridge. My girl and I had been on a steady diet of takeout the last couple of days, and we needed to re-engineer our life as just the two of us.

Priscilla and me against the world.

Mumbling, "Screw it," I poured myself a small glass of cabernet and sat at the kitchen counter. As I sat my butt in the same stool Mick had sat in the night before, my mind worked overtime.

I could cross off any relationship with my family. Tommy had asked me to discuss potential visits with Priscilla, and she'd firmly said, "No." He'd countered with an occasional dinner, and she'd said she would think about it.

Sheila was like the sister I'd never had. Even Dale had called to check on me, saying he'd spoken with Sheila, and now he was somehow in our inner circle of trust. Basically, I'd gone from keeping a secret life from my family, to having no family to count on but a motley crew of friends who were willing to die on the hill for me. Mick included in this group.

As if I'd conjured him up, my phone dinged.

Can I call? You up?

Remembering he was in New York City for the night, I responded with a quick *Yes.*

My phone rang, and I picked up with a wine-laden, "Hello." Setting the phone on the counter, I put it on speaker phone and toggled the volume to low.

"Hello there to you."

"I just got home a little while ago," I said with the comfort of a couple who'd spent decades together. I didn't know how Mick did that . . . he settled all my nerves and anxieties.

"Oh, right, the parents' meeting. Like the night we had the drink. Did you miss me sitting behind you at the bar?"

"Well, this time I was actually able to concentrate on what they were discussing."

"I'll bet. But still, I'd rather be there with you."

"How's the Big Apple?" I asked, then took a sip of wine.

My body flooded with warmth and my heart beat faster. Not sure if it was from the alcohol or Mick's voice, I decided it must be the latter.

"All business and no fun. This place sucks you up in the rat race. I did have a great meal prepared by this chef we wooed."

"Sounds busy and delicious. I'm downing a second glass of wine and telling myself to go to bed."

"How's Priscilla?"

I smiled at how kind Mick was being to my daughter. I didn't know if he genuinely liked her or simply felt bad for her because he understood her position.

"I can hear you drumming up arguments in your head through your silence," Mick said, calling out my pause.

"She's good. Resting. Wants to get back to school, so we're going to try on Friday. It's a half day, so a good day to try. Until then, they email all her work."

"When I get back, I'm going to bring sushi over. Tomorrow around seven?"

"Are you sure?"

"I've never been surer. I also can't wait to bring you here for a day or two with no work."

"That would be nice, but I think we are a little ways off."

"No rush on my part. Priscilla has to be settled, and you too."

"Do you have two more seconds?" I asked like an awkward teenager.

"I have all the time for you, Margo," he said softly into the phone, then it sounded like he took a gulp.

"Are you having a drink?" I blurted.

"Yep. A Macallan in the chair in my room. Nothing better. It's quiet, and there's only you to fill my ear."

"I'm having a wine. See? That's sort of what I mean . . . do you think this is crazy? How we met? Our dubious beginning? How in sync we seem to be, so compatible and easy?"

140

My mind spun, spitting questions out of my mouth faster than I could control them.

"No, how we met wasn't crazy. It was serendipitous. And if you ever tell any of my buddies that I used that word, I'll deny it."

This made me laugh out loud. "Okay, okay, I promise."

"While we're on the subject, we didn't have a dubious beginning because of what happened to you behind closed doors. Your marriage was over, just not on paper. And fuck yeah, it's easy, because that's how real feelings are. Easy."

"How do you know?"

"True, true. I'm guessing, but I'm usually right when it comes to my intuition."

"Cocky much?" I teased, the wine making me brave.

"My track record suggests I know what I'm doing. Moving on, I'll bring dinner tomorrow. And no pressure, but if you want to grab dinner this weekend just the two of us, we could."

"Like a date?"

"Exactly, smarty-pants."

"I'll check in with Priss, okay?"

"Absolutely," he said, his voice sincere yet gravelly with need.

"You know what? This may sound strange, but I need to redo this house. It's weird being here. It doesn't feel like me."

"You will, in time. Right now, it's about breathing and putting one foot in front of the other, just making it to the next day."

He was so right.

"You know," I said, "you really do know it all."

"Now go to bed, because I didn't forget you're meeting with your editor tomorrow. Remember, you don't owe her every detail, but you definitely should gun for some more articles. Did you work on your pitches?"

It was unreal how Mick remembered every detail we'd discussed on Saturday and Sunday. It was probably why he was so successful—his attention to detail. There was no denying that I liked being one of those details.

"Not as much as I should have, but yes."

"Then off to bed you go . . ."

"Night," I whispered.

"Back at you, Margo."

We disconnected, and I ran to check on Priscilla, wash my face, and crawl in between the covers and sleep like the dead.

Another side effect of no longer sleeping next to the enemy.

twenty-two

mick

After a quick shower, I was going through my closet to find a pair of jeans and a shirt when I came across something I'd forgotten about.

Shoved toward the back was an old navy suit, the one my dad wore to marry my mom. She gave it to me when I was about sixteen or seventeen, telling me it was the only thing of my dad's she kept. To her, it represented the union that resulted in me.

I didn't tell her that to me it represented the man I didn't want to become.

Clenching my fist, I took a deep breath. Violence wasn't a behavior I engaged in. Mental warfare was my weapon of choice. Although I used my mental prowess to win wars in business, but not life. In life, I tried to be true to who I was and wanted to be.

Running my palm over the sleeve of the jacket, I took in the cheap fabric, some type of poly blend. I'm sure it was all my dad could afford at the time, but it didn't make up for his poor choices when it came to my mom. He could have worn shorts and a T-shirt if he'd just held his temper in check.

Over the last week, I'd visited Margo and Priscilla twice, both times bringing food and dessert.

Margo denied it, but she walked around with a giant weight of guilt and fear on her shoulder. She'd told me in late-night whispers how she was upset with herself over our inappropriateness, but more disappointed in how long she'd made her daughter suffer. Then she would smile like the world was rainbows and unicorns when Priscilla was around. I reminded her that her soon-to-be ex-husband was the inappropriate one.

"I know, but I stayed," was always her response.

Pulling on my jeans, I made a mental note to tell Priscilla about the suit. How it loomed in my closet, reminding me never to be like that guy. She'd probably find it fascinating and derive a million hidden meanings from the story.

I liked Priscilla, and I believe she liked me too, which was why I was getting dressed to take Margo out for a drink. When Margo asked Priscilla if she minded having Penny back for a girls' night, so she could join me, Priscilla tapped out a text faster than someone calling an Uber after the Celtics game.

I didn't want to pressure Margo, but I also wanted to take her out and give her some happy moments. Of course, I asked if she'd prefer to come toward the Back Bay or stay in Brookline. She wanted to stay closer to home, so I made a reservation at a place called Barcelona. Neither of us had ever been there, so it seemed like a good choice for a fresh start.

"Hey, Mick," Priscilla called to me from the couch as her mother let me inside their house.

"You look hot," I whispered in Margo's ear as I gave her a kiss on her cheek. Moving away from her, I took in her black leather tank and dark jeans. "Smoking hot."

"Thanks."

"But the more important girl is calling for me," I said, winking.

"You know, you don't have to be so nice. She's so taken with you."

"We've discussed this . . ."

Another one of our late-night chats was about Priscilla and her fast feelings for me. Margo said she was always talking about *Mick this* and *Mick that*.

I told Margo that Priscilla was taken with our similar stories, and it was only natural. I didn't really know for sure, but it was what I suspected.

"Hey, look at you, downstairs," I said to Priscilla.

"Mom said Penny and I could hang down here as long as I don't fidget."

"Mom knows best . . . that I know. My mom always did," I told her, knowing

Margo was in earshot.

"I can hear you laying it on thick," she said, walking into the room.

Priscilla rolled her eyes. "Thank you, Mick, for getting her out of my hair."

"I heard that too," Margo called out.

"Seriously," Priscilla said, lowering her voice. "She's checking on me every second. I'm fine. I knew when I met you in Nike that I was going to be like you. You're strong."

If I could have said *oh shit*, I would have.

"I mean, I didn't know about this." She waved her hand between her mom and me. "But that night, I thought about it and said to myself, 'That guy knows something I don't.'"

"Maybe we shouldn't go," Margo said, looking at her daughter. "Maybe we should stay and chat."

"Mom!"

"Don't move around too much, Priscilla."

"Then don't say stupid things."

My head whipped back and forth between the two. I hadn't been in boardrooms this tense.

"Mom, go! You look too hot not to."

"Penny's not here yet," Margo said.

The doorbell rang, and Priscilla got in the last word, "Go! We don't need a big meet and greet."

I wasn't sure what that was all about, but I didn't think it was the time to ask.

After another resounding, "Go," from Priscilla, Margo kissed her on the forehead and said, "I love you."

Margo let Penny in, hugging her while she eyed me, and then told her to order pizza and to pay for it with the money on the kitchen counter.

I asked Margo if she had a coat, and of course, she did. She was a mother. After helping her put it on, I took her hand in mine and walked her out to the car.

"I was thinking of putting the house on the market," she said as we sped away. "Not right away. I mean, we have months of paperwork, or longer. But eventually. It's just not me."

"I think it's okay to think that, but not to rush."

"Eh, forget it. I don't want to talk about that all night. Or Priscilla. She's attached to you, and I can't even imagine—"

"Like you said, let's not go there," I said quickly.

I knew what she wanted to discuss. Where this was going? And what happened if it didn't work out?

As far as I was concerned, those answers were simple.

Far. And *not going to be a problem.*

Knowing Margo wasn't really ready for either discussion, I let it go, moving the conversation into safer territory. "Tell me about the new articles."

"Oh, it's really great. I'm going to do an ongoing series on teenagers and social media, and how to safely and effectively reach them."

"Wow, sounds like you found your calling."

"Honestly, thanks to Dale."

I couldn't help the rumbling growl that worked its way up my throat.

"Mick? Did you just growl?" She swung her head around, staring at me while I drove.

"It's a guy thing," I said, not looking at her as I tried to explain it away.

"You're upset over Dale?"

"No, I'm not. I'm here, and he's not."

The sky began to fade to black, and I was thankful for the cover of darkness. For the first time in a long while, I was being called out by a woman. While I was embarrassed, I loved Margo's spunk. It did something for me.

"Of course he's not. He's just a super-nice guy. A widower. But not you," she said. Her fingers made their way to my thigh, and she gave my leg a little squeeze. "Not you, okay?"

I glanced at her. "I like hearing you say that. I have to ask, though, are you going to thank him in your article?" I said it with a smile, and hoped she knew I was kidding. Sort of.

"Oh. My. God. Mick!"

"I was joking. Really."

"Now I'm going to," she said, lifting her chin stubbornly as we pulled up to the valet at Barcelona.

"We'll see about that," I said, chuckling.

"Wow, that was delicious," Margo said toward the end of our meal. We'd shared a bottle of Spanish cabernet and a bunch of tapas. "I need to try to make those potatoes aioli."

"I'm down for that. You could do it in my kitchen."

"That may be nice." Her gaze got far-off as if she were trying to picture it.

"With or without Priscilla. She's always welcome."

Margo simply nodded, and then the server showed up with the bill.

"I don't want this to end, but I need to get home," Margo said.

"I get it. Believe me. I applaud your priorities."

Unsure of what just happened, I still placed my hand at her lower back and walked her through the dark restaurant with Spanish music piping through the speakers.

While waiting for the valet, I pulled Margo into my side, and she came willingly.

"I'm sorry, I just got uptight. I still feel like I'm sneaking around." Her words were quiet and only meant for me, but they still hurt.

"You're not sneaking anymore, and I don't want you to feel like I'm a bad choice or taking you away from your daughter."

She didn't say anything in response, only stood on her tiptoes and brushed a small kiss across my cheek.

"Now, that I liked," I told her, squeezing her tighter against me.

With the car in front of us now, she slipped inside, and I walked around front, tipping the valet.

It was an abrupt ending to the evening, and I suspected it would be a long while before I was between the sheets with Margo again.

"I see your mind working overtime," she said.

"Caught. Honestly, I don't want this night to end."

"Neither do I. Let's see what Priscilla is doing. Maybe we can have some coffee or another drink at home? Let me text her to tell Penny to call for her ride."

"I'm in if you are. Do you want me to take her home?" I left it at that because pressure was a bad idea right now.

Margo laughed. "Um, no. I don't think a forty-year-old guy should be driving a non-related teen girl home. That's parenting one-oh-one."

"Hey, I don't claim to know everything."

"I got ya," she said as I turned on her street. "Pull in the driveway."

I did as I was told, hoping to steal some kisses or more. Happy to prolong the evening, I walked her inside the house.

"Hey, Mom," Priscilla called.

"Hi, girls," she said back. "Good time?"

I excused myself to the bathroom and let those three chat for a moment. When I got back, Penny was hugging everyone good-bye and heading to the door, headlights illuminating the outside of the house.

"Say hi to your mom," Margo said, and Penny was gone. To Priscilla, she said, "Want anything before I help you upstairs?"

Priscilla shook her head. "I'm tired. Sitting still is hard work," she joked.

"I'm here to help, baby," she said, leaning over to lend Priscilla a shoulder.

Margo must be exhausted, and here I was wanting to keep her up late. Why? Because I was a selfish prick . . . *or a selfish nice guy.*

"Mick?" Priscilla asked.

"Yeah?"

"Night. See you soon," she said before Margo helped her to her room.

I went into the kitchen and hunted for some decaffeinated coffee. Setting a pot to brew, I heard the two of them padding around upstairs. I was going to offer to help, and then thought of Margo's earlier advice.

"Oh, wow. Smells good," Margo said as she sneaked up on me.

"Hey, she okay?"

"Yep. Twelve and three-quarters going on twenty-three. Wanted to know if you were going to be here in the morning."

I felt my eyes bulging out of my head. "Ah, is that normal?"

"She's a young woman and knows all about the birds and the bees. What I didn't think she knew about was torrid extramarital affairs and divorce, but apparently, she's wiser than I thought."

I poured two coffees, grabbing the milk for Margo—yes, I knew how she took her coffee.

"I'm going to have to investigate all that . . . later." Taking a sip of her coffee, she let out a little moan of contentment. "Mmm."

I couldn't resist leaning over and kissing her. We were both standing, facing each other with a hip to the counter. My hand found hers, and I helped her shelve her mug on the counter before guiding her palm up my back and running mine down her back to her ass. We kissed, our tongues working their way into each other's mouths, and our lower bodies seeking friction. Her hand found my ass and squeezed it tight.

"God, I want you," I moaned quietly.

"Me too. I mean, I want you, but . . ." Her words trickled into my ear as she nibbled on the lobe, making her way back to my mouth.

"Don't worry, you don't need to explain. This is enough," I said.

Shutting up, I held her as close as possible, running my fingers down her side and to her jeans. I made quick work of the button fly and even faster time into her panties, my finger finding her warmth.

"No reason I can't leave you satisfied," I whispered.

"Mick . . ."

She started to protest, but then her head fell back and something like a purr came from her mouth as I added another finger and worked her over. My thumb met her most sensitive area, teasing the little ball of nerves while my fingers found the spot.

It didn't take long. Within a matter of moments, Margo was in full ecstasy.

Ask any guy, and he'll tell you what it does to him to get a woman off quickly with only his hand. It's a top-of-the-tallest-building type of feeling. Do that with a woman you actually care for, and it puts you on top of the world.

I continued to kiss Margo through her muffled cries until she was actually shivering in my arms. I pulled my hand out from her pants and brushed my lips over her forehead.

"Did that really just happen?" she asked breathlessly.

"That won't be the only time," I said before running my hand in front of my face, inhaling her intoxicating scent.

"I'm going to let you go to bed," I said, wiping my hand on my pant leg. I wanted to lick it clean, but we were in her kitchen with her daughter upstairs. We'd done enough for one night.

"What about—"

"Nope, don't even say it," I said, cutting her off. "Tonight was for you."

And with that, I kissed Margo good-night and was out the door.

twenty-three

margaret

After the night Mick took care of me in the kitchen, I woke up and decided to get a handle on my life.

Don't misunderstand, I liked what happened in the kitchen, and blushed when I thought about wanting it to happen again. But it had been impulsive and maybe a little reckless. I was a newly single mom with an impressionable almost-teenage daughter.

So, I decided to keep the evening as a frequent memory until the dust settled, or whatever they called it.

That's what I'd repeated to myself over the last few weeks. *When the dust settles, I'll get to do everything I've ever wanted.* I'm not sure I believed this positive-vibes mantra, but it helped move me forward rather than spiraling aimlessly.

First, I concentrated on getting Priscilla back to school, to and from doctor appointments, and helping her to see her friends. Hosting all her friends became a goal I was going to die on a hill achieving. There were pizza nights, manicure parties, and movie marathons. Between playing hostess with the mostest and working on my new series, I dealt with the specifics of my separation.

In an effort to keep up human connections and do well at my job, I asked a few of the school parents at pickup if I could interview them. We met at coffee shops and in the library at the kids' school.

Then there was Mick. I saw him, but we kept it to a quick lunch, just the two of us, or dinner with Priscilla. This was my doing, trying to reclaim a boundary that never existed. My stubborn daughter kept pushing for us to have a date, insisting she needed time away from me. Mick said it was up to me, but I was backpedaling, trying to turn back time and start our relationship over with harder limits.

"We need to do this the right way," I told him over my mug of coffee, dirty blond the way I took it.

Mick and I were at Stephanie's for lunch, and a group of businessmen had just walked out, reminding us of how we met. We laughed over our cliché bar meet cute, before I went and got serious.

"We're doing it our way," Mick insisted, right before the server dropped off our check.

But as Mick reached for it, I grabbed the bill. "This one's on me. Let me do this. You know, our way," I said, tossing his own words back at him.

He eyed me but didn't argue.

"I'm making the big bucks now with this series," I teased.

"That doesn't mean you should spend it on me . . . you should put it away. For Priscilla, for retirement, or shoes."

"I'll start doing that tomorrow. How's that?"

Bottom line, Mick worried about my security, thinking he was the catalyst for the separation. I'd told him Tommy was holding true. We'd hired a mediator because we had to, mostly to discuss custody.

Good news was Tommy didn't want much visitation, claiming teenage girls needed their mom. In reality, we both knew it was because she'd witnessed his absolute cruelty, and he didn't want to explain that one. We went through the motions, pretending to discuss and duke out arrangements.

In the end, Tommy agreed to dinner twice a month with Priscilla after her cast was off and she didn't need help in the bathroom . . . and every other Christmas. Thanksgiving would be mine and Easter his, not that Priscilla even cared about the bunny or the holiday anymore. He could take her on vacation, which I knew he wouldn't, even if she wanted to go, and he was welcome to watch any of her sports events, performances, or anything of the like.

"I found a therapist for Priscilla and me," I said while we waited for my receipt. "I'm sure it's a little odd how I'm sharing all this with you, but who else would I tell?"

Mick leaned in. "It's not weird. You can tell me. You can tell Sheila. She cares."

Mick had seen Sheila coming and going from my house a few times since the night at the hospital. She'd constantly gone on about his ass and forearms and back to his ass since then.

"Earth to Mar, where'd you go?"

"Uh . . ." I didn't know how to explain I'd been caught daydreaming about his ass.

"You've got a devilish smile going on, so I don't think you were thinking about therapy."

"I was thinking about you and Sheila."

The server interrupted the moment, and I was hoping Mick would let it go as I signed my name.

"Sheila? Wrong woman for me," he said when I looked up.

"Well, she was . . . commenting on you and certain body parts."

"Do tell." He winked at me, and I wanted to leap across the table and show him.

This man made me feel unbalanced. One minute, I was down about Priscilla and therapy, and the next, I wanted to strip naked and fool around.

"Maybe that's living?" I whispered aloud.

"Hmm?" Mick leaned forward again, his elbows on the table, the aforementioned forearms on display with his shirtsleeves rolled up.

"Sorry, my mind is all over the place. I was thinking that it's so awkward to sit here and talk about Priscilla and therapy. Which, by the way, she still insists she's fine and doesn't need, but it's a box I want to check."

I reached for his hand, lacing our fingers together on top of the table.

"For the record, I agree it's a box you should check," Mick said.

"Yes, I'm the parent, and I think so."

"I didn't mean to derail you. Tell me. Me, Sheila, living? What's it all mean?"

"Well, Sheila likes to dissect you when she sees you. Your arms," I said, eyeing his beautiful arms. "And your backside."

"Oh, really? Do you agree? Share the same view? Because, just so we're clear, I'm not concerned with what Sheila thinks."

"Well, I think you know I do, but that's not the point. What I mean is, one minute I'm uber serious, and the next I'm dreaming of your body. To me it feels off-kilter, but maybe that's really living?"

His hand abandoned mine and came to my chin, tipping my gaze toward his. "It is living, Mar. People who care for each other share the good, the bad, and the ugly. With no judgment or harsh consequences."

I felt a tear starting to form in the corner of my eye.

"Don't do that. You're living, and it's all good." Swiping his thumb under my eye, he whispered, "When can I kiss you?"

"Not here. Later."

"Let me walk you to your car, and maybe you'll let me kiss you there," Mick said while standing.

I didn't feel like he was rushing me. He was simply making the point that we were living in the moment. Serious for a second, fun the next, and everything in between.

"Speaking of later," Mick said, "tomorrow is going to be a good day. You know why? You're going to cook at my place and bring Priss for a change of scenery. Can you send me a list of ingredients so Rochelle can get it all?"

Caught off guard with his spontaneous request, or more like, demand, I stammered, "Ah, are you sure? I can buy the stuff. And are you sure you want Priscilla? We haven't really discussed it."

"Come on, don't play like that. Of course I want you both," he said. With my hand still in his, he added, "Let's drop this topic before it turns into a fight. Yes, I'm sure. End of discussion."

We stepped outside holding hands, and Mick walked me to my car.

"Maybe I should get a convertible?" I asked as Mick pulled me into his arms. "Fits the midlife crisis I'm having."

"You're not having a midlife crisis, babe. You're living, remember? Two very different things," he whispered before running his lips along mine. "And now I'm kissing you."

Making good on his promise, he pressed his lips to mine. A gentle kiss, yet full of promise. When he pulled back, I was breathless.

"I'm flying to New York and back tomorrow," he said. "I have a quick meeting, then I'll be back for dinner. Meet at my place at six?"

It should have felt heavy-handed, but it was different. Fun, lighthearted, just what I needed.

I was on my way to the lawyer now to sign the deed for our house. For one dollar, it was all mine, to do with as I wanted. What I wanted was to set it on fire—not really. I either wanted to drastically change it or sell it. It was one or the other, but first was therapy with Priscilla and making my own money, saving my settlement, and being independent.

Or maybe, first was another cup of coffee?

twenty-four

margaret

"This is really terrific," Jane said to me, holding a coffee mug in one hand and her phone in the other. She was scrolling through my notes, using her thumb. Writers and editors are stellar at multitasking when it comes to drinking coffee and anything else. "I wasn't sure how this would turn out, but it's really becoming way more than a passion project."

I took a sip of my own latte and looked down at the table. It had been a while since I'd been this excited, even more so than the gender-neutral clothing piece, which still hadn't dropped. It had been even longer since I'd been proud of myself.

"I could be wrong, but I rarely am," Jane looked up and said with a wink. "But this smacks of not only a series but a staff position."

"What?"

My mouth went dry, and it wasn't the coffee. Reaching for my water, I waited to hear what came next. I wasn't one to make assumptions.

Jane put her phone down and set her mug next to her tablet. We were in a small local place I preferred to the big-name coffee chains. The walls were exposed brick, and various sizes of planters filled with ivy lined the perimeter.

It felt like an inside garden, and typically was calming and soothing.

But not at this moment.

"I may have mentioned to Tony," the magazine's editor-in-chief, "that we were missing a market segment—parents and the companies who need to target them. Yes, we cover and cater to big toy brands and SAT prep, blah, blah, but we're missing floundering parents who need information on best practices. In the process, we gather data for all kinds of companies who want to reach parents. Yes, it's a bit like sticking our hand in both cookie jars, but quid pro quo and all that. If we help parents, then they can help us."

My head was spinning. Deciding against any more caffeine, I took another sip of water.

"I told Tony I would chat with you," Jane said, "but we quickly brainstormed and were thinking some sort of guidebooks and/or videos to start."

"I don't know what to say."

"To start, say you're flattered. You deserve this."

"I truly am. Flattered, that is." Swallowing my pride, I asked, "But this isn't pity?"

Jane sat back in her chair, leveling me with a serious expression. "I knew you were going to say that. Look, you didn't owe me any explanations, and I didn't expect a ton of details. You've been one of my best writers for a long time, and it's not typical for people to work together as long as we have in this world. I've always liked you, and I suspected things weren't so terrific at home for you."

"Oh," I muttered. I'd always thought I kept everything so buttoned up.

"No one stays like you did, doing freelance crap for me, biding your time. You were stuck, and now you're unstuck, and I want to hold on to you. So, no pity on my part."

I begged myself not to cry. I'd become such an emotional soul over the last few weeks. After my life had been in slow motion for years, everything was changing at light speed.

Holding back the tears, I simply said, "Yes, I'm in for that."

"Good. Now finish this story, and we'll set a meeting with Tony to discuss further. Payments and some added benefits, and all that."

My stomach was in my ankles. I wanted to rub my eyes and make sure this wasn't a dream.

"Can you come to the offices then? When we meet?" Jane asked, bringing me back to reality.

"Of course," I said.

Taking a deep breath, I went back to my coffee and celebrated with a long slug. Then I thought about dinner at Mick's later and celebrating with him.

And Priscilla.

Oh well, it would be G-rated—not everything could be fairy-tale perfect. But showing my daughter my success was a highlight.

Jane and I made plans to connect the beginning of the following week, and I noted in my calendar when I needed to finish the piece. I had one more interview tomorrow with another parent.

After Jane left, I closed my eyes and blew out a breath. Benefits. Staff position. Role model.

Words and titles floated in my brain until my phone beeped. I'd had an alarm set to go pick up Priscilla, but this was Rochelle texting me that she'd picked up what I needed to make dinner tonight.

"Hi, baby girl," I said to Priscilla as Annabeth helped her inside the car at afterschool pickup.

"Mommm," Priscilla said, giving me her standard frustrated response to that term of endearment.

Unfazed, I said, "You're always going to be my baby girl."

"Hi, Ms. Long," Annabeth said, opening up the back door and tossing in Priscilla's backpack.

One of her classmates had carried it around for her all day and helped her get situated in every class. In return, that person was able to take the elevator to their next class. Annabeth shared her last class of the day with Priscilla, so she typically helped her to my car.

"Say hi to your dad," I told Annabeth like I did every other day before she closed the door.

"Oh, he said he can't wait to read the piece you interviewed him for."

"Tell him I said thanks."

With that, Annabeth shut the door and blew a kiss to Priscilla.

"How was your day, sweetie?"

"Great. Except gym when I have to sit in the library. I don't know why I can't watch. They're worried I'm going to get hurt. Speaking of getting hurt, I'm going to hurt Maisey if she doesn't stop asking me questions. *Are your parents getting divorced? What's it like? Does your dad have a girlfriend?*"

I was grateful I'd been driving slowly, because otherwise, I would have wrecked the car. "Why would she say that?"

"She heard Penny and me talking and now thinks she's one of my friends. Apparently, her dad is having an affair with his assistant, and her parents are splitting up."

"Priss . . ."

"Mom, I know. Yours is a different situation. Dad was an asshole, pardon the language, and he deserved what you did. Plus, Mick is the bee's knees. I get it all."

I veered in front of a Starbucks despite just having a coffee.

"What are you doing? You never let me get the 'Bucks."

"Maybe today." I turned and looked at my daughter, her hair windblown, and a smidge of mascara on her lashes. I made a mental note to ask who applied it and to buy her a tube.

"You don't have to bribe me. I didn't say a word to Maisey about you. Or Mick. Or Dad. She's her own worst enemy. I'm not mad at you like how she's mad at her dad. It's all we hear about."

"I hear you, but we're still going to therapy."

"Ugh, Mom. I don't need it."

"We both do," I said, pushing the button to turn the car off. "Period. Now, what do you want? A sugary shake disguised as coffee?"

"Yep. A caramel frappuccino."

"You're skipping the whipped cream because I'm making cookie brownies at Mick's."

"With ice cream?"

"Of course."

"What are we celebrating?" Priscilla looked up at me as I opened her door to help her.

"Not much, but I may be getting a promotion at work. It's not a big deal," I told her, knowing in my heart it was a huge deal.

"Mom," she said while slipping her arm through mine, "It's a big deal. You're doing something for you for the first time. I'm not mad, even if it takes time away from me."

"That it won't," I said with a smile, leaning in and kissing her cheek, thinking how the heck did she understand relationships better than me.

As I yanked open the door, I thought, *The therapist is going to have a field day with this one.*

twenty-five

"This place is cool," Priscilla said like a starstruck teen when I took her to Mick's penthouse for the first time. She'd told me that Mick had told her about his dad, and what Mick had done to protect his mom, and now the pair was forever bonded.

"Oh, look. Penny's dad uses a bike like this." She ran toward the Peloton bike Mick loved so much.

Seeing his open floor plan, I was flooded with memories of the night we had sex against the door and then spread out naked on the couch. As my daughter strolled through, touching everything with her free hand, I wondered how many other women had been here.

Realizing my thoughts were getting away from me, I decided to busy myself in the kitchen.

"So cool," Priscilla said to herself. "Mick must really like us to let us come in by ourselves."

I wanted to agree, but a ridiculous niggling wouldn't allow me to.

I sifted through the ingredients on the counter and opened the fridge, noting the glass bottles of diet orange soda. "Priss, look at these."

"Oh, I love those. Did you tell them?"

"Rochelle may have asked what your favorite beverage was."

"We need a Rochelle. Then you wouldn't have to do as much." Priscilla reached around me and grabbed a soda.

"We can't afford a Rochelle. Although, with the promotion at work . . . maybe," I joked.

"What? That would be so cool!" Priscilla pushed herself onto the stool, leaning her casted arm on the counter like Mick had shown her a few weeks before. It made me a little sad to think her own father hadn't taken the time to show her anything like that.

"I'm kidding. I'm not even sure what this promotion means. I have a meeting next week to figure out all the details."

"Mom, it's gonna be great. I'm going to have to do a new interview with you and get all the details updated. By the way, you look amazing."

"Priss, I'm in jeans and a sweater."

"You look good. Smiling, your hair all wavy the way I like it. And that sweater is hot."

She grinned at me, and I felt a blush creeping up my neck, so I turned to wash my hands. Priscilla was becoming super pushy when it came to Mick.

"What's for dinner other than the brownies?"

I'm going to make my eggplant parm, and a side pasta and roasted veggies."

"Yum. You know I love it. Dad never ate it."

I nodded. "That's not why I was going to make it. It's just quick and also gourmet-ish."

"Mom, that article on TikTok is getting to you. Can you not say *ish*?"

"How about L-O-L?"

"Not that either, please," she said firmly.

We laughed as I turned on the oven, found a sauté pan, and went about prepping the eggplants. Washed, sliced, and salted, the lengthy pieces sat for fifteen minutes drying while I filled a pot with water and set it aside. Mixing the brownies, I added my secret ingredient—broken pieces of a Ghirardelli chocolate-and-caramel bar—and found a few more kitchen tools I needed. As soon as I finished flouring and frying the eggplant, assembled the dish, and popped it in the oven, the front door opened.

"Hey, I'm here. And you wouldn't believe what I found in New York."

Mick walked toward the kitchen, a black duffel over his shoulder, wearing jeans and a leather jacket, his hair a mess. But somehow he still looked fresh, and not at all like he'd taken a day trip to New York.

"Hey, Mick," Priscilla called from the stool.

"Don't get up," he told her.

"Hey," I said as I walked close.

He leaned over and gave me a lingering kiss on the cheek.

I was in the middle of thinking how domestic this all felt, and how that must have been Mick's play in inviting us over. But all that flew out the window when his bag moved.

"Did your duffel just move, or am I hallucinating?"

Mick chuckled. "Oh, no. It moved. Funny thing happened today in New York. First, I secured the chef, and then we went and secured the sous chef he wanted, who happened to be at home with her mother, who happened to be a dog breeder . . ."

He stopped talking and set the bag down in front of my feet, then leaned over to pull out a very tiny, shiny blond puppy.

"Meet Tito. He came with the name." Mick looked up with a silly grin on his face. With his hair falling over his forehead, he looked like a little boy.

Priscilla couldn't get out of her seat fast enough, maneuvering her way to the floor, her cast hindering her less and less. "Oh my God. Look at him."

She was on her knees, rubbing him all over with her available arm and hand . . . and falling in love with a puppy that wasn't ours.

"I hope you let Rochelle know about this," I blurted.

"Ha. You catch on quick, Mar. I most certainly did. She's thrilled, especially because her son has been wanting a puppy and she can't commit, but now they have one by default."

"Was this part of your master plan or spontaneous? I have to ask."

"It was one hundred percent on the spot. Honestly, I don't have time for a puppy, but I do like the fun of it."

"Well, welcome home, Tito," I said, taking in Priscilla, who hadn't moved since she got on the floor with the dog.

"What kind of dog is this?" she asked Mick while scratching the puppy's belly.

"A Lab. A yellow Lab. He's probably going to be around seventy-five pounds, so I'm glad I have the terrace for him to run on." Mick tilted his head toward the balcony doors.

"Your place is soooo cool," Priscilla said for the eleventh time since we'd arrived.

"I'm glad you're here. Did you get everything you needed?" Mick looked toward me and winked.

"I did."

"How about we pour you a small glass of wine? I know you're driving later, so a little one, okay? Then, Priss and I will take Tito to do some business outside . . . and then I'll be back to hang? Yeah?"

I went to put the water on to boil, and said, "Perfect."

As he took a bottle of white out of the fridge, I said, "You know what? Let me do that. You take care of Tito."

"It might be best for everyone," Mick said with a frown. "He's starting to sniff around."

I looked toward the floor, and sure enough, the tiny puppy was walking around, nose to the floor and butt shaking.

Mick held his hand out for Priscilla, and she stood before he picked up the dog.

"Rochelle is looking into a patch of AstroTurf for the corner of the patio, where he can do his thing," I heard him tell Priscilla on the way out. "She works crazy quick, so we're a good working team."

I took a larger gulp of my wine than expected, trying to calm my nerves over how natural this felt, and how my daughter was falling for my guy . . . but was he even mine? And what about her own father, did she miss him? Not to mention, what was Mick's commitment level? It would be easy to fall in love—even to fall in like—with this simple domesticity.

My head swam with questions as the oven timer beeped, letting me know it was time to uncover the eggplant. Welcoming the mindless task, I opened the oven and took a whiff of my cooking before closing it again.

Tommy never allowed me to experiment in the kitchen. He was a steak-and-potatoes guy, but Mick was much more easygoing. I tried to think back to Tommy in the early days. Had he been easygoing back then?

As I watched Mick and Priscilla over the rim of my wineglass as they came back inside, Mick carrying Tito, I decided it was unfair to compare the two men. Tommy was my past, and Mick was my present. I wasn't sure who would be in my future . . . certainly people who met under less than desirable circumstances like Mick and myself didn't build lives together.

Priscilla plopped back down in the stool. "Mom, we should get a puppy."

At least she wasn't talking about Mick being in our lives forever. Our own puppy was a good idea, I convinced myself.

"Oh yeah, with your arm in a cast for another week, and then physical therapy. And when that's done, are you wanting to go back to sports?"

"Will you still work from home?" Her head cocked to the side as she watched me bustling around the kitchen, throwing a salad together and checking on the pasta. "You know, when you get your big promotion."

I gave her a dirty look, telling her it was meant to stay between us.

"What?" she said, feigning innocence.

"Promotion?" Mick, who'd disappeared for a minute, reappeared holding a dog crate in one hand and the puppy in the other.

"Rochelle?" I don't even know why I asked.

"Yep," Mick said, setting the crate down and placing the squiggly puppy inside.

Tito whimpered for a beat or two and then immediately crashed.

"Is she Superwoman?" I asked as I whisked some olive oil with lemon juice to make a homemade salad dressing, thinking she'd picked up all these ingredients too.

"Who?" Mick poured himself a glass of wine and took a sip, before setting it down and rolling up his sleeves.

"Rochelle."

"She's just good at her job, like you are. Apparently, more than I know."

This guy knew exactly what to say—it was equally flattering and unnerving. Especially for someone like me who hadn't been complimented in over a decade.

"Well, it's only in the beginning stages. So, we'll see about this promotion business."

I gave both Mick and Priscilla my back, opening the oven and taking out the food. The kitchen flooded with the scent of garlic. Rochelle had picked up an Italian loaf on her own, so I decided a few extra carbs never hurt anyone.

"Let's eat," I said, changing the subject.

Priscilla popped up like she was starving. "I'll set the silverware out. I can do that."

Like a well-oiled machine and not the motley crew of unrelated misfits we were, we set the table and sat down to eat.

"What is that?" Mick looked toward the orange bottle Priscilla had brought to the table with her.

"My wine," she deadpanned, leaving Mick speechless.

The rest of dinner passed with the same easy flow. Tito asleep in his crate, and the three of us acting like we did this every night.

Mick insisted on a quick cleanup, which meant leaving the dishes in the sink for Rochelle, but I didn't like the idea of that.

"Mom, forget the dishes. Mick said it's fine. Can we have the brownies? Please?" Priscilla whined at me, batting her eyes.

"Yeah, listen to the girl," Mick said with a wink.

"Way to gang up on me," I said while reaching for the pan of brownies cooling on the counter.

"What are those?" Mick peered over my shoulder, his breath warm on my neck, making my whole body heat up.

"These are cookie-top brownies, but from scratch, not from a box."

"I think my little lady has a sweet tooth," he whispered along my neck. Sensing my hesitation, he quickly turned his head, looking for Priscilla. "She's over by the window, checking out the view."

Sure enough, she was looking out at the night, standing still, behaving with her cast as she should.

"I do," I mumbled back, cutting the brownies. "That's why I had Rochelle pick up some salted-caramel ice cream too."

"Hey, Mick, I want to try the bike . . . when I'm better." Priscilla had moved from her perch and was walking around the bike, checking it out.

"Of course, anytime. With your mom's brownies, I have a feeling I'm going to need an extra-long ride tomorrow."

"She has a sweet tooth. Bad," Priscilla said, the little narc.

Mick grinned. "I'm noticing."

"Here." I held a plate full of brownies out in front of Mick to quiet him down.

Priscilla sat back down, reminding me, "Don't forget the ice cream."

After a long duet of moans of ecstasy from Mick and Priscilla, and reminders of it being a school night from me, Mick said, "Let's take Tito out before you leave. Want to come?" he asked Priscilla, mindful not to make her feel left out, although her nose was stuck in her phone.

"No, I'm chatting with Penny about when I get my cast off. She's having a sleepover next Saturday. Can I go? Please, Mom? She said her mom will take great care of me."

With Mick opening the crate door, I told her I would think about it. He took my hand and ushered me outside.

The sky sparkled above us as he set Tito down in the far corner of the grass. The puppy didn't take long before squatting and relieving himself.

"One sec. Watch him for me," Mick said before dashing inside. He returned in a minute, holding a chenille blanket from the couch. "Come here."

I moved closer, and he wrapped the blanket around my shoulders, tugging me against him. He wrapped his arms around me and leaned in for a kiss, his lips gently touching mine, tasting like chocolate and caramel.

I hummed, and Mick took the kiss a little deeper. Another rumble escaped from me.

"Is that because I'm me or because I taste sweet and sticky?"

"Both." I couldn't look him in the eyes as I said it.

"I don't really give a shit, because I liked it. I like this," he said as he leaned in, his lips and words tickling my ear. "This whole night was good as hell."

I looked down, making sure Tito was staying close.

"He's fine. Don't avoid me using him," Mick said, running his face along my cheek, his nose brushing mine. "Point is, I like this. A whole hell of a lot."

"It was really nice. Easy. I liked cooking with no complaints," I said, then dropped my face in my hands for a second. "I'm sorry, I didn't mean to add that."

"You don't ever have to be sorry for being real. You don't have to hide your past from me as long as you're looking forward."

My heart sped up to a furious speed. Like a punch to the gut or a swat on the ass, how real this was getting hit me out of nowhere.

"Did you like the food?" I asked, wanting to change the subject and lighten the mood.

"Mar, I either eat out or enjoy whatever Rochelle picks up. It was fantastic, plus dessert. I'm happy."

His lips pressed to mine again with small caresses, telling me what the rest of his body would like to do to me, and I didn't disagree. Our hips met, seeking friction, and his tongue entered my mouth, sweeping against mine before he groaned.

"I want you, but now's not the time," he said, staring in my eyes. "But did I just hear you say you were going to think of a sleepover for Priscilla?"

This made me laugh. "I take it your mind went to dirty places over that?"

"Oh, it did. It absolutely did, Mar. Please say yes to Priss."

"I'll think about it," I said, leaning my head on his warm, hard chest.

"You're just toying with both of us now," he teased, kissing the top of my head.

"Maybe. Kiss me again, and I'll think about it on my way home."

Mick didn't argue, tipping my chin up with his finger and placing his mouth over mine, his lips brushing over mine. Then he pressed harder, digging in, trying to convince me to agree.

In my mind, though, I already had.

Priscilla is definitely going to that sleepover.

twenty-six

mick

Priscilla answered the door when I went to pick up Margo on Saturday night, which was a surprise.

I tried to hide my shock. I was embarrassed to admit it, but a small tinge of jealousy hit my gut. "Looking good, Priss," I said, noting her cast-free arm.

"All I got left is this sling for my collarbone."

"Snazzy."

I walked inside the door she held open, and before I could say anything else, Priscilla whispered, "My mom's on the phone. I'm still going on my sleepover, but she's been on for a while, and I need her to drive me."

I nodded. "No problem, but it's cool you're here. We can hang."

I was in uncharted territory, unsure what to say or do. The helpful side of me wanted to offer to drive her to the sleepover, but I knew better. Grown men who weren't related in some fashion didn't drive teenage girls anywhere . . . alone.

"Yeah, she said, but maybe let's go outside. It's been heated."

We both stepped back out the front door, and I thought it a bit odd that we didn't go to the sprawling backyard. I didn't have time to overthink it, though, because Priscilla looked at the ground, and I wanted to pull her in for a hug.

Another no-no, so I asked, "Heated over what? Work?"

I'd been in Chicago for a few days, helping put out a few fires, and I knew Margo was busy finalizing a presentation for her new boss.

"No. My dad. He's angry with her."

The urge to rush in and grab the phone from Margo hit me hard.

"He heard I'm going on a sleepover. Well, it's my fault. He actually called to say hello, which he's only done one other time. I didn't know it would be a mistake to tell him," Priscilla said.

"Of course you didn't know. Why wasn't he happy for you, though?"

With her free hand, she pushed her hair behind her hair, and it reminded me of her mom so much.

"He screamed at me to get her, saying just because she was single, it didn't mean she had to send me off so she could get . . . well, I don't want to say the last word."

Frowning, I said, "I can fill in the blanks."

Just then, Margo pulled open the front door. "Oh God, I'm sorry. I'm obviously running late." Her hair was tied in a knot on top of her head, and she wore leggings and an oversize sweatshirt.

"No biggie. It's the weekend."

"You told him," Margo said to her daughter through clenched teeth.

Priscilla nodded.

"Shit happens," I said. "Pardon my French."

This made Priscilla laugh, and Margo's shoulders relaxed.

"Can we leave now?" Priscilla asked.

"You know what?" I said to Margo. "Why don't I drive, and you can sit and decompress."

"I'm a mess." She waved a hand, gesturing to her outfit.

"I'm going to get my bag," Priscilla said quickly, seeming to sense we needed a minute.

I walked closer and pulled Margo in.

"Missed you," I said first, placing a chaste kiss on her lips. "How about we drop off Priss, go back to my place and grab Tito, take him for a little walk, and bring him back here? He's missed everyone after being with Rochelle for two days. Priss can see him tomorrow, and in the meantime, I can order takeout while you take a bath or shower."

"Really? Italian?"

"Really. Italian with dessert."

"You're okay with staying in?" Her hand came to rest right above my heart.

"More than okay."

"I'm ready," Priscilla said, bounding outside.

"Mar, lock up," I said. It was time to move forward.

"Thanks," Priscilla whispered to me when her mom went back inside.

"I've got you covered."

"She really needs to let it go. It wasn't her fault."

I didn't know where this kid came from, but I was going to bring her on as a partner when she was old enough. "You know, your insight is beyond your years, so I hope you know it wasn't your fault either."

"I guess. I just want to be with my friends right now."

I decided to leave it alone. I wasn't a therapist or an expert.

"Ready," Margo said, walking out the door with a long cardigan sweater wrapped tightly around her.

"Can we stop at Starbucks?"

"Absolutely," I told Priscilla with a wink, while her mom elbowed her good side.

A sucker was born every minute, and today that sucker was me.

"Um, we can turn that off right this very second," Margo said with a smile as soon as we dropped off Priscilla.

"You mean you don't like Justin Bieber?"

"Oh, I'm so sorry. I didn't know you were a huge fan. Please, let the Biebs play."

This had me laughing as we pulled away.

When we dropped off Priscilla, Sheila had come out to say hello, and asked what we had planned.

Margo had said, "Not much."

Knowing better than to chime in, I kept my mouth shut.

Sheila glanced between us, then grinned at Margo. "Oh yeah. Let's have coffee on Monday so you can tell me the truth."

"'Bye, Sheila. Call me if you need anything at all with Priss," Margo said.

Now, as we pulled away from the curb, my laughter faded. Margo looked pensive.

"What's up?" I asked, not trying to downplay her emotions but showing I noticed.

"Is it wrong of me to leave her? I know she told you about Tommy. What an ass. He never cared what she did before. Now all of a sudden, he's my judge and jury, saying I'm sloughing her off. I mean, he didn't even want to see her until she was out of a cast and able to care for herself. That's who I share a last name with, the kind of person who I married . . . God, I'm not making any sense."

Throwing her head back, Margo let out an exasperated breath.

Glancing at her, I didn't speak right away. Not because I didn't have thoughts, but in case she had anything to add.

"Sorry," she said with a huff. "I didn't mean to dump all that. I'm sure you're ready to escape."

"No, I was making sure you got it all out."

"I did. I swear."

Resisting the urge to pull over, I drove toward my place to pick up Tito, trying to get the puppy as quickly as possible so I could help Margo relax.

"You're quiet again," she said.

"Yes. I was thinking that a bath, some self-care, is what you need. Time for you."

"That's what you were thinking?"

"Yep." I nodded, taking a quick peek at her profile. "Hey, I had a single mom. I know women. I see your mind churning."

This time, she laughed. "If this whole business-savior thing doesn't work out for you, you could be a fortune-teller. I'm thinking you read people's minds."

"Look, a bath, a glass of wine, some pasta, maybe a foot rub . . . it will all do you wonders. You've been going nonstop. Making a new life, getting promoted at work, taking care of Priscilla, who in no way did you ditch. She wanted to see her friends tonight because she's a normal kid."

"How do you know?"

"I have a sixth sense. Even if I don't know, what I do know, is your ex—"

"He's not my ex yet."

"On paper, not yet. In matters of the heart, for years. What I was going to say was your ex had no right to accuse you of that or say that. He's going to be angry. He got caught being an asshole, and now he has to pay. He even has to ignore your indiscretions, since I know that's what you're going to say."

"Ha-ha," she said.

"Hold that thought," I told her as I pulled in front of my building and pressed the hazard lights. "Be right back."

I hustled into my building, relieved the elevator was empty, and was back down with Tito in minutes. He peed right away and snuggled right into Margo's lap afterward—who wouldn't want to do exactly that?

As we pulled away, I picked up right where we'd left off. "As for your name, change it back. It's not that hard. Get rid of that piece of shit and everything that's attached to you from him."

"Well, I can't get rid of Priss."

"No fucking way, and I never would ask you to. You know that?"

She nodded. I caught her head moving out of the corner of my eye.

"I didn't mean that. I just meant, I don't want her to feel left out."

I glanced her way. "For the record, if you wanted me to turn around and go back and get her, I would."

"No, I kind of like the idea of staying in with you. And a foot rub."

She quieted as she concentrated on the puppy, petting his fur, seeming to be deep in thought.

With that, our collective mood turned a corner just in time as I pulled into her driveway.

"Come on," I said before slipping out of the driver's side and hurrying to open her door. "Let's get you settled." I stole Tito and his leash, keeping him by my feet.

Margo leaned against me, almost collapsing, the weight of her day seeping into me.

She opened the door, and as soon as it closed behind us, she held on to me tighter.

I turned her toward me and ran my lips over the top of her head. Her hair a wild mess, I brushed it over one shoulder and bent to kiss her neck. I wasn't sure if she was up for it, but the humming coming from her throat was a good sign.

My lips ran up and down her soft skin, tasting a tinge of salt as I inhaled her scent. A discreet hint of perfume and the rest all Margo. Not Margaret.

"Let yourself go," I whispered as I made my way up to her mouth.

I brushed over her supple lips and gave her a closed-mouth kiss. She responded with more humming, and a moan escaped my own throat. We didn't waste time, taking the kiss deeper, eventually our mouths opening and tongues exploring. Somehow, we ended up maneuvered with her back against the door and my hips pressing into hers.

"Huh-uh," I said as Tito gave a little yap. "We aren't doing the door thing. First, you're taking a bath and I'm tiring out the dog, then I'm feeding you, and then I'm going to take my time with you."

Back on her tiptoes, Margo pressed her lips to mine. She kissed me with a fervor I'd never known, like she wanted to devour me.

"Thank you for being there," she murmured.

Breaking the moment, I took her hand and led her up the stairs. "Where to?" I asked. I'd been over a lot, but not inside her bedroom.

"Last door on the left." She motioned with her free hand to the left of the T at the top of the stairs.

I looked around as I walked her toward her room—the one she'd shared with her ex-prick—but I couldn't bring myself to care. On one wall was framed children's artwork, and I assumed they were Priscilla's. A portrait of Margo holding a newborn Priscilla and an antique-looking photo were hung side-by-side.

"Your grandma?" I asked.

"Yes. A far cry from my mom, but who I hope I'm closest to being like."

As we approached the door, I said, "You're one of a kind, Mar. One of the most giving and caring persons I've ever met."

"I don't know . . ."

"I do. Don't let self-doubt creep up into this moment."

Our hands still intertwined, I turned to face her and placed a kiss on her lips. I couldn't keep my mouth or hands to myself.

"I made some changes, by the way."

Raising an eyebrow, I wasn't sure what to make of what she was saying.

She turned toward the bed. "I didn't say anything because I didn't want to presume, but I took an afternoon for myself while Priss was at school and redecorated. I got new bedding and replaced some of the pictures."

I turned to take in the full room. The bed was done in shades of blue, and the nightstands both held black-and-white photos of Priscilla. The lamps had books as the stems.

"Those lamps are cool. I take it you read?" I asked, realizing how much I had to learn about Margo, and I wanted to learn every single thing about her.

She chuckled. "I do like to read. Mostly science fiction. I know, I know . . . weird choice."

"No," I said as I gathered her in my arms. "I think it's perfect. Margo, my little Martian."

This got me more laughter.

"I actually bought those lamps recently too. On the same day. I found them in a little store over by the Paula."

"I'm glad. You deserve your own space."

She didn't say anything, only leaned on my chest.

"Come on," I told her. "Bath time."

She led me into the bathroom, and I released her hand to start the bath in her large claw-foot tub. I checked the temperature of the water running in, and let it start to fill. Margo was rummaging under the sink when I turned. Her perfect ass was in my sight line, but I shook off any desires. This moment was for her to relax.

"Got it," she said. "Priss got this for me last Mother's Day. A bath bomb."

"Bath bomb? Looks more like a baseball."

"You drop it in the tub and it fizzes, releasing a skin-softening type thing. She found it on Amazon."

"Well, it sounds like the perfect thing for right now."

"Don't make fun of me. It's a thing. I don't know what to call it."

"Aren't you the writer?" I teased her, moving close and pulling her shirt over her head.

I ran my mouth over her shoulder, placing kisses along my route. Goose bumps broke out along her skin, and I ran my palm over her rib cage, brushing her side cleavage, finally warming her shoulder.

"Mmm." She hummed as I unclipped her bra, and allowed my palm to take its time running over her supple flesh.

"Give me that." I broke free and took the bath bomb from her hand. After dropping it in the tub, I beckoned her over. "Come here."

There was an intimacy between Margo and me that I couldn't define or understand, especially since I didn't know she read science fiction, but I wanted to know everything about her. I was forty years old, and I'd worked like a dog on my career. I was a millionaire several times over, pushed by pride and suffering, proud that I wasn't at all like my sleaze of a father, But being with Margo made me want to be even greater a man.

I only wished my mom were here to see me and meet Margo. I knew what I wanted, and she was it.

"You're really off in la-la land," the woman of my dreams said, running her palm down my arm.

"Just thinking how much I'm loving this moment. Now, let's get those pants off and dunk you in."

We'd somehow remembered to kick off our shoes by the door, so I whisked her pants down while we were both standing. All I could see was a nude silk boy short.

"Oh my," I said, swallowing hard. "This could derail everything."

This time, her laugh was husky and throaty, further crushing my willpower to get her in the tub.

Dropping to my knees, I set her legs free from the pants bunched at her ankles, and rose to place one quick kiss to the front of her panties before stripping them off. "In you go, before I get any ideas."

While I held her hand, she dipped a toe in the water and said, "Just right." Then she swung her other leg in and let go of my hand to step in the water.

I turned the knob to stop it from filling and took her in, leaning her head back, her eyes closed.

"How's the bomb thingy?" I asked, smirking.

She opened her eyes and caught me. "It's pretty freaking good. This is . . . I don't have words. Thank you. I'm not sure how we found each other and why there seems to be this chemistry, but I'm really happy."

It didn't matter how many successes you had as a businessperson or how many affairs of the heart you've had, when something makes your blood pressure rise and your whole body hum, you know it's worth holding on to— forever.

"Me too," I said simply, not revealing my deep thoughts, then rushed back to Tito.

Much later, we sat on the couch, our bellies full. Margo wore only her robe, and had her feet up on my lap.

"This is nice. Thanks for knowing what I needed."

"This," I said, squeezing her foot, "is more than nice."

"Okay, maybe you're right." She stood and took my hand. "Come on, isn't this supposed to be a sleepover?"

I didn't argue, but I did worry she was thinking about her argument with Tommy and trying to appease me at the same time.

When I stood, I squeezed her hand. "You know there's no pressure from me, right?"

"Yep, I know." Giving me a come-hither look, she made her way to bed, sliding off her robe before she slid under the covers.

There wasn't much more talking after that, only a lot of moaning.

twenty—seven

"Mommm, we don't need to go. I want to go to Penny's. Pleeease?" Priscilla pleaded with me after school. Seated in the passenger seat of the Volvo, she pouted and aimed her death glare at my profile.

"We can't cancel now."

"Is this because Dad was mean over the weekend? Mick said to forget it."

"Let's leave Mick out of this," I said firmly.

I cracked my window, desperate for some fresh air. In reality, I wanted to roll it all the way down and stick my head out of it. My heart was pounding in rhythm with my head, and I could feel the vein in my temple pulsing.

Focusing on the road, I spoke again. "Look, I'm not excited about going either, but we need to."

"I. Am. Fine," Priscilla said, scowling as she crossed her arms over her chest.

"I know, honey."

"Then why? I'm going to have dinner with Dad next week. I'll tell him that you didn't do anything wrong."

"That's exactly why we're going. You shouldn't have to tell Dad anything of the sort." I made a left turn, then glanced at her. "And the way we lived, we shouldn't have had to live that way."

"Mom, please. Is this about Mick? I'm fine with it. You know that."

I pulled into a small parking lot and cut the engine. "Let's save it for in our session. We need to go, Priss. Period. Then you can see your friends."

Not waiting for a response, I grabbed my keys from the center console and tossed them in my purse. Remembering that today was Priscilla's first day without the sling, I walked around to open her door for her. She got out a little less gingerly than I would have liked, but I kept those thoughts to myself.

Sophie Schroeder, PhD, greeted us as we walked into the waiting room, then ushered us inside her office.

"You must be Priscilla," she said, extending a hand toward my frowning daughter.

When Priscilla extended her left hand, Dr. Schroeder slapped her own forehead. "I forgot. How is your arm? Your mom told me about your injury over the phone."

"Oh," Priscilla said. "It's better now, thanks," she added, adjusting her attitude.

"Please sit," Dr. Schroeder said, and we did.

I grabbed the chair while Priscilla sank into the loveseat. Her mood was too big for us to sit next to each other.

"So, like I said, your mom filled me in a little over the phone, and I know the last few months have been stressful. I'd like to hear from you, though."

I crossed my legs and waited. Truthfully, I didn't know the therapist was going to dive right into it so quickly.

Priscilla sat silent for a moment, which was the first indicator that we were in trouble. My daughter was never quiet.

"I don't think we need this," she finally said. "I mean, we're finally good. I always knew my dad was a jerk, but I couldn't say it. Now I can."

When I opened my mouth, Dr. Schroeder quickly lifted her hand, telling me with her eyes to keep quiet. "Were you worried for your mom?" she asked nonchalantly.

Priscilla sat quietly again, then cut right to the chase when it came to everything that was going on. "I was, so I tried to be at friends' houses. That was wrong, but now I don't have to worry anymore. Weird thing is, I don't think my dad would hurt me. He won't, I mean, and Mom is safe now. I just want to move on. You know this thing with Mick, she's letting it get to her, but she shouldn't. I mean, I know about . . . *you know*, and it's fine. I want her to be happy."

"I'm glad you feel safe with your dad. I'm sure that gives everyone a good feeling, but you need to know this—if your mom feels you're unsafe, that's her job."

"I know. My mom would never do anything bad to me," Priscilla said, then crossed her arms over her chest. "Except make me come here."

"Of course she wouldn't, and somewhere deep inside, she must believe this will be helpful. Like when you say *you know*, what does that mean?"

I closed my eyes for a beat, wanting to transport myself to a desert island somewhere, fearful of what might come out of Priscilla's mouth.

"It means like . . . this girl in my school . . . you don't know her, but her dad had a girlfriend. While he was married, and my mom did too. Not a girlfriend, but you know what I mean. Mick. But I don't blame her, and I'm not mad at her. My mom wasn't happy with my dad. Neither was I. What I mean is . . . my mom should be happy, and now she is. With Mick. We learned in English class about choices and making the best choice using situational awareness. This is like that."

"I understand," Dr. Schroeder said, encouraging her while nodding.

"So, we don't need this."

Priscilla moved to stand up, but Dr. Schroeder stopped her.

"Not so fast. I understand you want to leave, but let's hear from your mom."

This only earned Dr. Schroeder an eye roll, which she ignored.

Clearing my throat, I gathered my thoughts. "I'm sorry. Sorry to you, Priss. I'm sorry I didn't realize you thought I was in danger, or knew I was. I'm sorry it took the whole scene at the hospital to move things along. I really am sorry. I'm also sorry that you need to know this about Mick, and how he came to be in our lives. It's too much adult stuff for you to know."

"Mom, it's fine."

I glanced at our therapist, hoping she could make this right.

Dr. Schroeder leaned forward in her chair toward Priscilla. "I think your mom needs this. She needs to figure out how to say good-bye to the past and the things she's sorry for. It's called closure, and while it may feel like you have it—and you may have—we need to do this for your mom."

Somehow this seemed to resonate with Priscilla. She sat quietly, and a lone tear slid down her cheek.

"I'm sorry, Mom," she muttered. "I'll do this, it's just I want to put this behind me. I want to be normal with my friends and have fun. Play soccer again."

"You will do all that. This is one hour of your time and will mean the world to me," I said, and it was sealed.

We talked a bit more with Dr. Schroeder. I tried to avoid the affair conversation, but knew it was coming soon.

A week later, I sat at Mick's kitchen bar, sipping a glass of wine.

"I'm sure it's fine," I murmured into my glass.

"Mar," Mick said, coming around my back and kneading my shoulders. "There's no one tougher than Priss, and I'm not just saying that. She knows right from wrong, and she's not going to allow anything wrong to happen."

"I know," I said, still not fully satisfied with the truth, glancing at sweet little Tito asleep in his crate.

"It's a terrible burden. I know that too." He moved to the side of me, hip to the bar, in dark jeans and an untucked black dress shirt, open at the collar. His hair tousled the way I liked, still damp from his shower after his workout. "Look, it's not fair, but she's at her dad's because she has to be. Soon, she'll be able to say whether she wants to be there or not. It sucks, but it's going to be over soon."

Sighing, I said, "The therapist said not to pounce when she gets home. To let her process."

With his palm warm on the nape of my neck, underneath my hair, he held my gaze. "Then that's what you will do. Have your wine and relax. I'll take you home later, and you'll go take a warm bath and let Priss process, yeah? I can even bring Tito, and she can play with him."

"Okay."

"Good. Now, let me tell you about my day," he said while his hand slid to my earlobe.

"I want to hear."

I meant what I said. I'd become enthralled with Mick's business dealings. The way he became so entrenched in an industry, studying it, and yet relinquishing his power when he didn't know something.

He fiddled with my earlobe, standing close enough that I could smell his soap. Man and pine was what it brought to mind.

"Well, a sucker is born every day, and now this chef has about seventeen ideas he wants me to back him in."

"Of course he does," I said with a laugh. Taking a sip of my wine, I asked, "No drink for you?"

"Driving safe cargo later."

"Ah, maybe it's because you may see Tommy?"

"That too," Mick said, shaking his head, "but I'm seeing you now. What shall we eat?"

"Thai?"

"Definitely, but before I forget, I made a small stop today in New York."

My eyes widened. "Please tell me you don't have another puppy stashed around here."

"Better." He moved to the other side of the kitchen and picked up a tiny box.

"Um, what's that?" A chill of excitement ran down my spine while my gut churned with fear.

This was getting serious, right? *Should it be?*

Mick caught my eye. "Don't get stuck in that overactive mind of yours. Save that for your writing."

He popped open a box, revealing the most gorgeous pair of earrings. Two little eyes stared back at me, blue in the center and outlined with crystals. Or diamonds.

My gut churned again.

"Now all the bad will be cast away," Mick said, handing me the box.

When I took it with shaky hands, he reached for my ear, gently removing the small hoop I had in.

"Put them on," he said with authority.

I did what he asked without arguing, willing my hand not to tremble while I took off the backing to slip the post into my piercing.

"Thank you," I whispered.

Mick shook his head, telling me not to say it, but I couldn't help it. I thanked him again.

With both earrings in, I stood and kissed him. Maybe it was just my imagination, but I felt their protection like a cloak wrapped around my body.

Our mouths fused and then opened, our tongues exploring. His minty breath, coupled with the wine in mine, lit a fire in me. We stayed that way for a while . . . until my stomach growled, and Mick took it upon himself to break free and order Thai for delivery.

"Now, where were we?" he said, smirking.

"You were telling me how you're becoming a restauranteur?" I said coyly, leaning back into the bar.

"That was earlier, and while I didn't think the restaurant biz was for me, I like this guy. The chef. So I am. But I meant when my mouth was on yours and my hand was itching to be underneath those clothes."

A jolt ran through my body. Classic Mick. He didn't need to be explicit to set all of me on fire. All I needed was a promise of his hands or mouth on me, and I was primed.

"Oh yes, now I remember."

He pounced on me, lifting me onto the bar. Wedging himself between my thighs, he kissed me senseless before tugging off my sweater. It fluttered silently to the floor as Mick's lips traveled down my neck and over my breastbone, landing on the fabric of my bra, directly over my nipple. He nibbled on the satin before breaking free and blowing warm air across the dampness. Chills ran through me as he repeated the same pattern on the other side, my heart beating furiously underneath where he was working voodoo with his mouth.

"Love every inch of you," he murmured.

I didn't know what the hell he meant, but I liked hearing it.

Mick gave me no time to overthink it. No wasting a second, he unbuttoned my jeans and lifted my butt so I could wiggle out of them. Then he was on his knees, tugging them down before placing his mouth over my satin panties.

I'd never thought of myself as wanton, but all of a sudden, I needed more, and I wasn't too shy to ask. Panting, I breathed out, "More."

Mick tugged my panties to the side and gave me more. His breath on me was hot, yet shivers ran down my legs and back up my thighs as he expertly used his tongue on me.

"Oh God." My head fell back on a moan as I started to come apart.

"Let go, Mar," Mick murmured against my most sensitive spot, and I did.

For a moment, I forgot about Priscilla being with Tommy, and how horrible the last decade or more was. Even better, I believed the next decade could be different.

As Mick knelt between my thighs, making me shatter, I dreamed of a better relationship. One built on affection and great sex and admiration . . . and respect.

Lost in a world of possibilities, it took me a second to catch on that Mick had traveled back up my body and was nudging my face, smelling like me, and I didn't mind. It might seem naive or juvenile, but I'd never been with a lover who actually cared for me.

"God, I want you, Mar," Mick whispered in my ear.

"Take me," I said, pulling him closer and kissing his mouth.

With one hand behind me, holding on to my hip, he used his other hand to undo his jeans and push them down.

"Shit, no condom," he grumbled with his hand on his length, pumping, and his eyes feral.

"IUD," I said, biting my lip.

I'd had it put in, not wanting to have any more kids with Tommy. Considering we hadn't been together in forever, I was clean, and for some strange reason, I completely trusted Mick.

"You sure?"

I nodded, afraid of what he would say.

Mick released himself and pushed my panties all the way to the side before guiding himself in. "Ah . . . you feel so fucking good."

He pushed into me, starting with slow, leisurely thrusts before speeding up. With my butt on the kitchen bar, I threw my head back as beads of sweat broke out along the nape of my neck, under my hair.

"I'm going to go again," I yelped. I couldn't believe it. That had never happened before.

Mick took his time, pulling out, every nerve of mine feeling him, and then he pushed in hard and deep. He only had to do it once more, and we were falling apart in each other's arms.

"You good?" Mick asked moments later, cradling my head against his chest.

Speechless, I nodded.

"I think we're going to have to disinfect this counter before we eat."

He lifted my chin so my eyes met his gaze. He was smiling, and this caused me to giggle.

"Oh, that feels pretty fucking good," he said, looking down to where we were still roughly connected.

All at once, my stomach growled and Mick's phone buzzed.

"Time to eat." He slipped out of me and yanked up his jeans . . . it was then I noticed he'd been commando. "Hello," he said into the phone, assuming it was our takeout, but waggled his eyebrows at me.

Warmth crept up my cheeks and I slid down from the counter, hiding my face with my hair.

Mick set aside his phone. "I'm going to take Tito with me downstairs to get the food, let him stretch his legs and maybe lift his leg on the sidewalk."

"I'll be here," I said, thinking I'd go clean up while he was downstairs, but decided to check my phone first.

I'd missed one text from Priscilla. In the time it took for face recognition to unlock the phone, my heart jumped into my throat and then back down to my ankles.

I'm good. It's fine. Don't worry.

That girl. I didn't deserve her.

twenty–eight

margaret

"She's decided to wait a few more weeks before another visit," I told Tommy. Dr. Schroeder had said it was fine for me to advocate for Priscilla. A girl her age shouldn't have to find herself in the middle of custody negotiations, so I went for it.

"It's not a big deal," he said. "You were the one who was always close with her."

"Okay, I'll let you know when she's feeling up to it," I said, trying to end the call. We'd scheduled fifteen minutes to discuss school tuition and anything else related to Priscilla's bills, and we'd finished minutes earlier.

"I guess when she's sick of your new guy," Tommy said snidely, "she'll come crawling back to Dad."

I squeezed my eyes shut and counted to five, then to ten. Hoping he would disconnect the call, I went for fifteen, then gave up. "Tommy, don't do that. Priscilla doesn't deserve it."

"Oh, look at that, we're out of time," he said. "'Bye, Margaret. Tell the school everything will be paid in full."

He disconnected before I could respond.

185

Dr. Schroeder also said the only trick Tommy had left in his bag was to emotionally torment me, and she was right. He did it in spades. While it hurt my heart to hear him talk so poorly about our daughter, it was better than him physically hurting anyone.

I put my phone on the table and pulled my earbud out, then looked at the time. I still had an hour before picking up Priscilla at school and taking her to walk Tito.

It had been three weeks since the sleepover battle and the night Mick took care of me, and two weeks since her dinner with Tommy. Her shoulder was mostly healed, and she'd grown much too attached to the dog. Mick was always bringing him over, and then he decided, why pay a dog walker to come in twice a day when Priscilla could do it a few afternoons a week?

Mick had asked Priscilla in front of me, and then of course, said if it was okay with me, but Priscilla was already jumping for joy. This would be our second time this week, and she'd texted me at lunchtime to make sure I remembered.

With the minutes ticking by, I decided to get to work. My actual promotion started in two weeks, but I was already doing a lot of preliminary work. Tony and Jane were both big believers in self-starters and self-motivation, so I didn't have to punch a clock. I would work at my own pace, which as a single mom was a real perk.

Lost in my latest writing piece, I startled when my alarm went off, signaling it was time to pack up and go. I downed the last dregs of my coffee, shoved everything in my tote, and put on my coat.

As soon as I was seated in my car, the phone rang, and I pressed accept call.

"Off to walk the tyrant?" Mick asked.

"Well, first, I have to pick up the walker."

"You do that. I don't think I'm going to be able to see you later. I have to take a later dinner meeting to go over some documents with my lawyer."

I smiled to myself. This is how it was with Mick. Easy. So easy that a frown started to push my smile away.

What if this is a game? Or a trick?

"I'm sorry," he said, drawing me out of my anxiety and self-pity.

"Oh no, it's fine. I was lost in my thoughts."

"Tomorrow? I can have something brought in for all of us," he said, so sweet to always include Priscilla. "Tell me, what kind of panties are you wearing?"

"What? I almost just wrecked my safety-first SUV."

He laughed into the phone, and just hearing it reverberate through the Bluetooth gave me all the feels. "Just wanted to make sure you were listening."

"I am. Dinner tomorrow. Good."

"Okay, now there's one more thing. I left something for Priss at the condo on the kitchen counter."

"What now?"

Mick had started buying little things for Priscilla. A speaker for her phone, then a Kindle. It was too much, but when I protested and asked him to stop, he wouldn't hear of it.

"Oh, just a spring break trip for ten of her friends, chaperoned."

"No. You didn't." My heart dropped. How was I going to tell her no?

"I'm kidding. But this gift requires you to go, so be warned."

"I don't like surprises, Mick. Prepare me for the teen angst about to come my way."

I imagined his eyes crinkling and a smirk lifting his mouth on the left side while I talked to him from the car.

"Okay, okay. Justin Bieber tickets. Four of them."

Luckily, I was at a stoplight. "No, you didn't. She's gonna float through her dog walk."

"And backstage passes."

"You owe me," I said firmly. "You know the shrieking that's going to be involved in that evening?"

"I don't mind owing you," he said.

"Yeah, yeah. Now, I'm almost here to grab your dog walker."

"Be safe. You girls are precious cargo."

"I will," I said, and then added, "Oh, Mick?"

"Yes?"

"Navy lace." Grinning, I ended the call before he could respond.

About thirty minutes later, Priscilla and I walked into Mick's condo.

Tito whined from his crate as soon as he heard Priscilla come in. Remembering Mick's instructions, she waited for him to quiet, and plucked the note from the top of the crate from Rochelle.

I took Mr. Bossypants out at one. He did #1 and #2. Lots of luck getting him to cooperate on a walk later. Also, Mick left something for you on the kitchen counter by the blender.

— Rochelle

I rolled my eyes while Priscilla read the note aloud. How was this my life?

My daughter, being the best kind of person ever, said, "I'm going to walk Tito first and then get the thing from Mick." Before I could say anything, she was kneeling on the floor and scooping Tito out of his crate. "There you are, you good little boy."

His tail flapped in her face, and she just moved her head out of the way.

"He's going to get big, ya know?" I said.

"Mom, don't ruin it for me."

Then she grabbed his leash from the hook and slipped out to the hallway toward the elevator.

Sitting down at the kitchen bar, I pulled in a deep breath, thinking maybe I should try Mick's bike when Priscilla came to walk Tito. I'd been running three or four days a week, but I shouldn't just sit here.

I was thinking about my new exercise routine when I spotted a note on the bar that read mar on the front. Taking the envelope in my hand, I opened it with shaky hands.

Pulling out a piece of paper with my right hand, I touched my ear with my left. So far in a few months, Mick had done more for me than Tommy ever had in our marriage.

Mar—

I know you're sitting there overthinking. You're probably looking around my condo thinking why you're there, what else you should be doing, and how this happened.

It just did. Nothing we can do. We met under unusual circumstances, but sometimes the happiest of endings have the ugliest roots. That's us.

So, go over to the fridge, get yourself a sparkling water, and relax. Sit down on the couch and make yourself at home. Don't worry about Priss and Tito. They're looking out for each other.

Like I want to look out for you. Always.

Mick

How did he know I was doing that? For someone who had never really been in a serious relationship, Mick knew women. Or did he just know me?

Then I saw a small arrow at the bottom of the page and turned over the paper.

How do I know?

I was a momma's boy.

Awestruck, I folded the paper and stuck it deep inside my tote and went to the fridge. Gulping a sparkling water, I felt like crying and jumping up and down like a lottery winner.

Confusion settled in my chest, making me feel woozy. I thought about Sheila's latest advice.

We'd been on the phone, and she told me not to be too hard on myself. Things happen for a reason. Then she'd told me that Peter had an affair a few years back.

I couldn't believe it, and then I imagined her curled up in the couch while talking to me, a glass of wine in hand, sharing this painful time for my benefit. While her story hadn't turned out the same as mine—it ended up reinvigorating Peter's commitment to the marriage—it helped me to know I wasn't alone. Peter had gone to counseling and wrestled with the guilt, along with the reasons behind his actions, and Sheila had forgiven him. My situation ended up differently, but Tommy and I were never meant to be.

Apparently, Dale was a real source of strength to her during that time. He'd been a widower looking for a platonic friend, and Sheila was a mess. What amazed me was how much was happening in the world while I was stuck in my own torturous bubble.

"Tito, hold up!"

I looked up to see Priscilla chasing Tito as he raced through the condo, and she glanced my way.

"I let him off the leash in the hall, and he went nuts."

"Well, let's not to do that again."

I didn't have time to say anything more because he was at my feet, begging for attention.

"Hey, there, little fella," I said, bending over to pet him. "Although you won't be little for too much longer."

"Oh. My. God!" Priscilla shrieked, and I knew she opened her gift, which was probably procured by Rochelle.

"Mom. Mom! Justin Bieber! I can't breathe!" She was jumping up and down, and I had to admit it was a bit contagious. "I have to text Penny. Oh. My.

189

God. I said that already, but still."

"Why don't you put Tito in his crate and call Penny from the car? I need to get home and make dinner."

"What about Mick?" she asked, cocking her head to the side.

The woozy feeling was back with how attached she was getting to Mick.

Was I messing up?

Tucking away my emotions, I decided to call Sheila or make a therapist appointment. Then I simply said, "He's working late," and we hit the road.

twenty—nine

"How is Annabeth?" I asked Dale.

"Much better after she spoke with you. I wasn't prepared for that . . . it's embarrassing."

Annabeth got her period for the first time on Friday night, and poor Dale panicked. Now he sat red-faced across from Sheila and me at the coffee shop, where we were finalizing the order of speakers for the holiday banquet.

"Don't be. None of us are," Sheila said, consoling him. "When Penny told me, I accused her of lying to get attention. I was fifteen . . . I mean, how much hormones are these poor kids ingesting?"

"Don't give it a moment's thought," I said, wanting to change the subject. I didn't think Dale wanted to hear about Sheila's menstrual cycle.

"Also, sorry about the SOS text during your date," Dale said, bringing up the elephant in my living room.

"No, no bother. It wasn't a date. I was cooking my tortilla soup, and Priss was home. Of course she was home. It's her house. Ugh, this is coming out all wrong."

"What's wrong?" Sheila tossed her hair behind her shoulder and turned to

191

face me.

"Nothing."

"That's not a nothing face." She raised an eyebrow at me, and I felt hot with shame.

"Do you want me to go?" Dale said, looking like he'd rather walk on fire than sit in on this conversation.

"Stay," Sheila said, and he did. "Now tell us. You give Dale a woman's opinion all the time, and now it's his turn to pay up."

I tried to swallow, but my throat was as dry as sawdust. No chance burning-hot coffee would make it better, so I just spoke.

"It's . . . everything is going so fast. Mick is too good for me. He's totally cool with Priss, and she's gaga for him. She barely wants to see Tommy, which I know isn't hard to imagine . . . but it's all *Mick this* and *Mick that*. My past is so messy, and I feel like he's wasting his best years on me."

Sheila shook her head and clucked her tongue, and Dale joined in with the head shaking.

"Dale, tell her," Sheila said.

"He doesn't see it as wasting his best years. No man would spend time with you and your daughter . . . shlep his dog over like I know he does . . . and not want to do all that. As for Priss, she's a good judge of character—"

"Maybe better than me," I said, interrupting.

"That's a topic for another day," Dale said. "Look, she likes Mick, and that's a good thing. He's not interested in your past but your future. So that's it."

I knew better than to argue, so I decided to cool things down a bit. "Thanks. That helps, but let's do this, because the banquet isn't waiting for us."

"It's going to be fabulous," Sheila said, clapping her hands with enthusiasm.

I knew any mention of the event would get Sheila back on track, but it didn't stop me from breathing a sigh of relief.

A few days later over a drink at the Oak, I turned to Mick and said, "This feels too calm."

Dale and Sheila's advice lingered in my mind, but my own negative thoughts overpowered it.

Mick set his Scotch down, drawing my attention to his forearm, his dress shirt rolled up. His Rolex was like a shiny beacon on his olive-toned skin, taunting me for a million reasons I wasn't even sure of.

"I think calm is good," he said matter-of-factly.

"I don't know. It's just too quiet. Almost unsettling," I said, and he slipped the stem of my wineglass out of my hand and set it on the bar.

We were in our corner. Mick had asked me if I was okay coming back here after the last time, and I was. It held a few really momentous memories, but now reality was crashing down on me hard.

"I can see your mind chugging a million miles a minute," he said, taking my hand in his and massaging my fingers. "We should have gone somewhere else."

"No, it's not that. Yes, everything is still fresh in my mind, but it's just this is too good."

He laughed and squeezed my hand. "Mar, don't do this. You're overthinking."

My racing mind had me pick up my phone and check it. "Sorry, you know Priss is home alone."

He nodded. "I don't mind. I didn't mind having a drink in your kitchen or mine."

Priscilla was at our house—with Tito. Mick asked if I wanted to do happy hour, and my daughter being my daughter volunteered to dog sit.

"Did you get that dog for her?" I blurted. Sweat was forming on my neck, and my chest was tight with anger of some sort.

"What?" Mick schooled his face, but his tone let me know he was hurt.

"The dog. Did you get it to bribe Priss?"

"No." Mick's answer was firm, but I didn't believe him. After all, he was a ruthless businessman.

"Us. When we met at the bar, did you just mean to sleep with me?"

Another firm *no* came from his mouth.

"And now we're sitting here having a drink, like we've been doing this for decades."

"Is that a bad thing?"

"It is, considering how we met, and then Priscilla's fall, and then Tommy, and then just everything."

"It's not a bad thing."

I gulped down some wine, my throat raw with emotion and my skin on fire with my feelings. "I've spent most of my life with a dark cloud following me. Now it's all rainbows and glitter. I can't trust it. It's too good."

Mick gathered me close enough that our foreheads touched. Classic Bee Gees started piping through the bar, and I pictured us in a cheesy eighties rom-com.

"Mick," I whispered. "It feels too fast, too good. I'm scared."

"I hear you. I don't want you to think I'm ignoring your feelings, but you're wrong."

"What if Tommy changes his mind and reverses our agreement?"

Mick ran his thumb over my cheek, and I caught his bartender, Wes, looking at us. "Contracts, I know. When someone rushes a deal and gives the person everything they want, they're hiding something themselves."

I shook my head. "I don't know."

"I do," he said firmly.

Blinking at him, I froze. "You do because of your experience, or you really do know?"

My mind ran through a range of possibilities. Had Mick interfered in the proceedings? Did I misjudge him? If my anxiety was high prior to this conversation, it skyrocketed in this moment.

"This isn't turning out to be the relaxing night I'd hoped," Mick said, still holding my hand.

"I'm sorry."

"Don't apologize. I don't want you to hold in your feelings. That's not fair, but I should be honest. A while back, I was at a business dinner and heard Tommy talking at the table behind me . . ." Mick went on to tell me about not knowing who Tommy was at first, but then putting it all together. "It was a gross display of behavior for anyone, let alone who I came to know as your husband."

A lump the size of a cantaloupe formed in my throat, and I could barely swallow.

"You never said anything?" I asked, unable to understand why. "I thought we were being one hundred percent honest with each other?"

"Mar—"

Whirling inside, I pulled away. "I mean, I told you every embarrassing detail."

"That's why I kept quiet. I didn't want to cause you more pain or shame. The man is slime, and you deserve better."

"Like you?"

"Don't say that."

My heart didn't beat a million miles a minute from excitement but rather apprehension. I had been wrong to think this would be fun or okay—and right to think it was way too easy. My life was meant to be twisted in complications, and this reeked of that.

I grabbed my purse. "You know what? I want to go home. I left Priss, and for what? This? I need to think."

Mick grasped my hand gently. "I'm not going to grab you or squeeze you or keep you from what you want to do, Mar. That's not me. But know this—I'm sorry, and right now my heart is cracking. I was damned if I said anything, and screwed if I didn't."

"I need to think," I said again. "I just need to think."

I kept saying the same thing, forgetting my words. I was a writer, so that didn't happen often.

"I understand, but I'm not going to wait long before coming back to get you. Take your time to think. I won't take that away from you, but know I'll be here waiting to get you back."

I stood and so did Mick, his hand coming to my lower back. He tossed a hundred-dollar bill on the bar and said, "I'm still driving you home."

I simply nodded, knowing there was no point in arguing. In fact, I sat silent for the entire ride. When we were in front of my house, I debated just getting out of the car without saying another word, but I couldn't.

Despite hurting me, Mick still meant something to me. I knew better than to stay. I'd learned that lesson with Tommy. If something was hurting me, I couldn't stand idly by. But I didn't know how to reconcile this whole situation.

"I don't mean to run away," I told Mick, not meeting his eyes. "I do need time to digest all this. Do you understand?" My voice wavered at the very end, part of me wanting to change my mind.

"I do," Mick said with confidence. "I told you . . . I won't force you to do anything. Ever. But I care about you deeply and I'm not going to lose you."

All I did was give him a quick nod and jump out of the car, mostly out of fear of jumping over the center console and into his lap.

thirty

m i c k

One thing I knew was that my beautiful Mar needed to feel independent and in control.

Her ex had taken away that feeling from her. I knew she knew this, but I didn't think she realized that I hadn't given her sense of independence and control back to her. She had given them to herself.

Yes, when she decided to have an affair with me, she was grasping for control. Of course, it wasn't her best moment or mine. Definitely not one we would get a gold star for, but it happened. Margo needed to understand all of this on her own, and maybe, just maybe she would feel that way soon.

I texted her every day, and told myself after ten days, tops, I was going to talk sense into Margo.

I'd say something like . . . "Mar, how are you today? Kicking ass at work?"

Or . . . "Mar, I'm thinking of your beautiful smile today as I fly off to NYC. Wish you and Priscilla (but not Tito) were with me."

Or even better . . . "Mar, I think—no, I know—I don't want to be without you. No matter what, that won't change. Also, you picked me!"

I knew I was making headway when I got a text back from her on day five.

I miss you.

That's all she wrote until about fifteen minutes later, when she sent another text.

And Tito too.

Then I really knew.

I'd flown to New York and agreed to some Asian fusion concept because I was a sucker for the guy I'd affectionately begun to call Chef. His drive and passion reminded me so much of me, he was like the little brother I'd always wanted.

I'd also decided to lighten my workload by not buying a construction company in dire straits.

I knew Margo and Priscilla were going to be a bigger part of my life, and I wanted to be a part of theirs, which was why I called Sheila and bought a table at her fundraiser. I told her to donate all the seats to teachers, but to save me a seat next to Margo.

Of course, she snickered, then oohed and aahed over the phone, promising not to tell Margo a thing. Those two had become close friends ever since I'd first come to know of Sheila the Great at the Paula.

I had plenty of money, so I wasn't worried about passing on one business opportunity. In fact, I was concentrating more on making more passive income.

Today was going to be the last text I sent to Margo. The event was tonight, and I'd reached my limit for waiting.

She'd had time to think and realize that my not telling her about what Tommy had said was nothing more than a bad judgment call on my part. The first of what would probably be many . . . it was how I'd reacted that mattered. That's what she needed to know.

I kept my text light today, because later I was going to lay on the heavy.

Tito found a glove of Priscilla's and sleeps with it. He misses her.

I wasn't expecting the crying emoji I got back. It twisted in my gut as I put on my tuxedo. Time to get Mar back where she belonged.

thirty-one

margaret

Decorated for the holiday gala, the ballroom was a kaleidoscope of colors. The tablecloths were various jewel tones, and the walls were draped in purple fabric with twinkling lights twisted along the molding. The chandeliers sparkled, lighting up the dance floor, and an oversized Christmas tree had a place of honor in the center. It was exactly the vision Sheila had talked about at our second meeting.

Only last week, I'd discovered the forthrightness I'd originally made fun of was what I most admired about Sheila now. Her passion and vision of what she wanted was something I needed healthy doses of, so I no longer poo-pooed those character traits.

Except now I was missing Mick and didn't know how to get him back. How to say I was sorry for being unforgiving.

Drowning in my melancholy, I took in the stage area, candelabras representing Hanukkah and Kwanzaa lined up in front of where the band played. I especially loved the electric violin, and how its sound reverberated in my chest. Glittery confetti in the shapes of symbols from all three winter holidays littered every surface, making everything sparkle and bringing out the brightness of the season.

I wished I felt brighter as I watched couples mingle through the room, air kissing others and toasting to a wonderful holiday season. This would be my first holiday season alone. Well, not alone, with Priscilla, which was typically how we celebrated. Tommy had often escaped to the office to do some paperwork.

Although after Mick's story, who knew what Tommy was up to when he took off. I didn't really care anymore. He and I had been done for a long time in affairs of the heart, even if on paper we were still married.

The auction table was a flurry of activity with bidders. And then there was me, trying to reconcile my relationship status.

I stood next to the bar, leaning my elbow against it as I held a glass of wine, watching life pass me by, drowning in my mistakes. For a second, I considered pretending to be sick so I could leave early, but I knew Sheila would come and sniff me out. No way would she let me miss this event, even if I were really under the weather.

My heart pounded, wanting Mick by my side, but my brain argued against it.

"Can I buy you a drink?"

The words radiated to my core as they rang in my ears.

My gaze dropped to the floor, catching a pair of Gucci loafers, striped socks, and flat-front black dress pants. Not lingering there for very long, my gaze worked its way up to a pair of fuck-me eyes and messy black hair. Like that night so long ago at the Oak, Mick wore his tux, but tonight the tie was properly affixed.

Although this time, the tux was for me—presumably—and not for a clandestine affair.

"I have one," I said, my words hoarse and throaty, my emotions clogging my veins.

"How about one I bought you? You know I'm big on that."

I smiled. It was a reference only I could get, and while the memory itself was bittersweet, it had been the start of something new for me.

"What if I buy you one?" I asked, and he smirked.

Mick came close, leaned in, and ran his hand up the side of my dress. "I don't see the likes of a wallet on you, but nice try. Are you taking lessons in negotiation from anyone I know?"

I opened my mouth to answer, but he interrupted.

"Not that I don't like what I'm seeing. That dress, those shoes, you just standing there looking gorgeous." His gaze dropped to my heels and ran back up the length of me. "But I like that smile the best. I've missed it. I don't know what you were thinking this week, but wipe it from your mind. Whatever overtime that brain of yours is doing, it's over."

I swallowed, willing myself to speak. "Mick," I said, but couldn't continue. I cleared my dry throat and saw Mick flick his hand at the bartender, who promptly appeared with a sparkling water.

"I don't know how you do that," I said after a sip. "You seem to so easily command the world around you. And yourself. I don't have that. I'm learning, but I'm finding my way."

"I don't want you to be anything but who you are," he said before leaning in and running his lips along my cheek.

A quick glance around the room revealed that no one seemed to be noticing his PDA except for Sheila, who was smiling like the cat who found the spilled milk.

"I'm sorry." My body naturally leaned into Mick's, seeking his warmth.

His arm came around my back and held me snug. The event carried on in the background, but my world shrank to our little corner of the bar.

"I overreacted. I don't know if I was just plain hurt," I said softly, "or maybe I was embarrassed that he'd treated me even more poorly than I'd thought."

Mick's hand ran the length of my back. Up, down, and up again. "It doesn't matter. To me, that is. I know it hurts you, which is why I didn't say anything. But I agree, we shouldn't have secrets."

"Because of how we began?" I asked like a lovesick teenager.

"No. Because I love you," Mick said.

Gaping at him, I was grateful his arm was around me. Otherwise, I would have slipped to the floor in my midnight-blue gown.

I was about to protest when Mick said firmly, "Don't you dare overthink this."

I laughed-cried. You know when you're teary-eyed, but a laugh comes out and you have no idea what's happening?

Looking up, I said, "Now, how about that drink?"

"On me? For sure."

"On me," I said with a smirk of my own. "After all, the drinks are included in your ticket."

"Then I need to get a table's worth of drinks."

"You didn't," I said, knowing he must have.

"I did. See table number twenty-two? Two of those seats are for us if we want."

"Oh. My."

Mick wave his hand in the air, catching the bartender while repeating, "No overthinking." He was about to give our orders when I took over.

"A sauvignon blanc and a Lagavulin?" I looked toward Mick, and he nodded, murmuring, "And she knows my drink."

With our drinks in hand, he said, "To you being you, and me loving you."

"To my sunny sky. Thank you for giving me that," I whispered back.

"Always."

It was time to sit for dinner, and despite threatening to make us sit at table twenty-two surrounded by nosy teachers, Mick joined me at the event planners' table, where he also had a seat.

I faked a scowl at Sheila, who only winked and went to grab the mic. Dale sat on the other side of Mick, and I couldn't be sure, but I swear I heard him threaten Mick if he hurt me.

Is this really my life? I'd gone from someone who had no one in my corner to several someones, and my heart was fuller than I could have ever imagined.

It was then I felt Mick's palm slide up my dress and over my bare leg, his pinky drawing figure-eights on my thigh. My skin broke out in goose bumps, and my core heated.

Reaching for my water, I brought it to my lips.

"Later," Mick said, his voice rich with promise. "And don't play coy. Sheila told me Priss is spending the night at her house."

I decided a gulp of water was needed while I enjoyed the beginning of the next phase of my life. The first was a nightmare, but the second promised to be a wonderfully weird fairy tale.

epilogue

m a r g a r e t

Two and a half years later

"Happy birthday, Mar."

Mick grabbed me in the kitchen and pulled me into his arms, running his lips over my cheek and kissing the small sliver of skin right below my ear.

"I love you," he murmured, and I felt those three words deep in my belly. He backed me into the counter and continued to kiss my neck.

"Love you too," I told him, and meant it.

My life had done a one-eighty, and even though he wouldn't take credit, Mick was the reason. Of course, he'd say it was all me, his momma's boy instincts not letting him take the credit. Dr. Schroeder agreed with him too, when I told her about all that had happened since our last session, but I knew the truth.

"Do we have to do this whole birthday thing? I like this . . . kissing." Admittedly, I was whining, but I would prefer a quiet night. With Mick. In bed.

"You're only forty once, babe. We have to do it."

"I'm not sure I want to be forty, so if we don't celebrate it, then maybe I won't be."

"Nothing you can do about it now," he said back. He slid his palm around my body, lightly spanking my butt. In a delicious way—to be clear. Then he smirked and did it again.

We didn't get much further because the doorbell rang and Tito went crazy, barking and dancing in circles. After he learned a lot of bad habits from Priscilla, we sent him to doggie boot camp, but that didn't help him much either. His biggest trick was he sat for treats now.

"I'll get it," Priscilla called, running down the stairs in a miniskirt and a very off-the-shoulder sweatshirt.

"What is she wearing?" I asked Mick, squeezing my eyes shut.

"Underwear disguised as a skirt?"

"Oh my God. Why does she do this to me?"

I wasn't sure how I'd survive the high school years with her. I mentally reminded myself what Dr. Schroeder had said, that Priscilla was headstrong and firm in her beliefs, but good at heart.

"Let it go. She's a good kid," Mick said, reminding me of what I already knew.

She'd been the light for me all those years I suffered, and so letting go of the miniskirt ban was the least I could do. Maybe.

About to start her high school years, Priscilla was still happy at the all-girls school and wanted to stay. She had a great friends group and brought them over to the house often—which we welcomed.

A while back, we'd thought about moving but ended up staying in my house and putting on an addition this winter. We expanded the back of the house to include an office for Mick and a workout room (also mostly for Mick), plus added a pool. I'd painted the whole house a warm shade of almond that soothed my senses every time I walked through the house. What used to be my prison was now my sanctuary.

Well, everywhere but Priscilla's room, which was painted purple, trimmed in twinkly lights, and covered in clothes.

"Hi," I heard my daughter call to Penny and Sheila in the foyer.

They were making small talk in the background. It was only when I heard a lot of girly whispers that I told Mick to go light up our new firepit in the back—just like the one that Priss had asked about way back when. As always, he was happy to have something to do. It was early June in Boston, and the evenings were still cool, but we were all eager to enjoy the outside.

"Take Tito," I told him, and he obliged.

Walking to see what all the excitement was about, I caught Penny shrieking, "You did?"

"What?" I asked.

"Nothing, nothing," Priscilla said.

I knew she was lying but would interrogate her later, another habit of mine she complained about. *Too bad.*

I hadn't told her my secret, but clearly, she had her own. We'd have to come clean sooner or later.

"Come in," I told them, and Sheila kissed my cheek and handed me a bottle of red wine.

"Happy birthday, Marg."

Everyone had their own nickname for me these days, and it stirred a private warmth in my belly. With no love lost over the soured relationship with my parents, I'd made my own family.

"You've come a long way since being Margaret," she said without prompting.

"Were you reading my thoughts?"

"Nah, you're just wearing all your secrets on your face today."

The girls ran up the stairs toward Priscilla's room. Surely to paint nails or braid hair or talk about boys.

Sheila's gaze dropped to my belly, and I said, "What?"

"All your secrets are starting to show."

"What? Do I smell funny?"

I tried to scowl, but she stood there looking pretty in dark jeans and a camel-colored sweater.

"You've got that glow. You're almost as bright as those old yellow walls in here."

"I'm forty." I frowned at her, still not reconciled to entering a new decade of life.

"So? Forty is the new thirty. You'll be fine."

"What about Priss? She'll be affected, right?"

"You sound like Dale with all that worrying. That girl is a rock. She's seen the worst, and she'll be thrilled to see some good."

We were standing close enough, I could smell Sheila's Chanel No. 5 as we whispered so no one would hear.

Sheila smirked at me. "Have you told Mick?"

"Not yet. Later."

"Secret's safe with me."

"Ladies, what can I get you to drink?"

Mick appeared out of nowhere, and I hoped he hadn't heard a thing.

"Vodka and soda," Sheila said.

"Wine," I said, knowing I'd only spill it out slowly in the yard. "White," I added, noting my own white sweater over pleather leggings. No reason to spill on my sweater and give away any clues.

"Let's go," Mick said as he herded us through the kitchen and out the patio door.

"Looks great back here," Sheila said.

"We finally got the fence up." I pointed toward the enclosure for the pool. "Tito was going wild, trying to get in. That dog needs a full-time nanny."

Sheila spun around, taking in all the changes we'd made to the backyard. For a moment, I remembered sitting out here and talking to Mick on the phone—secretly—so long ago.

"It's our little oasis," I said with a smile.

"I'm so glad you stayed. I do think Priscilla is happy about that," Sheila said.

She was right. With a little time, I'd come to think of the house as mine. I'd deserved it as my safe haven, and when Mick and I moved in together, it was my contribution to our household. He refused to use or take any of my work money, insisting I buy shoes, stocks, or a little of both.

"To the beautiful birthday lady," Mick said when he returned, juggling three drinks. Handing everyone their beverage, he said, "Cheers. To another forty or eighty."

"That's a lot of birthdays," I said, holding up my glass.

"I'll toast to that." Sheila tapped her glass to mine and took a long sip.

"Sit." Mick was pulling out chairs around the firepit. "Chef is bringing out appetizers."

I'd wanted to cook or order in sushi. Mick, however, insisted on flying Chef—what he affectionately called his now business partner—in from New York to cook for the five of us. There was no arguing when Priscilla got involved, saying she loved his wagyu sliders and asked if he would make them.

I didn't even know what had happened to that girl. After a few trips to New York with Mick and me, now she was a foodie.

"So, Dale had his fourth date last night," Sheila told us. "Your Rochelle. I think this could be the one."

Sheila continued to be obsessed with Dale and acting as his matchmaker. She claimed to have made a promise to his late wife a long time ago, but I knew better. He'd been such a good friend to Sheila that she felt forever indebted to him. If there was one thing about Sheila, she kept her promises.

We'd put her up to introducing him to Rochelle, who was still with us. I'd decided my job was too important to me to give it up, and Mick agreed, although he insisted that Rochelle stay on to help me. She did the shopping and cleaning, waited for contractors, and occasionally picked up Priscilla for me. Rochelle and I also shared coffee a lot of afternoons, and we hosted her and her son over for dinner many times. He loved Tito, way more than Rochelle did.

"Apparently, she's crazy for Dale, and wants to go away with him in a few weeks. It could be a quickie marriage with them both having kids."

Mick cleared his throat at the mention of them both having kids and a marriage in sight.

He'd asked once if I was ready, and I said no. I wasn't opposed to us moving in together, but combining everything with something that scared me was too much.

Even though that didn't make much sense, it felt like I'd be giving up a lot of newfound, hard-fought freedom. At least, initially. That was before I'd fallen even deeper in love with Mick's soft side and the way he looked out for Priscilla.

Oh, and I was carrying his baby . . . which he didn't know.

"Oh my God, Sheila, stop with all that," I told her, thinking she was only going to prompt a lengthy conversation between Mick and me later.

Mick chimed in. "Everyone has their own way of living, Mar."

"Don't get all philosophical on me," I joked, knowing he was making his own silent point.

Chef appeared then, and I whispered, "Saved by the bell," to myself. It was my birthday, after all.

"I heard you," Sheila muttered.

The rest of the evening went like that. Jokes, food, drinks, laughs, and more food.

When it came time for cake, Mick told me to sit and close my eyes.

I did as I was told and heard the girls approach while singing "Happy Birthday."

"Open up," he told me.

When I did, there was a giant cupcake made from regular-size cupcakes, each with a candy ring in them, until a single cupcake at the very top, where a real ring sat atop the pink icing.

There were no birthday candles, only the candles on the table twinkling around us, as I stared wide-eyed at the cake and the sparkling gem at the top of the tier. No one spoke for a moment, especially me, as I took a moment to register what all this meant.

"Mom."

Priscilla nudged me, and I looked up at a patiently waiting Mick. He stood next to my chair, his eyes locked on me.

"Marry me?"

I swallowed, but was still speechless.

"Mom!" Priscilla stood bouncing on her toes on the other side of me, as Sheila and Penny looked on with expectant expressions.

"Is this what you were whispering about earlier? You little devil," I said to Priscilla.

"Mom. Answer Mick."

There he was, my Mick, steadfast as always. My rock, the yin to my yang, the sun to my dark cloud, my pink and purple sunset.

"Yes, yes, yes," I said on repeat.

"One was enough," Mick said, pulling me up and kissing me in front of our three guests. He kept it closed-mouthed before breaking away and taking the ring out of the cake, then licked off the icing from the band before slipping it on my finger.

"Now, let's eat cake," he said, and that's just what we did.

Crawling into bed that night, I curled onto Mick's chest.

"Have a good birthday?" he asked.

"The best to date," I said, looking at the shiny ring on my hand.

"You like it?"

"Love it." It was the perfect ring for me. An emerald-cut sapphire flanked by two smaller emerald-cut diamonds in a platinum band.

"Priss really loved that one. Said you would love the dated sophistication. You sure get your money's worth from that school. Her vocabulary is better than mine."

I could have mentioned Tommy getting his money's worth, but I was over it, and for that matter, him. He was a part of my past, and Mick was my future.

My therapist's words rang in my mind. "It wasn't traditional, and some may say it was illicit when your past and present merged for a brief period of time, but some stories are messy. It's not how neatly they were packaged but what they look like when they're unwrapped."

I'd told her, "For me it was when the sun faded, and Mick was still there when it rose. Too many times, I'd watched the sun fade and rise, not knowing what version of Tommy I was getting. With Mick, I always got Mick-Mick." Maybe my words weren't as eloquent, but they worked for me.

"She'll be off to college soon. I'll really miss her," I said.

"We'll miss her, but it's not for a long while. When the time comes, though, Tito will be distraught. Who will keep him busy or give him a hundred treats a day?"

"Well, I may have someone in mind . . ."

Mick sat up and looked at me. "Who?"

I slid up my pillow and said, "Someone we haven't met yet, but we will in about seven months." I glanced toward the lower portion of my body.

"What?" His fingers intertwined with mine. "What are you saying?" He leaned over me and kissed me.

"I can't tell you if you're kissing me," I murmured, and he moved back an inch. "I'm pregnant. At forty. And up until a few hours ago, I wasn't even engaged to the baby daddy."

"Fuck, Mar." He shoved his hand through his messy hair.

"You're not happy?"

"No way. I'm fucking ecstatic. It's just I shouldn't have waited to marry you. I should've done it the minute I moved in here."

"I wasn't ready," I told him. "But now I am."

"You'd better be, babe. Holy shit, I'm going to be a dad. I know, I kind of already am, but I never did this stage. Do you think Priscilla will mind sharing me? She's used to all my attention."

"No. She'll probably be happy to have less eyes on her."

His hand came to my belly, his palm finding its way under my tank. "This one is going to have all the eyes, but Priss doesn't need to worry. I'm very smart and have my ways."

We both laughed before kissing, and our clothes found their way into a pile on the floor.

As Mick slipped inside me, I moaned, "I love you," while silently thanking God, Buddha, and whoever else had willed me to walk into Stephanie's that day not so long ago.

acknowledgments

As always, these are increasingly difficult to write.

With every book (and this is book number sixteen), I realize the effects of the romance world on me. There's no separation between who I am in my daily life and when I step into Romancelandia. These people are my family.

Huge thanks to Sarah Hansen, who created this beauty of a cover. I usually just say, "Work your magic," but I didn't say one single thing this time. This is what she gave me on the first try.

To Pam Berehulke, where would I be without you? Together since day one, we've gone through so many of life's ups and downs. I appreciate your editing expertise more than you know, and thank you for squeezing this baby in.

Thank you to my team of forever-by-my-side ladies—Michelle R, Jenn D, and Virginia. I'm sure you have me on Do Not Disturb at this point, but your feedback is essential.

Queen V, when are we going to another signing again? I hope soon. I can't express enough gratitude for your eagle eye when it comes to proofreading and, of course, for your saying I LOVE THIS BOOK!

To Emily Tippetts and gang (and Stacey, who is ignoring me right about now). Without you, I can't upload a thing. Thanks for making it all work.

Special thanks to Nina at Valentine PR for breathing life into me again, telling me I could do this. Thanks for getting me back to regular writing and, wait for it: PLANNING!

To Nic, my PA. For helping me with three book babies during a pandemic and dealing with frantic scattered emails from me, you deserve a medal.

Christy Pastore. My daily text, call, yell for help, you always answer me, and if you don't, I find you. Thank you for being part of my world. At least we have a plan for 2022. Get ready!

Fabi, you continue to inspire me with your grit and hard work. Our lives are better with you in it. Thanks for channeling my inner cowgirl and setting an example.

To my family. Just thanks for being you and loving me (M-W-F).

To THE ELECTRIC READERS, I love you eternally. See you for coffee tomorrow.

And to YOU, for reading.

about the author

Rachel Blaufeld is a bestselling author of Romantic Suspense, New Adult, Coming-of-Age Romance, and Sports Romance. A recent poll of her readers described her as insightful, generous, articulate, and spunky. Originally a social worker, Rachel creates broken yet redeeming characters. She's been known to turn up the angst like cranking up the heat in the dead of winter.

A devout coffee drinker and doughnut eater, Rachel spends way too many hours in local coffee shops, downing the aforementioned goodies while she plots her ideas. Her tales may all come with a side of angst and naughtiness, but end as lusciously as her treats.

As a side note, Blaufeld, also a long-time blogger and an advocate of woman-run anything, is fearless about sharing her opinion. To her, work/life/family balance is an urban legend, but she does her best.

Rachel has also blogged for The Huffington Post, Modern Mom, and USA TODAY, where she shared conversations at "In Bed with a Romance Author" and reading recommendations at "Happy Ever After."

Rachel lives around the corner from her childhood home in Pennsylvania with her family and two beagles. Her obsessions include running, coffee, basketball, icing-filled doughnuts, antiheroes, and mighty fine epilogues.

To connect with Rachel, she's most active in her private reading group, The Electric Readers, where she shares insider information and intimate conversation with her readers:

Tunnel VIPs
As well as:
www.rachelblaufeld.com
Twitter
Facebook
Newsletter

If you liked this book, feel free to leave a review where you bought it or on Goodreads. Send me an e-mail when you do, and I will thank you personally!

Made in the USA
Monee, IL
08 October 2021